The Coldness of Killers

When the body of a young dropout is discovered at a downtown school in a West
Yorkshire city, is the motive mindless racism
or something more complex but just as brutal?

The ensuing violence and racial tension test
loyalties to breaking-point across a mixed
community, and no one is more involved than
liberal teacher Joanna Robertson, who finds
that not only are personal loyalties strained in
ways she could never have envisaged, but she
is herself suspected of murder.

Christmas approaches, and Detective Chief
Inspector Harry Huddleston, who had
planned to end his police career in his home
town on a convivial note, has several suspect
killings on his hands and no clues to any of the
perpetrators. But as his tenacious investigation
gets under way, neither Huddleston nor anyone else foresaw the violent conclusion which
was to disrupt so many lives.

PATRICIA HALL

The Coldness of Killers

THE CRIME CLUB
An Imprint of HarperCollins *Publishers*

First published in Great Britain in 1992
by The Crime Club, an imprint of
HarperCollins Publishers, 77–85 Fulham Palace Road,
Hammersmith, London W6 8JB

9 8 7 6 5 4 3 2 1

For Michael and James

A catalogue record for this book is
available from the British Library

ISBN 0 00 232403 2

Photoset in Linotron Baskerville by
Rowland Phototypesetting Ltd
Bury St Edmunds, Suffolk
Printed and bound in Great Britain by
HarperCollins Book Manufacturing, Glasgow

CHAPTER 1

The first scream ripped through the busy hum of the school reducing it to an eerie unnatural silence within seconds. At the front of her fifth-year class Joanna Robertson was reduced to immobility at the blackboard, chalk in hand, half way through writing up a quotation from a Dylan Thomas poem.

At the back of the room, Darren and Steven, two inattentive, gangling youths who had to her knowledge kept up a constant and unquenchable chatter ever since she had first met them as relatively deferential eleven-year-olds, were reduced to speechlessness. The rest of the class appeared frozen by the chilling sound coming apparently from beneath them and unnervingly close at hand. Twenty-seven adolescents sat rigidly at their desks, mouths slackly open, pens poised over books, and one hand, which had been waving urgently in the air, subsiding nervelessly back to its desk as shocked horror took hold.

The first scream had been piercing and intense and was followed by several seconds of total silence. Then, as a thousand in-drawn breaths around the school were expelled and a murmur of horrified surprise spread through every classroom, laboratory and office in the sprawling old building, there was a new and equally disturbing noise. At first Jo thought it was laughter, but as the class of fifteen-year-olds fell into horrified silence again, she realized that it was simply a different sort of scream, a choking, sobbing noise, rising and falling rhythmically as if whoever was making it was rocking to and fro in intense distress.

Jo swallowed hard, put down her volume of Thomas poems on the desk and met the twenty-seven pairs of anxious eyes in front of her with the surface confidence which comes from years of practice in front of thousands of children, but which on this occasion was paper thin.

'It sounds as though there's been an accident,' she said

quietly, finding her mouth so dry that it was unusually hard to project her voice to the back of the room.

'I'm going to see if I can find out what the trouble is and if anyone needs any help. You can all obviously help by staying here quietly. I know it's a lot to ask, but try to carry on reading where we left off, will you? For homework I want you to do a comparison of this poem and the one we read last lesson. If you've got time before I come back you can make a start on that.'

The class shuffled its feet and its book uneasily.

'Will you tell us what's happened, Miss?' came a voice from the back. The question came from a plump, pasty girl, her pale eyes popping with anxiety. Jo Robertson shrugged slightly and brushed a hand through her short fair hair.

'I'll tell you whatever I can when I come back,' she said noncommittally. 'Now please get on with your work.'

She went out, closing the classroom door quietly but firmly behind her, though without any real conviction that the group would find the concentration to follow her instructions. Even at fifteen, self-discipline came hard to most of the school's pupils and she felt rather than heard the rising mutter of astonished curiosity behind her.

In the corridor she found several colleagues also leaving their classes, and one group of children, apparently unsupervised, spilling noisily from their room in a hubbub of excited chatter, almost but not quite blocking out the hysterical screams which, it was now clear, were coming from the stone staircase which led to her basement cloakrooms one floor below them. Glancing at her colleagues, Jo realized at once that she was by some years the most senior teacher there. With an urgency made more acute by every dreadful sound from below she took charge.

'For goodness' sake, Tom,' she said to the young geography teacher who was standing in the middle of the corridor looking pale and horrified and almost as young as the children surrounding him. 'Get those third-years back into their room and keep them there. 3P, go back into your classroom at once! Mr Pearson is going to look after you until we find out what's going on.'

6

She cast a speculative eye over her other three colleagues —Sue Darnley, a pale, crop-haired young mathematician who looked on the verge of tears, Jane Davies, a competent enough member of the history department, she had heard, but also looking severely shaken by the screaming, which continued unabated, and David Macgregor, a burly and taciturn Scot whom she did not know well but who looked relatively unmoved by the unprecedented events unfolding around them.

'Will you come with me, David?' she asked. 'We seem to be nearest to whatever's going on.'

Macgregor nodded.

'Down there, d'you think?' he asked, indicating the staircase.

'Right underneath my classroom, I'd guess,' Jo said, turning on her heel quickly and leading the way down the stairs.

Sutton Park School was housed in a motley collection of buildings on a steep hillside overlooking the small manufacturing town of Bradfield. Its core, now much added to as the original boys' secondary school had been comprehensivized, extended and eventually amalgamated with a neighbouring girls' establishment, was an uncompromisingly grim stone pile of four storeys built into the slope of the hill and almost as old as the century.

The original bleak stone staircase with dark brown tiled walls at each corner of the building, one of which Jo Robertson and David Macgregor now somewhat nervously descended, had not been softened by time, modern theories of education or the depredations of generations of Bradfield teenagers. The bottom flight led into a basement which, because of the nature of the terrain, occupied only half the floor area of the upper storeys. It provided gloomy cloakrooms for all the school's thousand youngsters, and two sets of changing-rooms and showers, one for boys and one for girls, at each corner of the building. The boys' showers, which lay immediately beneath the classroom where Jo had been taking her GCSE English group, had been out of order for the best part of the autumn term.

Yet the boys' showers were the undoubted source of the hysterical screams which increased in volume as the two teachers descended the stairs. Jo Robertson took a deep breath as she reached the bottom step and turned towards her colleague outside the half-glazed door which led into the changing-rooms. She felt hot and slightly sick and she ran a nervous hand round her neck to loosen the collar of her shirt. The sound had reached a crescendo now. Close to, it had a terrible intensity which made coherent thought difficult.

Her eyes met Macgregor's for a moment and she saw her own fear reflected there. They were both, she realized, quite terrified of what they would find behind the door.

'Come on,' she said, her voice husky, and taking another deep breath, as if only oxygen could carry her through the ordeal, she opened the door and led the way in.

The changing-room was divided into sections by elderly wooden benches topped by rails and rows of hooks to take discarded clothing. Empty and unused at the moment, and smelling mustily of old wet towels and sweat, the benches still made it difficult to see across the room, which was dimly lit by small windows of frosted glass set high in the walls so as to prevent anyone looking in from outside. They let in little of the rapidly fading daylight and Jo clicked the light-switch inside the door impatiently. Nothing happened. The room remained as dim as only a late November afternoon could make it.

On the far side, beyond the benches, a little additional light filtered mistily out of the open door which led into the double row of showers. The screaming, undiminished still, came from there. Jo led the way round the benches to the open doorway, with Macgregor close on her heels. She hesitated for only a moment to accustom her eyes to the brighter light before darting across the slatted passageway between the uncurtained shower cubicles to where a girl in school uniform was pressed rigidly against the tiled wall, her hands at her own throat, as she screamed now with hysterical monotony.

When it comes to the point, Jo thought afterwards, you

8

do what you have been conditioned to do more often than not. She took hold of the hysterical girl and slapped her hard across the face. She heard David Macgregor's sharply in-drawn breath behind her in the total silence which followed, although whether his reaction was one of simple surprise or horror at the breaking of the taboo on violence in school she did not know. For a long moment the girl simply stared at Jo blankly before her face crumpled and she sagged slowly into the teacher's arms and burst into heartbroken but normal sobs.

Jo Robertson led the girl into the changing-room and sat her down on one of the benches. She was a small, rather dumpy girl, plump-faced and with a mop of untidy brown curls, her regulation school skirt too short and her blouse and sweater too tight, as if she had grown too fast for her clothes. She was not a member of any of Jo's classes but Jo knew her name and that she was a member of the fourth year, and therefore about fourteen.

'What is it, Tessa?' she asked, brushing the girl's tangled, damp hair away from her face, which was screwed up and blotchy with emotion. 'Whatever is it? You're upsetting the whole school.'

The girl shuddered convulsively against Jo and mumbled something she could not understand. She looked helplessly at David Macgregor who was standing anxiously by.

'Tessa,' he said, with unexpected firmness. 'Can you tell us why you're so upset? Have you hurt yourself?'

Whether it was the effect of a double dose of adult sympathy or an ingrained response to a male voice of authority, as Jo suspected, David's question at least evoked a response from the incoherent girl. She visibly made a dramatic effort to calm her sobs and straightened up, freeing herself from Jo's comforting arm. For all Tessa's podgy pubescent body, which looked as though it might burst out of the constraints of her school uniform at any moment, she gained a certain dignity, which demanded to be taken seriously as she struggled to control her emotions. There was not a moment's doubt in Jo Robertson's mind that Tessa was telling the truth.

9

'He's dead,' she said quite clearly. 'I found him dead.'

'Who's dead, Tessa?' Jo asked sharply.

'Him, in there,' Tessa said, glancing back towards the showers behind them. 'The Paki lad. I don't know his name. I found him dead.'

Jo felt her stomach tighten and her mouth dry. She glanced at David Macgregor, who suddenly looked very young and had turned a distinctly green shade of pale. She took hold of his arm firmly, feeling very old and very tired.

'Look after Tessa for a minute,' she said quietly, as she got up and walked far more determinedly than she felt towards the shower room again.

Inside everything looked normal, but it was not possible to see clearly into every cubicle from the doorway. Very slowly she walked the length of the pale, water-washed duckboard which covered the tiled floor, glancing carefully into every individual shower. She found him in the end cubicle, a tall, slender and very young body, fully clothed, and curled into an almost foetal position, on his side with his knees tucked up towards his chest, so that he fitted neatly into the square tiled space at the base of the shower.

There was no doubt in Jo's mind that the boy was dead. One hand had clutched unavailingly at the only part of the shower which was not smooth and white. He had broken his nails on the small round grating which drained away the shower water into an open channel running the length of the room. His long black hair spread untidily over the tiles at the back of the cubicle, where they curved upwards to meet the wall. And from underneath the left side of his dark blue sweatshirt blood had oozed into a pool, roughly the size and shape of a dinner plate, but congealed now into a dark, sticky, almost geloid mass.

Jo put a hand against the edge of the shower wall for support and took a couple of deep breaths to steady herself. Gingerly she knelt down and reached out to touch the boy's cheek. It was cold, almost as cold as the tiles on which he lay. Very gently she pushed the hair away from his face, and nodded as her suspicions were confirmed.

She knew him. His name was Karim, and the sight of

10

him lying there brought her last frustrating contact with him back to her mind with astonishing clarity as she sat back on her heels, trying to come quickly to terms with what she had found. There had been problems with Karim Aziz, she remembered. She had spent an hour one hot and sultry summer afternoon with his father, a small, mild man with dark anxious eyes whose ambitions for his only son were being disappointed at a cruelly early stage.

Karim had apparently lost interest in school, his work was falling away and he declared himself determined, unusually for an Asian boy, to leave school at the earliest opportunity, which eventually, as the examinations approached and his prospects of passing them diminished, he did.

Neither the school nor, apparently, his family had understood what had been going on behind Karim's nonchalant façade as he had drifted almost insouciantly away from them both that sunny summer term. Whatever hopes Mr Aziz still entertained for Karim would turn to dust and ashes now, Jo thought sadly.

David Macgregor's anxious voice, asking from the doorway if she was all right, jerked her back to reality. She got up slowly, and went back into the changing-rooms. Tessa was still sitting on the bench, shaking convulsively occasionally and twisting a paper tissue in her small plump hands, but quiet now. David, still pale, looked at her inquiringly and she nodded.

'It's a former pupil,' she said very quietly. 'He's quite dead. Don't go in. There's no point. There's nothing we can do for him.'

She stood for a moment trying to order her own thoughts.

'Ought we to call the police?' David asked tentatively at last.

Jo nodded, collecting herself.

'Stay here, David, and don't let anyone in. No one at all, until the police come. I'll take Tessa with me and get help.' She spoke jerkily, the shock taking effect now. Quickly she helped the girl to her feet, while up above them she heard the bell ringing for the end of the first afternoon lesson and the thunderous scraping of hundreds of chairs on wooden floors. For the next five minutes the school corridors would be a milling mass of youngsters changing classrooms.

In less than an hour the final bell of the afternoon would sound and the basement itself would be filled with the best part of a thousand pupils stowing books in lockers, putting on coats or hoping to get changed for whatever sports activities were scheduled for the late afternoon. Some of the boys, she thought, in panic, would be wanting to change in this very room.

She guided Tessa along the basement passageway lined with banks of lockers which ran the length of the school and up the stairs at the far end which brought them out on to the relatively quiet corridor which served the school offices and the head's study. As they walked, Tessa let loose a pent-up jumble of disconnected information which only gradually fell into a coherent explanation of what had just happened.

She had gone to the boys' changing-room to hide, she said, so that she wouldn't have to play hockey. She had fled into the showers because she thought she heard the games mistress looking for her. She had not seen the body immediately as she had hidden in an adjacent shower, but when she ventured out, thinking the coast was clear, she had spotted Karim's foot protruding over the tiled sill of a cubicle. When she had investigated more closely she had found his body and begun to scream and could not stop.

With her arm around the still distraught fourteen-year-old, Jo marched unceremoniously into the office of the head's secretary, Jean Phillips, a woman of more than middle age and more than average dignity who regarded it as her prime duty in life to protect her mistress from the importunities of everyday life in the large school which she ostensibly ran. Jean looked up askance from her conversation over some papers with one of the junior secretaries and her brow darkened even more when she saw that Jo was accompanied by a pupil. In Mrs Phillips's book, staff were a nuisance, pupils a downright inconvenience.

12

'She's very busy . . .' Mrs Phillips began, but Jo let her get no further.

'There's an emergency,' she said flatly. 'I need someone to look after this child. She's had a dreadful shock. She needs tea, warmth, someone who knows about first aid. Will you see to it, please? And I need to see Margaret straight away . . .'

Jean Phillips made as if to argue, pulling herself up to her full five foot four of outraged dignity, but something in Jo Robertson's expression made her hesitate. Jo had been at the school for barely two years but had earned herself a reputation for not suffering fools gladly.

'Someone is dead, Jean,' Jo said, more harshly than she really intended, and flung open the communicating door between the secretary's office and the head's study.

Margaret Jackson turned almost as pale as her white silk blouse as she listened to what Jo Robertson told her. She was a tall, slim woman, her fair hair turning silver rather than grey. She favoured rather formal tailored suits in the style of the 'eighties, which had been when she had achieved, rather late in her career, her long-standing ambition to become one of the very few women to run a large mixed comprehensive school.

In spite of her somewhat austere appearance, with more than a touch of the style of the long-vanished spinster teachers of the girls' schools of her own youth, she was much loved and it distressed Jo Robertson to have brought Margaret Jackson news which had clearly upset her deeply and had shattered her normal calm authority.

'We must get the police,' Margaret said hesitantly, at last, after considering the situation in silence for a time. 'Could you ring them, please, Jo?'

Jo did as she was asked, her own self-control beginning to feel ragged now that she had passed responsibility for the situation up the line. Her hand was shaking, she noticed, as she picked up Margaret's phone and dialled 999.

Mrs Jackson looked at Jo speculatively when she had finished the brief call.

'You think the boy was murdered?' she asked.

'I didn't touch the body, once I'd made sure he was dead,' Jo said slowly. 'But, yes, I should think it's murder. It looked as though he had been stabbed and that's not a normal way for people to kill themselves, is it? And could hardly be an accident.'

'But you say he's left school? So what was he doing on the premises, for goodness' sake? And who could have killed him? Surely not one of our students . . .'

Margaret Jackson stared out of the window for a moment, a frown creasing her brow as she obviously tried to work out the implications of what had happened.

'It won't do our reputation any good, with the primary children just about to choose their secondary schools,' Margaret said at last, almost inconsequentially.

Jo stood up and went to the window where she pressed her forehead against the cool glass and looked out at the muddy playing fields where a class of girls was playing a desultory game of hockey, the game Tessa had been avoiding. The image of the boy's body curled up so apparently peacefully in its chilly tomb seemed to be etched on her retina so clearly that she doubted whether she would ever be able to erase it. It was almost as if a flash bulb had gone off at that moment, creating a stark, shadowless image of death which would survive for a lifetime.

'I wouldn't have thought that was the first consideration,' she said suddenly, with unexpected vehemence. Margaret Jackson looked at her blankly for a moment, fiddling with the fountain pen on her desk. Then her face sagged and she looked suddenly much older and on the verge of tears.

'You're right, of course,' she admitted. 'That was stupid of me. You get so bogged down in management that sometimes you risk forgetting about the people it's all in aid of. The children will be upset, of course. We need to think what to do about that, especially for those who knew the dead boy. I'll talk to the senior staff at the end of school. It will need to be dealt with in assembly tomorrow, too. I'll see to that myself.'

She joined Jo at the window and put a hand lightly on her shoulder.

'I'm sorry, Joanna. It must have been a shock for you, too,' she said.

As the two women watched, two police cars with lights flashing urgently in the gathering gloom of the afternoon drove around the corner of the building and drew up outside the school's main door.

'Here comes the world of anger and telegrams,' Margaret said, with forced lightness. 'You'll be first on the interview list, Jo, I expect, in the circumstances. Come with me and let's see what they want us to do.'

CHAPTER 2

'What time does school finish, Mrs Robertson?' asked Detective Chief Inspector Harry Huddleston, looking anxiously at his watch. He and what seemed to Jo to be an unnecessary large contingent of policemen, some in uniform, some in overalls, some in plain clothes, were packed into the changing-room and shower area. There were, she noticed, fingerprint officers, photographers and a large, almost rotund civilian with a medical bag and an air which combined arrogance and boredom in equal measure.

The centre of their attention, the curled and apparently awkwardly situated body of Karim Aziz, was causing them all enormous difficulties as they tried to carry out their routine tasks in the cramped space available around the tiny cubicle where he had been found and where, she supposed, he must have died.

Jo glanced at her watch.

'We finish in half an hour,' she said. 'At four o'clock.'

'Right. I don't want anyone to leave,' the Chief Inspector said flatly. Jo looked at him, astonished.

'But we can't keep a thousand children in,' she said.

'You must. I want a register taken so that I know exactly who is here before they're allowed to go home. Can you organize that?'

'Well, I suppose we could,' Jo conceded, thinking

quickly. 'We could ask them all to go back to their form-tutors and send the registers around again, like we do at the beginning of school. I'll have to consult the office.'

'Do that, then. When they have all registered again, they can go. I'll want a list of staff who were on the premises today as well, and anyone else, secretaries, cleaners, visitors and so on. And I need to talk to the girl who found the body this afternoon. Can you get her parents to come to school to be with her?'

Jo found herself faintly irritated by the policeman's tone —not simply authoritative, as she would have expected from a senior police officer, but slightly preremptory with it.

'Will there be anything else, Chief Inspector?' she asked, with the slightest trace of irony in her voice. It clearly washed over Huddleston, though she thought she saw the good-looking young sergeant who seemed to attend on his every move give the slightest twitch of the lips.

'Sergeant Mower here can go with you to help with the arrangements,' Huddleston said, indicating his colleague, who straightened his face with unnerving promptness. 'I don't want anyone to leave until we know exactly who's been here today. And if you are passing a message round to all the classes, you might also ask anyone who has seen this lad—what's his name? Karim?—anyone who's seen him recently, or seen anything suspicious on school premises, to contact me before they go home.'

Jo nodded and turned to go, when Huddleston summoned her back again.

'How are your race relations here?' he asked brusquely. 'You've a fair number of Pak . . . Asians, haven't you?' He corrected himself without any sign of being abashed. 'Any problems?'

'Race relations in school are very good,' Jo Robertson said icily. 'We take good care of all our young people.'

'I'm sure you do, Mrs Robertson,' Huddleston came back heavily. 'Which doesn't mean they take good care of each other, does it? With a death like this, the most likely scenario is a feud inside the community—some Moslem girl's brothers didn't like the liberties he was taking, perhaps.

16

Second most likely, some white lads didn't like Asian lads, full stop. You may not like it, but that's how it most usually works out.'

Huddleston turned away to meet the pathologist, the bulky man in a crumpled grey suit who was his match in age and weight, and who had found some difficulty manœuvring himself out of the narrow space in the shower cubicle. He came into the changing-room mopping his brow with a large handkerchief and breathing heavily.

'Now then, Amos,' Huddleston said almost jovially. 'Are we looking for Norman Bates, then, or what?'

Jo winced and felt Sergeant Mower's eyes on her again, with that same flicker of amusement.

'A single knife wound to the heart,' Amos Atherton said brusquely, ignoring Huddleston's attempt at humour. 'Instantaneous, or as good as. Very little blood.'

If that heart-stopping pool was considered to be very little blood, Jo thought with a shudder, she hoped she would be spared the sight of a lot.

'Any idea of a time?' Huddleston persisted.

The doctor shrugged.

'It's very cold down here,' he said. 'No heating, as far as I can see. At a guess I'd say he was killed either late last night or early this moring. But you'll have to wait for anything more definite.'

'Not in school time, then?' Huddleston asked.

'No, not in school time, I don't think.'

Jo Robertson, who had hovered on the edge of this exchange with the Detective-Sergeant, neither of them apparently willing to move until they had gleaned whatever information the pathologist had to impart, felt the first slight lightening of her spirits since that first appalling scream had shattered the calm of a dull November afternoon. She turned on her heel and went back upstairs to make the arrangements that the police had requested, with Mower close behind her taking a not entirely professional interest in the swing of her skirt and the turn of her ankles as she hurried up the stairs ahead of him.

By five o'clock that afternoon, Jo Robertson felt she had

been put through a wringer. She was sitting on the opposite side of a table from Chief Inspector Huddleston, with Sergeant Mower crammed uncomfortably on to an upright chair to her left in a room in which one adult and a child would have felt like a crowd. The makeshift office had until an hour ago been the medical room, the only available space where the police could sensibly set up a temporary office while the whole school was still on the premises. The folding bed had been stacked away to accommodate a spare table and three chairs. Even so, with his boss behind the desk, Sergeant Mower had to make notes with his notebook on his lap and his left elbow likely to jab the person who was being interviewed in the ribs.

On her way to the interview room with Sergeant Mower, Jo had found herself pushing and shoving her way through an excitable mob of young people who had gathered outside the door of the school office apparently seeking information. Vinny Barnes, the tall, black dreadlocked lead singer in the fifth year's rock group and a natural leader of a much wider constituency, placed himself deliberately in Jo's way.

'Who's dead, Mrs R?' he asked. 'There's all sorts of rumours.' The hubbub around them subsided slightly as the whole crowd of teenagers waited breathlessly for an answer. Jo glanced at Sergeant Mower, who had become separated from her in the mêlée and he raised an eyebrow and shrugged imperceptibly.

'It's a boy called Karim Aziz, Vinny,' Jo said. 'He left last summer. You may remember him.' Vinny looked at Jo for a long moment, some of the anger fading from his dark eyes and the tension perceptibly draining away.

'Karim,' he said softly. 'So it's Karim. I do remember him.'

'And the rumours?' Jo asked.

'No, the rumours said something else, Mrs R, something else entirely.'

'I think it's time to go home, Vinny,' Jo said. The boy nodded gravely, in an almost formal acceptance of her reassertion of authority.

'Sure,' he said. 'We'll all be going home now.' And as if

18

by some prearranged signal the jostling crowd took their cue and moved amiably towards the main doors.

As Jo came into the medical room, Chief Inspector Huddleston glanced at her with the massive imperturbability which she, her nerves ragged, found faintly irritating. He was a big man, who seemed bigger in this cramped space, with the build of a rugby forward, iron grey hair clipped short at the back and sides, and eyes of a clear, cold blue which appeared to take in everything and give nothing away. They were eyes which had seen it all, Jo thought, and had reached certain conclusions about the human race which she neither shared nor wanted to share.

Huddleston had not allowed the school's pupils to be dismissed until half past four, after satisfying himself that each and every one of them had gone back to their form-room to register for a second time that afternoon. By that time Karim Aziz's body had been zipped into a plastic bag and taken away by mortuary van, leaving the changing-room and showers to the attentions of the scene of crime officers Huddleston had drafted in and the object of intense curiosity to the thousand adolescents, most of whom contrived, with determined nonchalance, to pass by the half-glazed doors as they made their way out of school.

Huddleston had taken charge of the lists of adults who had been on the premises from Jean Phillips, and had spent half an hour in the tiny medical room with Tessa Brown and her mother, who had been summoned to school by telephone to take charge of her still tearful daughter. Not once, as far as Jo was aware when she was summoned to the Chief Inspector's presence, had he thanked anyone for the massive organizational effort that had been made on his behalf.

'I'm sorry to have kept you waiting,' Jo said, sinking wearily into the third chair into which Huddleston waved her brusquely. 'I had to telephone my husband to tell him I'd be late.'

He nodded noncommittally and for a moment they appraised each other silently. She found the effort unrewarding. She was as used as he was to making instant assessments of people, and Chief Inspector Harry Huddleston, she concluded quickly, was not a man she would turn to for sympathy in times of trouble. There was cold stillness about the broad face, a professional and dispassionate watchfulness around the big man's eyes, in spite of the occasional outbreaks of joviality which she had witnessed, which she disliked.

For his part, he faced a woman half his age, her fair hair slightly dishevelled, soberly dressed for her job in a dark red shirt and a navy sweater and skirt with flat, 'sensible' shoes. An attractive woman, nevertheless, in an understated way, he conceded reluctantly, in spite of the faint lines around her eyes, which could be the result of laughter or of stress, it was impossible to tell.

What threw him, he was honest enought to admit, and what had thrown him at his brief meeting with the school's head, whom he had not expected to be female, was the confidence of a woman perfectly well-adjusted to taking charge of a situation. He had caught the momentary amusement in Sergeant Mower's eyes when he had walked into Margaret Jackson's room and looked around for the headmaster he had expected, and it had annoyed him enough for him to remain slightly off balance as this new interview commenced.

'I hear you have been broadcasting information about today's victim without my say-so, Mrs Robertson,' Huddleston began at last. Jo looked at Mower, who dropped his eyes to his notebook and avoided her gaze. Sod you, she thought angrily and turned back to meet Huddleston's accusatory stare.

'There were a lot of rumours flying around,' she cried. 'Some of the boys were getting very agitated. I didn't think it was a good idea to send them home in that state.'

'I think I should have been the judge of that,' Huddleston came back quickly.

'And I don't think you'd have thanked me if you'd had to call the riot vans out tonight,' Jo snapped. 'You've already said you think the murder might be racially motivated. If those boys had gone home with that in mind, not knowing who the victim was . . .' She shrugged.

'A murder inquiry takes precedence over race relations, Mrs Robertson,' Huddleston said heavily.

'Of course,' she said, her agreement clearly disconcerting him, though he switched tack with a speed which brought an admiring glance from Sergeant Mower who had been following the exchange with barely concealed enjoyment.

'So tell me what it involves, this counselling you do,' the Chief Inspector asked. 'This is on top of your job as an English teacher?'

'I teach English for about half my timetable,' Jo said. 'The rest of the time I'm responsible for counselling the fifth-year students on what they should do after they've taken their GCSE exams. I arrange work experience for them, help them with job applications if they're leaving in the summer, advise them on courses if they want to stay on into the sixth form, or go to college, all that sort of thing.'

'That's a half-time job, is it?' Huddleston asked with more scepticism than he really intended. He was genuinely curious. In his days as a Bradfield grammar school boy more than thirty years before, Sutton Park had been a school written off locally as a sort of educational slum serving the run-down end of the town. In all his years as a policeman he had never penetrated beyond the forbidding iron railings which separated it, now as then, from the outside world.

'It's more than a half-time job in a school like this, Chief Inspector,' Jo answered with some asperity. 'A lot of these youngsters have problems.' They looked at each other in silence, his faintly hostile blue eyes meeting her cool grey challenging gaze for a moment before he decided not to pursue that line of questioning any further.

'And Mrs Jackson says you're the person who knew Karim Aziz best, is that right?' he went on at length.

'Well, I suppose it is. His form tutor left at the end of the summer term. He would have been the best person to talk to, of course . . .'

'We'll follow him up later, if we need to,' Huddleston said. 'Go on, Mrs Robertson.'

'Well, I did have quite a lot of contact with Karim when he was in the fifth year—mainly because he was having some difficulties.'

'What sort of difficulties?' Huddleston jumped on the word quickly.

Jo hesitated. She found it curiously upsetting to be interrogated about the dead boy's private life. It felt like an intrusion into the world of someone so recently dead, although she knew that was an irrational reaction, that the policeman's questions were not only legitimate but essential. Even so, she felt uncomfortably as if Karim Aziz were watching her with that look of mocking amusement in his brown eyes with which he had more often than not left their inconclusive and, for her, frustrating sessions together.

'His work fell away quite sharply,' she said. 'He'd been doing quite well lower down the school, but in the fifth year he seemed to lose interest. He began to take time off. It happens sometimes but it's unusual with the Asian boys. Generally they do very well academically. Their parents are very ambitious for them. Indeed, Karim's father is—was,' she corrected herself quickly.

'But the boy himself seemed to have lost interest in school. He was determined to leave even before the exams last summer and nothing I could suggest in the way of jobs or further education seemed to interest him. I think when I came to do my report on where the fifth-year students had gone next, he went into the Unknown category.'

'He played truant, you said?'

Jo nodded. 'Not persistently, just occasionally. But even when he was here, all his teachers said the same thing on his reports—he wasn't working, he seemed to have lost interest in his GCSEs. School seemed to have become a bit of a joke to him—he wasn't disruptive, or awkward or anything like that, he just seemed to be laughing at us. In the end he skipped most of his exams, too, as far as I can remember. Except for art. He was very keen on art.'

'Did you like him?' Sergeant Mower broke in unexpectedly. 'You sound as if you had a soft spot for him.'

Jo looked at the Sergeant consideringly. She found the question surprising and rather touching. It was not one which she thought the unsmiling Chief Inspector would have thought of asking and she wondered what had prompted this sharp young man, with his fashionable jacket, his colourful, un-policeman-like tie and an accent which placed him far to the south of Bradfield, to ask it.

'Yes,' she said quietly. 'I did like Karim, oddly enough, in spite of all the hassle he caused. He had a sort of *joie de vivre* that isn't that common in kids of that age. The usual adolescent angst, the moodiness and awkwardness, seemed to have passed him by. But quite why he was enjoying life so much I have no idea—it certainly wasn't because of school, that's for sure.'

'He wasn't known to us,' Huddleston said, matter-of-factly. 'That was the first thing I checked. Do you think he was involved in anything delinquent we didn't know about?'

'Not in school,' Jo said quickly. 'He wasn't troublesome in that sense, as I say. Just uninterested, completely turned off. I talked to his father and he was at his wits' end to explain it. He was worried to death about the boy. There were three or four younger children, all girls, I think, so the father set great store by Karim doing well.'

'What are they? Pakistanis?' Huddleston asked.

'Most of the Asians round here come from a very small area of the Punjab, the Pakistani Punjab. We offer the language at GCSE. And Urdu, which is the official language.'

Huddleston grunted, a sound just short of contempt, and Jo resisted the temptation to respond angrily. She was conscious of Mower's eyes on her again and wondered what he was thinking.

'Moslems, then?' Huddleston went on, and Jo nodded.

'Not particularly fundamentalist about it,' she said quietly. 'A few of the girls have started wearing headscarves recently, but not many.'

23

'You allow that, with their school uniform?' Huddleston asked, his surprise showing.

'Of course,' Jo said. 'We've always allowed them to wear trousers. If it's a matter of conscience . . .' She gave an almost imperceptible shrug. She saw no reason to justify the school's policies to someone who clearly had little sympathy with them.

Huddleston grunted again.

'So not a girl then? Or likely not a Paki—an Asian girl, anyway? He wasn't in love?'

'If he was, it wasn't anything he would have talked to me about. But he didn't really give any sign of that. I've seen plenty of love-sick adolescents in this job.'

'What about a white girl? Could that have annoyed some of the other kids?' Huddleston persisted.

'The children here mix well,' Jo said, sharply this time. 'In school time, anyway. As far as romantic attachments are concerned, it happens sometimes—not involving the Moslem girls much, of course. They tend to be well protected by their families. But the other way, with the Asian boys sometimes, and with the Afro-Caribbean youngsters. There's been no trouble on that score while I've been here.'

Huddleston looked at Jo for a long time without speaking.

'You know what's been going on with some of the white youngsters in town,' he said at last, sceptically. 'We've had trouble with extremist groups. Are you telling me that there's nowt like that here, that you succeed in keeping politics out of school?' His tone was frankly disbelieving.

'There was an attempt to distribute leaflets at the school gate—oh, about six months ago, I suppose. We called the police,' she said ironically. 'The material they were dishing out was pretty inflammatory. Your uniformed people moved them on and they haven't been back.'

'But none of them were your pupils?'

'No, they weren't. They were considerably older, on the whole. Early twenties, I should say, rather than teenagers. In school, we treat racial abuse of any kind as a serious offence. We send the pupil home and don't have them back

24

until we've talked to the parents about what's happened. So far that seems to have worked very well.'

Huddleston leaned back in his chair and stretched his shoulders and sighed heavily.

'You can see my problem, Mrs Robertson,' he said. 'Asian lads do get stabbed. That's not my prejudice—it's a fact of life. What's odd about this case is that he should be stabbed here, at school, when officially he left the place months ago. I'm not trying to cast doubt on what I'm sure are the admirably high standards of behaviour you impose on your pupils, but the fact that he was killed here must lead me to ask whether there is any reason to suppose someone here was involved. This is a run-down area of town, a school which in my day had a run-down reputation to match, and you're telling me, in effect, that every one of your pupils is a little angel. I find that difficult to believe.'

'I'm not telling you that at all, Chief Inspector,' Jo Robertson replied coldly. 'We have more than our share of truants and delinquents, as your own records will show if you check them, as I'm sure you will. All I'm saying is that as far as Karim Aziz is concerned, I don't know of anyone here, black or white, who would have a motive for killing him. Nor can I give you a handy list of racist thugs who might have stabbed him simply because he's Asian. We don't, to my certain knowledge, have a chapter of the Ku Klux Klan here, or even the National Front.'

'So what happens about drugs, then, Mrs Robertson? Do you have a problem there?' The Chief Inspector changed tack suddenly but if he hoped to take Jo Robertson by surprise he must have been disappointed. Her cool gaze did not waver.

'What school hasn't had?' she said more quietly. 'But again, not on the premises more than a couple of times over the last two years, which is the time I've been here. And just small amounts of cannabis, nothing harder than that. If you want to go further back than that you'll have to talk to Mrs Jackson. But we know there's plenty of cannabis around the neighbourhood, as I'm sure you do. And worse.'

'So could that explain Karim's sudden lack of interest in school work?' Huddleston persisted.

'I thought of that. In fact, on one occasion I even asked him. But he just laughed and said he wasn't so stupid, and I was not to worry. Even so, I did worry,' Jo said slowly, Karim's almost mocking smile flashing disconcertingly across her mind's eye again, leaving her unsure of her ground. 'If a boy of that age suddenly appears to imagine that he can survive out there without much effort, without qualifications, without any serious plans for finding a job, then you know as well as I do that dealing in drugs is one way he could do it.'

'But you had no evidence?' The question hung in the air like an accusation.

'Absolutely none,' she said. 'We jump on drugs just as hard as we jump on racism, Chief Inspector.'

'The post-mortem will show us if he was on drugs,' Huddleston said heavily. 'But the pathologist found no obvious signs when he examined him down there. I asked him specifically.'

Jo suddenly felt infinitely tired, but although she squared her shoulders against the hard back of her chair, anticipating that the interview would continue, Huddleston glanced at his sergeant, who nodded and closed his notebook with a snap.

'I may need to talk to you again in a day or so, but I think that'll be all for now, Mrs Robertson,' the Chief Inspector said. 'You've been very patient after the shock you had. Thank you.'

Jo stood up wearily.

'I'm sorry I can't be more helpful,' she said. 'If I think of anything else, I'll let you know.'

The school appeared deserted when she left the medical room and walked slowly back to the staff-room down a half-lit corridor. At the end she caught a glimpse of the cleaners working in the gym, but the staff-room itself appeared to be empty as she crossed to her desk to collect her brief-case and a bundle of fourth-year essays which had to be marked that night. It was only when she had gathered her things together and picked up her coat that she noticed a tall, thin figure sitting hunched over a desk in the corner of the room.

Peter Masefield turned, becoming aware of her presence suddenly.

'They gave you bail, then?' he said softly, his face lighting up at the sight of her.

Jo dropped her belongings on to the desk and crossed the room swiftly to meet Peter's open arms.

'Oh, Peter,' she said, burying her face in his shoulder for a moment to hide the tears which had sprung into her eyes unbidden.

'It was awful?' he asked, kissing the top of her head.

She pulled away from him and sank into a chair next to his, keeping tight hold of his hand.

'It was awful,' she said. 'First the body, and then the questions. All awful.'

'Do you want to tell me?' he asked, his eyes full of concern.

She looked at her watch and shook her head.

'Not now,' she said. 'I must get home. I rang Neil but you know what he's like.' She shrugged dispiritedly, and Masefield took hold of her shoulders and pulled her towards him and kissed her gently and passionately on the mouth. For a moment they were lost to their surroundings until Jo pulled away and disentangled herself from Peter's embrace. He turned away to conceal the look of pain which flashed into his eyes and was wiped clean as quickly as it appeared.

'Have you got your car?' he asked, fully in control again, and when she shook her head wearily went on: 'I'll take you home.'

Neil Robertson was sitting at a computer screen in the tiny cluttered bedroom that he used as an office when his wife came home. He was head to head with a boy of about fourteen, his dark brown curls showing their first touch of grey up against a brush-like sandy crop with a wavy pattern razored into the short hair at the nape of the neck. They

27

were scrolling a complex program down the screen and did not turn round when Jo walked in. She brushed Neil's cheek with a perfunctory kiss, nodded to the boy, a fourth-year pupil at Sutton Park who gave her an uncertain grin, and went into the kitchen to start preparing the evening meal.

It was half an hour before she heard the front door slam as the visitor left, and Neil spun his wheelchair expertly into the small kitchen behind her.

'So what's the emergency? Young David wasn't at school today so he didn't know anything about it,' he asked expectantly. Jo looked at him blankly for a moment before she remembered that when she had telephoned him a couple of hours ago she had simply said that an emergency would keep her at school late. Neil was looking at her accusingly, his eyes unfriendly, as they often were these days.

'It was more a tragedy than an emergency,' Jo said, draining the potatoes into the sink in a cloud of steam and wondering now why she had chosen that particular word. As she set the table for two and gave Neil a glass of whisky and water she told him briefly what had happened. The kitchen was specially adapted for the needs of someone in a wheelchair but Neil seldom made use of it if Jo was there. He pulled his chair up to the table in the living-room with an impatient jerk, watching his wife as she dished up their meal, and sipped his drink thirstily. He was a big man, whose broad shoulders looked out of proportion in the narrow confines of the chair, and whose impatient thrusts at the wheels with well-muscled arms made it seem almost incredible that he could not push himself to his feet and cross the room with the sort of stride to which he obviously aspired.

'What on earth was he doing in the building, anyway?' he asked at last, his dark eyes bright with curiosity and his colour rising as the whisky took effect.

'I simply can't imagine,' Jo said. 'He hardly came to school during his last term, so why he should turn up now is a complete mystery. Margaret wants me to go and see his parents after school tomorrow. I can't say I'm keen, but someone should pass on the school's sympathy.'

'So I suppose you'll be late again?' Neil's angry reaction was swift and not unexpected. 'Just as well I asked young David to come round again. We're working on a new game. He has real talent, you know, that boy. He'll be better than I am in a year or so.'

Since illness put him into the chair that he regarded as a prison, Neil Robertson had struggled to turn what had been a hobby, writing computer games, into a living, with only modest success in commercial terms. But the high-powered machine that they had invested in had its benefits in providing a world where his bitterly resented disability lost its power to frustrate him. Not one single substitute world, but many, lay at his fingertips, worlds where wrongs were invariably righted in a way which Neil had bitterly ceased to believe was possible in reality.

David, the computer obsessed teenager Jo had intro-duced to him, aided and abetted these flights of the imagin-ation in time and space with increasing skill of his own. Although she would never put the thought into words to Neil, the relationship between the two was becoming more and more like that of father and son, some small comfort, she thought, in a house where the possibility of having children was no longer mentioned.

'Did you got out today?' Jo asked. 'You said you would.'

Neil looked away and did not reply. That morning he had insisted angrily on keeping their car, specially adapted so that he could put his wheelchair on board and drive without foot controls, leaving Jo to go to school on the bus. He needed to visit a computer shop in town, he had insisted. It was a trip he was quite capable of making on his own, but which he more often than not deferred until Jo could do the errand for him.

'I'll need the car tomorrow,' she said.

'Then you can get the discs for me, can't you?' he came back quickly. Her lips tightened but she nodded wearily and said nothing. Tonight, of all nights, she thought, she could not stand a row with Neil.

Neil picked up the remote control for the television and switched on the news. That, Jo knew very well, was a signal that conversation was at an end for the moment, possibly for the whole evening, and her own face reflected a mixture of anger and pain.

The Robertsons lived within two miles of Sutton Park school in a bungalow which had been specially converted for the use of a someone in a wheelchair. The house had been the deciding factor in their move to Bradfield from London two years ago. In the city Neil had been virtually imprisoned by his disability, trapped in a third-floor flat after an illness as sudden as it was devastating had put him in a wheelchair at the age of 30 and effectively ended his own career.

Neil Robertson was not a patient man. He had picked up the virus which crippled him, and which had thrown the medical profession into a frenzy of curiosity which produced nothing in the way of a cure, on a business trip to the Far East. He had flown home feeling unwell, had been rushed to hospital with a rocketing fever within hours of his return, and had railed against an unjust Fate ever since he had regained consciousness, unable to use his legs, after three days and nights in intensive care.

Jo finished her meal in silence, half-watching the flickering images on the screen with her mind on the horrific sight she had seen at school. She got up at last with a heavy sigh and stacked the dishes in the sink to wash later. Leaving Neil in front of the television in the living-room, she set out her evening's marking at her desk in their shared study and put a tape of Schubert's Trout Quintet on the stereo. She sat for a moment with her head on her hands listening to the familiar melody.

She remembered going to a concert on the South Bank with Neil to hear this very piece soon after they were married. She had loved him then, she thought, with all the passion she had been capable of at twenty-three, loved his physical strength, his dark, sturdy body, his slightly manic humour and his fierce determination to succeed.

She might, she thought, in her darkest moments have predicted the tragedy which befell him five years later, though with his unapologetic love of speed and ex-

30

citement a car accident would have been a more likely scenario than the virus which had actually struck him down. What she could not have foreseen was that the loss of his mobility would reduce him to a surly, uncooperative, moody shadow of his former self. It was not the loss of her husband's ability to walk which caused Jo Robertson's anguish, but the loss of the man she had loved and married.

CHAPTER 3

Chief Inspector Harry Huddleston was not happy. He had looked forward to his last couple of weeks in the police force as a time of winding down, a period for many a convivial and nostalgic drink with colleagues he had worked with for more than thirty years. He had hoped for sufficient leeway to visit some of the outlaying police stations in the county where he had old friends of all ranks to whom he owed a pint of Tetleys or two and who would, he anticipated confidently, return the compliment and more. He had hoped, in fact, to go into his retirement gently, and if he had thought at all about the possibility of a major case arising before the end of the year when he would finally depart, he had perhaps dreamed, in so far as he, as an often self-proclaimed realist, ever permitted himself to dream, of a dramatic murder case which he would solve swiftly with the sort of insight which he knew came rarely in real life, though common enough in fiction, and even more rarely to him personally.

All that, it seemed, was not to be. What he assumed must be his last murder case had taken a very different form and one which he disliked intensely. He knew his own limitations, and one of them was that as a Bradfield man born and bred, as the local phrase had it, he had watched its transformation from a self-confidently bustling northern manufacturing town into a depressed multi-racial community with some resentment. Many of those who had originally found a welcome of sorts in Yorkshire when there

31

was work to be had were now washed up on the margins of society, unemployed and disenchanted with the country to which they had travelled with such high hopes for themselves and their children.

If pressed, as Huddleston sometimes was by colleagues in the lounge bar of the Woolpack after he had left police headquarters for the day, he complained that too many allowances were being made, by the police among others, in the interests of 'good community relations'. For himself, he would add, he would behave as if colour-blind: 'they' would get the same treatment from him as any other citizen of Bradfield, nothing more and nothing less.

His view was quite firm: if strangers came to live on his patch—whether they came from the other side of the Pennines, the other side of Europe, from where many an immigrant had sought refuge in the town's dark stone terraces when he had been at school himself immediately after the war, or from the other side of the world, their first obligation was to learn the ways of the natives and live as inconspicuous a life as possible. They should learn the language, learn to play cricket, if they didn't know already, and keep a low profile else.

In his experience, this was what the Poles and Lithuanians and Jews who had moved into the decaying Victorian heart of the town in his childhood had successfully done. And good luck to them, he said, as they moved out of the multi-occupied terraces and into the suburbs to become his neighbours. But it was what the most recent newcomers, with their even more obtrusive dress, and food and religion, so resolutely refused to do. He was far too cautious ever to call the area where Asygarth Lane took a sharp turn over the canal bridge into the town centre Little Asia, as many in the town did, but it was what he thought, as he and Sergeant Mower drove into Water Street and pulled up outside the corner shop owned by Karim Aziz's father.

'Should we have brought a WPC?' the Sergeant asked cautiously, having known Huddleston long enough to be aware of his prejudices, and that it was wise to tread around them carefully, though he did not share them.

32

'What for?' Huddleston asked sharply. Young Kevin Mower, with his dark good looks and his Londoner's sharpness of dress and attitude, was not his favourite partner on a case. He was, he knew, a young man with ambition but he was not sure yet whether that ambition should be met in the Yorkshire force, particularly as canteen gossip had it that he had left London under a cloud, the precise nature of which Huddleston had not yet prised out of his tight-lipped superiors. On the future of young Sergeant Mower Huddleston still reserved judgement and suspected he might continue to reserve it beyond the end of the year.

'Well, if the mother is there on her own she won't want to let us in,' Mower said, reasonably enough. 'You know —strange men and Moslem women. She might not even speak English . . .'

'I thought you were learning Punjabi, or whatever the lingo's called,' the Chief Inspector said.

'Yes, I am,' Mower said defensively. 'But I've only learned a few words. I'm not in the interviewing league yet. No way.'

'Aye, well, let's go and see, shall we? It looks as if they've got visitors already.' Huddleston nodded at a sleek black Mercedes sports car parked incongruously outside the small brick shop where the windows were still covered by an overnight security grille. The door stood open, though, and the two men went through to the cluttered interior, the shelves piled high with a mixture of European and Asian foods, and the air smelling strongly of spices. There was no one in the shop but they followed the faint sound of voices to find themselves at a curtained doorway which obviously led into living quarters at the rear.

They were met, to Huddleston's evident irritation, by a tall, good-looking young man, his gleaming dark hair expensively styled, wearing a suit of a cut and material which Mower recognized—and envied—as very expensive indeed. As if that were not enough, he was glancing at a Rolex watch which was clearly not a Far Eastern imitation as he made his way towards them across Ahmed Aziz's tiny living-room.

'Ah, Chief Inspector Huddleston,' the young man said with total self-confidence. There was no trace of an accent in his voice, either that of Pakistan or of Bradfield. He held out his hand to Huddleston who took it briefly and without enthusiasm.

'Sammy Arif,' he said. 'I think we have met before at one of those joint Rotary-police charity do's at the Clarendon, isn't that right? I was there for my father, who I think was in Pakistan at the time. And didn't I see you at Headingley last summer, at the Test?'

Huddleston nodded grudgingly at that. Cricket was not just a passion but a religion with him, and he took his annual leave to coincide with the two test matches which were played in the north of England.

'They were on good form at Leeds, your lot,' he said.

Sammy Arif smiled delightedly, although Mower wondered whether his pleasure was the compliment to the Pakistan team or the Chief Inspector's automatic assignment of the anglicized young man to the non-English camp. Politicians were not the first to apply the cricket test as a measure of where allegiance lay. Arif glanced slightly guiltily at the anxious figure of Ahmed Aziz, who was standing close behind him, apparently hanging on his every word.

'As I think you know, I am legally qualified, although I don't practise. I came down to see if Mr Aziz and his family needed any help. We have contact with many of these small shops through the business, you know.'

'Very thoughtful of you,' Huddleston acknowledged without warmth. Sergeant Mower shot a glance at him which mixed the faintest trace of amusement with concern. He had been in Bradfield long enough to know Arif's name, and his father's reputation, as one of the wealthiest and most powerful men in the Moslem community, head of an import-export business which traded all over the world, and for a time a member of the city council and the first Asian to be elected mayor.

Sami Arif, inevitably known since his student days as Sammy, did not disguise the appraisal in his look now as he faced the two policemen in the doorway. His dark eyes were watchful rather than friendly, Mower thought, and it was Huddleston who broke the moment's tension by turning away from the young man and addressing Aziz, who was looking anxiously at the confrontation in his doorway.

'It is convenient to talk now, is it, Mr Aziz?' he asked, in a voice which was just a fraction too loud. 'You did say last night that it would be convenient.'

Aziz was a small man and it was clear to both policemen that he was still in a state of shock. The skin around his eyes was dark and puffy, he wore no tie and his suit looked crumpled and dusty, almost as if he had slept in it. He had not shaved, and for a moment his eyes wandered almost vacantly from one of his visitors to another as if uncertain to whom he should respond.

'Yes, yes,' he said at last. 'Yes, I am expecting you, Chief Inspector, sir. I am telling Mr Arif here that I am expecting you now. Please come in.'

Arif spoke again, this time in fluent Punjabi to Aziz, and when he had finished he turned back to Huddleston with a brilliant smile.

'I was just telling Mr Aziz that he is welcome to contact me or my father if there is anything we can do,' he explained blandly. 'Now I really must dash. I wish you the best of luck with the case, Chief Inspector, and a speedy conclusion. This sort of thing does no good to community relations at all, does it?'

Without waiting for a reply he swung the dark navy overcoat that he had been carrying on his arm over his shoulders and swept out through the curtained doorway to the dimly lit shop, leaving behind him on the disturbed air only the subtlest trace of his after-shave.

Sergeant Mower actually saw Huddleston grit his teeth with annoyance. We're going to have to tread carefully on this one, he thought to himself. Please God we get a quick result—and a clear-cut one, at that. Anything less could be very messy indeed.

'Well, that didn't get us very far,' Huddleston said grimly half an hour later as they got back into their car. In fact

Ahmed Aziz had been able to tell them very little that was of help to their inquiries. Six months ago, he said, Karim had left home, and they had not seen him since. The admission was made with obvious embarrassment on the father's part, and both Huddleston and Mower knew how unusual it was for the children of this Asian community to run away from home. What in an English context would have been a commonplace enough tale of family rows followed by an angry departure by the young man was told by Aziz with still lingering disbelief and obvious pain. With four younger daughters to provide for, the boy's departure was obviously not merely an emotional trauma but threatened the family with financial difficulties as well. Throughout the interview Mrs Aziz, who, as Mower had suspected, spoke little English, had sat beside her husband with her head-covering pulled half across her face, dabbing ineffectually at the tears which trickled down her cheeks.

'So where now, guv?' Mower asked, starting up the car, watched solemnly by a small group of little girls on the street corner, bundled up in winter coats and scarves over their traditional bright satins.

'Time to have a word with that nutcase Regan,' Huddleston said.

Mower nodded, and accelerated fast into a gap in the traffic on Aysgarth Lane.

'Do you think that's a serious possibility?' he asked. 'At the school? It's an odd place for a murder, and a long way from Regan's usual patch. That teacher, the Robertson woman, she's right, you know. There's not been much race trouble on that side of town.'

'Well, there's always a first time,' Huddleston said. 'It's not that hard to get from the Heights to Sutton Park, is it? Anyway it'll not hurt to put the fear of God into young Regan and his friends. He's an evil little toe-rag at the best of times.'

Mower took them through the town centre, where what was left of the mellow stone Victorian heart of the town seemed to cower apologetically in the face of the brash twentieth-century additions: rain-streaked 'sixties concrete blocks, now outfaced by the glittering glass and coloured steel and brick palaces of the 1980s. They passed the central police station, an uncomfortable boxy neighbour of the gothic town hall, and swirled round the one-way system until they found the exit which took them climbing swiftly to the west side of the town where the tower blocks of the most avant-garde of the town's council estates, The Heights, known more colloquially simply as Wuthering, glowered down at the changing industrial scene in the valley below.

Geoff Regan still lived, surprisingly, with his parents and a younger sister in a fifth-floor maisonette. Taking a deep breath of fresh air to clear the smell of the lift from their nostrils as they walked along the access deck to the front door, Mower glanced down briefly to where they had parked the car a hundred feet below.

'The sociologists aren't far wrong,' he ventured, to a sceptical grunt from Huddleston.

'How's that, then?' he asked grudgingly.

'If you put people in pig sties you'll tend to produce pigs,' Mower said.

Huddleston looked at the sergeant sharply, but unusually there was a hint of amusement in his eyes.

'When I were a lad . . .' he said, and they both laughed. It was a conversation they had had too many times for either of them to expect any change in the other's attitude. Seven years in the police force had not dented Mower's conviction, strengthened by three years at university but born of his own schooling in a racially mixed inner suburb of London, that to a large extent human beings were the product of their environment, while Huddleston, who had struggled out of an equally impoverished working-class home with no father, put all his faith in the ability of anyone to pull themselves up by their bootstraps as successfully as he had done himself.

'I don't see that even this dump is any excuse for this laddo,' Huddleston said flatly as he banged on the next front door they came to. 'And his parents seem inoffensive enough to me.'

37

Geoff Regan opened the door to them himself. He was a tall youth, his hair cropped almost to the skull, the stubble over his scalp and face glinting a faintly metallic red over the white and slightly mottled skin. He wore dangling metal ear-rings in both ears, one in the shape of a skull and the other a militaristic design incorporating a swastika. His muscular body filled his skimpy black T-shirt, decorated with another version of a death's head, and his baggy blue jeans were turned up at the bottom to half-way up his calf to reveal a pair of heavy red boots, tightly laced, and menacingly metal-tipped at the toe. Regan kept one boot firmly behind the door so that he could block their entrance.

Chief Inspector Huddleston looked at him with an expression which barely masked contempt with professional impassivity.

'A quick word, if you don't mind, lad,' he said, putting a hand firmly on the door-handle. Regan appeared to hesitate for a moment before giving a shrug and moving back into the hallway to let the two men in.

He led the way into the living-room where a large television set was relaying a film from a video-recorder. A jumble of video-films and lager cans, some empty and others full, lay on the floor where years of grime and cigarette ash had turned what might have been a patterned carpet into a dull grey felt. The screen was filled with the noise of gunfire and the sight of what appeared to be a helicopter attack on a Vietnamese village.

Regan used a remote control to turn the sound-track down slightly but did not switch the set off. He waved a hand at the imitation leather sofa at the other side of the room by way of invitation to the two men to sit down but seemed to find it difficult to drag his own eyes away from the screen. On the other side of a door which Mower assumed must lead to the kitchen a dog began to bark menacingly and scratch ferociously at the paintwork, shifting the flimsy door in its frame.

'Shurrup, Cæsar,' Regan snarled in the direction of the door and the frustrated animal fell silent, contenting itself with occasional lunges at the woodwork, which shuddered under its assaults.

'You're not working, then?' Huddleston said. It was more a statement of the obvious than a question.

'Nah,' Regan said, and reluctantly switched the sound off completely and turned his attention to the policemen.

'So what's it to you, then?' he asked. 'My probation officer's a happy man, so what the hell do you want?'

'Just a little chat about community relations', Huddleston said, with the slight distaste in his voice which always surfaced when he was compelled to use that phrase. Regan laughed.

'Devoted to them, I am, didn't you know? Bad relations, any road.'

'This isn't a joke, Regan,' Mower said sharply. 'We need to know where you were the night before last, you and any of your NF mates who are still on the streets.'

'Wednesday night?' Regan asked. 'Where'd you think we'd be Wednesday night, you pillock? United were playing away, weren't they? We was in Manchester for the match.'

'I thought you'd been banned from United's games,' Huddleston said, registering the insult but content to let it ride.

'Yeah, well, there's ways of getting round these things, ain't there,' Regan said with a satisfied smirk. 'Any road, that's where I was, and Terry Garford and Boots Hendry. We had a few drinks after the game and got back here about midnight I should think. Is that what you want to know, Inspector? Me mum'll vouch for when I come in, won't she? What do you want to know for, any road?'

'So how did you travel?' Mower asked.

'In Terry's car.'

'Did anyone else see you in Manchester, anyone from Bradfield see you at the match?' Huddleston persisted, his face still a picture of professional scepticism, his eyes cold. Regan turned the sound up on his film slightly and his eyes flickered back and forth between the screen and his interlocutors restlessly. He's not worried enough, Mower decided and Huddleston seemed to come to the same conclusion because he did not press for an answer to his final question.

'We'll check it out, Geoff lad,' he said, but the warning lacked any serious threat. He got to his feet. 'And I'll be having a quiet word with my friend Inspector Purcell about your attendance at football matches. No doubt he'll be around to see you later on.'

'Eff you,' Regan snarled. 'That wasn't why you came. Can't you leave it out?'

'No, it wasn't why we came,' Huddleston agreed. 'But it'll do to be going on with. I'm watching you, lad.' The two men left the youth slumped on the sofa again with the volume turned up to its maximum, filling the whole flat with the thunder of battle. On the walkway outside they bumped into a small middle-aged woman with the same dull red hair as Regan carrying a heavy shopping-bag.

'Good day, Mrs Regan,' Huddleston said with enormous bonhomie. 'Your lad keeping his nose clean now, is he? That's what he tells me.'

'What do you want?' Mrs Regan asked sharply.

'Where was he on Wednesday evening, Mrs Regan?' Mower came back quickly. The woman looked at him with slightly watery blue eyes which showed no hint of fear.

'He went to t'match, didn't he?' she said. 'I told him he shouldn't, but I might as well talk to t'floor. With Terry and Boots. To Manchester. He can always find brass, you know, when it's a case of going to a match but if I ask him for owt for his keep, he's always skint.'

'Right, Mrs Regan, that's fine. We may be back, but then again, we may not,' Huddleston said enthusiastically and pushed his not inconsiderable bulk past the bemused woman and strode off towards the lifts.

'Effing pigs,' Mrs Regan muttered under her breath as she picked up her shopping and resumed her slow progress along the deck to her own flat. 'Can't you leave anyone alone.'

As the stinking lift lurched back to ground level, Mower, trying to hold his breath as long as he could, looked quizzically at Huddleston but said nothing. The older man eventually raised one eyebrow.

'He's not our laddo,' he said finally. 'I remember the day the magistrates banned him from United's games. He was that furious he put a brick through the cop-shop window and got ten days inside for it. He's a true supporter, in spite of being a pain in the bum every time he gets inside the ground. Someone'll have seen him at Manchester. He's too well known not to have been noticed. You'd better get one of the lads to check it out, but it'll be a waste of time.'

'So you reckon that lets him out?' Mower asked as soon as he had taken a deep breath of almost fresh air as the lift door reluctantly creaked open.

'Given what old Amos Atherton said this morning about the time of death, aye, I'd say that lets him out. And thank God for that. If it's a choice between putting that yobbo away for a race killing and digging around among the Pakis to find which of them put a knife into young Karim I know which I'd rather do. I'd rather have Geoff Regan banged up again any day. But if it's a choice between the race riots that might follow and a nice quiet bit of ethnic family revenge or summat like that, then you have to admit we'd be better off looking for cousin Achmed or Mohammed or whoever. Much less trouble in the long run. You know I'm right.'

Mower grinned in spite of himself.

'Right, guv,' he said.

CHAPTER 4

An all-embracing and only half-controlled excitement gripped the whole of Sutton Park school that day. Time and again Jo Robertson fended off questions about the murder from inquisitive children with sparkling eyes. Had she seen the body? Was there a lot of blood? Did she know who did it? In desperation, she decided that at the beginning of each of her lessons she would tell the class the facts, as she knew them, and as Margaret Jackson had outlined them to the whole school at assembly that morning, and then firmly close the subject. That seemed to work, although it was much harder to deter the youngsters, their faces avid with curiosity, who stopped her in the corridor demanding more information as she moved from class to class.

Down in the school basement the boys' changing-room and showers had been sealed off by the police, but were still the centre of interest to children as they came and went to their lockers. At break Jo chased a group of third-year boys who were trying to peer through the glass panels of the door into the locked room.

'Vanish!' she said sharply. 'The bell's gone, you should be in your classrooms by now.'

'We were just looking, miss,' one boy said ingratiatingly. 'Ali here's Karim's cousin and he's right upset.' He indicated a small Asian boy, impeccable in his school uniform, who had been hanging back on the edge of the group of white boys.

'I'm sorry, Ali,' Jo said, taking the boy's arm and leading him away from the changing-room. 'You must be very upset. Should you be in school today?' The boy looked back at her impassively, giving nothing away.

'My father said come today, stay off for the funeral,' he said.

'Well, fine, if you feel you can cope. But I should keep away from the changing-rooms, if I were you. That's bound to make it worse.'

The child nodded, looking very small and vulnerable, although Jo knew that he must be at least thirteen.

'Do you have any other relations in school?' she asked, knowing that many of the Asians in the town belonged to large extended families who had emigrated originally from the same group of villages, fathers and brothers in the first wave, wives and older children, cousins and even elderly parents later.

'Only my sister Ayesha,' the boy said. 'She's in the lower sixth.'

'Yes, of course,' Jo said, seeing the family resemblance,

42

the fine bone structure and the eyes of an unusually pale brown, now it was brought to her attention. 'I teach her. Well, if you're feeling very miserable, I should find Ayesha later on and ask her to take you home. Have you told your form tutor that Karim was your cousin?' The boy shook his head, and Jo realized that such a confession would be more than he could cope with.

'Don't worry. Whose form are you in? I'll tell them for you.' That settled, she chased the whole group of boys to their next lesson, wondering how long it would be before the previous day's horror sank into the school's collective memory and lost its power to excite and shock. The resilience of children, who in this part of town faced family breakdown, violence and occasionally worse with heartbreaking regularity, never failed to astonish her, but this was something new. For many of Sutton Park's pupils school was a haven of order in a cruel and capricious world. To find violence intruding so grotesquely here, she knew, would disturb many, with unpredictable consequences for the school's own fragile stability.

She watched while the boys scuffled and pushed their way up the stairs to their next class. Then she too stole a glance at the locked door and shuddered as the memory of the icy coldness of Karim's huddled body sprang unbidden into her mind. She tore her eyes away and turned on her heel, forcing herself to concentrate on the mysteries of punctuation which she was about to explore with a group of slow-learning twelve-year-olds. A full stop is what we need for this, she thought grimly as she followed Ali and his friends up the stairs.

At lunch-time Jo ate a hasty sandwich in the staff-room and then caught Peter Masefield's eye across the room. He nodded and they left together to walk to the school hall where they were due to supervise a rehearsal for the Christmas entertainment. The corridor was quiet, with only a small group of pupils gossiping at the far end, well out of earshot, but even so Peter spoke quietly. It was the first time they had been able to exchange a private word that day.

43

'Are you all right?' Peter asked.

She nodded. 'I'm fine,' she said. 'I even slept soundly, which is something of an achievement in the circumstances.'

'Come round to my place after school,' he said.

'I can't, Peter. I have to go down to the police station to sign a statement, and then Margaret's asked me to go round and see the Aziz family.'

They turned into the narrow passageway which led into the small drama changing-rooms at the back of the stage in the main hall. Peter spun on his heel and stopped Jo in her tracks with a hand on her arm, his face tense with suppressed emotion and his eyes full of pain.

'I don't think I can stand this much longer,' he said, his voice harsh.

Jo put her hand over his and felt the familiar urgent pang of desire which his touch induced. She took her hand away again as if stung and drew back, leaning against the wall slightly breathlessly.

'Not now,' she whispered. 'The kids . . .'

Masefield nodded, and with an obvious effort of will composed himself and turned away.

She followed him into the hall. It was a high, gaunt room, with tall windows grimy with years of unattended dirt which in any case let in little light as the curtains were in most cases impossible to draw fully open because the sliding rails had either rusted or silted up long ago. In one corner the ceiling and walls were stained with rainwater which continually leaked from the flat roof above, however many times it was pronounced sealed by the council's maintenance staff. Sutton Park was housed in buildings which had been designated for replacement in the 1950s. Forty years later the school was still waiting to move.

Traditionally, with its multi-racial mixture of several different religions, the school celebrated Christmas with an entertainment which all the children could share. This year there were to be several comic sketches of school life, a selection of Christmas music performed by the school orchestra and choir, a pop contribution from the school's latest fifth-year 'group', if the volatile black vocalist, Vinny Barnes, and his backing instrumentalists had not fragmented by the time the day of the concert arrived, and for the first time a musical contribution by three elegant young Asian girls, including Karim Aziz's cousin Ayesha and two friends who had just begun their sixth-form studies and had revealed themselves as accomplished players of the sitar and a small drum called a tabla. This lunch-time roughly half the performers were supposed to be prepared to run through their performances so that Jo and Peter could time them and advise on costume and presentation.

They walked into a deafening cacophony of noise and activity. Every instrumentalist in the room appeared to be tuning up, with the amplified guitars and the thunderous extroversion of the pop drummer drowning the delicate sounds of the Asian girls' instruments, and gales of laughter attending the antics of a group of fourth-year children who were apparently rehearsing their comic sketch with the assistance of a row of upturned chairs and some incidental music on the piano.

Peter jumped on to the stage, deftly unplugged three electric guitars from their amplifiers and imperiously waved the energetic drummer to a cymbal-clashing standstill, after which the boy collapsed in mock exhaustion over his kit. The sudden diminution in the noise level in itself attracted attention to the stage and Peter stood on the edge of the platform, rocking to and fro gently on the balls of his feet, waiting until the hubbub below slowly subsided and he had the attention of everyone in the hall.

'Right,' he said at last, with total authority. 'Now if you want this concert to go ahead, this is what is going to happen next.'

At the back of the hall, Jo stood next to Ayesha and her friends, Farida and Safia, as an excited silence fell. These were not the submissive young Asian girls of European preconception, but self-confident young women who cheerfully adapted the basic rules of Moslem modesty to their own more westernized fashion sense. They all wore trousers in the school's regulation navy, but with a selection of cream and white tunics and shirts which meant that they would not have looked out of place at a fashion show. None of them favoured the traditional headscarf that some of their co-religionists at the school wore, and their gleaming dark hair was if anything more elegantly styled than anything their fairer contemporaries could boast.

'If you're not needed until the end, do you want to go and practise in one of the music rooms while you're waiting?' Jo asked the three girls. They glanced at each other with unusual uncertainty and Jo thought that she caught a glimpse of strain pass across Ayesha's classically beautiful features.

'Could you time us straight away if we played to you somewhere else?' she asked. She hesitated for a moment. 'I'm not feeling very good, Mrs Robertson,' she admitted at last. 'Things at home are a bit—you know?'

'Of course, that'll be fine,' Jo said. 'I'll just tell Mr Masefield what we're doing.'

In the tiny practice room Jo listened dreamily to the girls' performance. She knew little enough about Asian music, she realized, and suspected that what they were playing had been adapted to suit European sensibilities, though she could not be sure. She watched the girls closely, fascinated by their absolute concentration on their instruments. They were all sixth-formers, among the brightest of the school's students. Farida and Safia were both studying science and Safia hoped to become a doctor while Farida had set her heart on going to Oxford, though more because her brother went to Cambridge than for any positive attachment to the dreaming spires, Jo thought.

Farida Arif, unlike the other two, was the daughter of a wealthy family where encouragement to do well at school came particularly from her mother, who taught at the local college of higher education, as well as from her successful businessman father, one of the school's governors. Farida had come to Sutton Park to join the sixth from at her own insistence, after a time at a private boarding-school which, she had told Jo, she had hated. There had been more prejudice among those well-heeled young ladies than she had ever met in Bradfield, she had complained bitterly.

Ayesha and Safia, though, were the daughters of two of the families from remote Punjabi villages who had flocked to Bradfield in the 1960s to take jobs in the textile factories and on the buses. If her parents had remained at home, Ayesha had told Jo once, she would be married by now, and probably a mother, expected to work long hours in the fields by day and then in the house until the rest of the family had gone to bed, as her cousins who had remained in Pakistan already did. She had visited her parents' village when she was twelve and had come back to England determined that she would never return.

Most musicians in Pakistan, they had told her, were men, although there had been female musicians in the old days at the courts of the Moghul emperors. But in Britain few boys were showing much enthusiasm for traditional instruments and all three girls had began to play with the encouragement of Farida's mother, who had been saddened to see one of the oldest musical traditions in the world lost to their generation.

The girls played for six minutes exactly, which is what they had been asked to do, and when they had finished, with a haunting note which died away slowly into the oppressive silence of the sound-proofed room, Jo clapped her hands with genuine enthusiasm.

'Great,' she said. 'That's just right—and you played it beautifully. I don't think you need to hang about any more. I'll tell Mr Masefield that you're well-rehearsed.' The girls packed their instruments away silently, but as her friends went out ahead of her Ayesha hesitated for a moment in the doorway.

'Do you want to talk?' Jo asked quietly. The girl looked at her gravely, her unusual hazel eyes troubled, but in the end she shook her head.

'I'm all right, thanks,' she said and closed the door quietly behind her. Jo did not believe her.

*

Anxiety about the murder and its effect on the school took the edge off the day. In class even the most conscientious children were fidgety and unable to concentrate, those who seldom concentrated anyway verged on the uncontrollable. Tired and irritable herself after a day trying to maintain precarious order in classes and corridors, Jo found herself staring in tearful disbelief at a copy of the local evening paper she had bought on her way to the central police station to sign her statement. The huge front page headline, which read RACE KILLING AT SUTTON SCHOOL, leapt from the page. She sat in the car for a moment with the paper spread out in front of her over the steering-wheel, reading the heavy type of the news item and feeling slightly sick. The details of what had happened the previous day were accurate enough. What shocked her was the implication that the police had already decided that there was a racial motive involved in the murder—that Karim Aziz had probably been stabbed by white youths while engaged in some sort of break-in at the school.

She drove on slowly, parked in the centre of the town and walked to the police station where Detective-Sergeant Mower welcomed her with an appreciative look which was just the safe side of offensive and took her to a small interview room and read her his typed version of how she had found Karim Aziz's body. It was a fair and accurate summary and she signed it without hesitation. But instead of getting up to go, she sat back in her chair for a moment and looked at the detective across the table. She saw an intelligent face, dark and undeniably attractive but with a stubborn set to the chin and mouth, and, in spite of the ready smile, a look of caution in the brown eyes. He was dressed carefully in a dark polo-necked sweater under a grey bomber jacket, and his slacks were neatly pressed. An ambitious policeman, she guessed, and sharper, she suspected, than the ponderous chief inspector for whom he worked.

She took the newspaper out of her briefcase and spread it out in front of him. He glanced at it interestedly, as if he had not seen it before.

'Is that what you really think?' Jo asked.

Mower looked down at his hands, as if deciding whether to speak while he inspected his fingernails.

'They quote your chief inspector,' Jo said angrily. 'He must have some evidence to go on before making suggestions about race killings and stirring up trouble in the community.'

'I don't talk to the Press,' Mower said, apparently stung into an embarrassed response. 'It's not my job. As far as I know, the paper's pushing that issue further than anyone here thinks is reasonable. As far as I know, there's no evidence for it. The boss seems to think that it was probably someone the boy's own age, his own community—an argument over a girl, something like that. Or conceivably the race thing. But there's nothing definite.'

He shrugged gloomily, as though the 'race thing' was a wild card which no one could account for, as in some senses, Jo thought, it probably was. A force that was irrational and violent and unpredictable.

'But we didn't want to play that up at the moment because of upsetting the Asians,' Sergeant Mower went on, glancing at the headline again. 'There's bound to be a reaction.'

'Of course there will be, if that's what it comes down to,' Jo said. 'They'll be very angry—and very frightened. And I really didn't think there was that level of hatred among the youngsters on our side of town. I've never seen any evidence of it at school.'

'Yes, well, let's hope it was one of theirs, then,' the Sergeant said dismissively, getting up from his seat. 'And let's hope we make a quick arrest. It's easier all round, you know, if white sticks to murdering white and black kills black.'

Dear God, is that what we've come to, Jo thought as she followed the sergeant out to the front entrance.

She drove back towards Sutton Park, but before the busy main road began to climb towards the school and the council estate which surrounded it, she turned into a side-street of modest Victorian brick houses, each with a narrow strip of garden separating front porch from pavement, inter-

49

spersed with the occasional small shop, which was where many of the school's Asian families lived.

She pulled up outside the corner grocer's which was owned by Karim Aziz's father, and went in. An elderly man she did not know stood at the till talking in a language she recognized as Punjabi to two middle-aged women in traditional dress with loose scarves pulled well forward across their hair. They all turned to look at her with a mixture of curiosity and suspicion as she approached.

'Can I help you?' the old man asked politely, but without warmth. Jo explained who she was and was waved through a curtain into a rear room, where she found the Aziz family, parents and four huge-eyed little girls, sitting silently together with a tall bearded man in a round white cap and traditional dress whom she took to be an imam. The tall man acknowledged her presence gravely and got up to leave.

A single tear crept down the brown cheek of Mrs Aziz. She wiped it away with the corner of the veil of soft material which covered her hair, and her husband took her hand awkwardly.

'It was very good of you to come, Mrs Robertson,' he said. 'We do appreciate it. My wife appreciates it. Her English is not good, you understand, and at a time like this . . .' Mr Aziz shrugged helplessly. 'At a time like this it is difficult to know what to do,' he said.

'All the school send their sympathy,' Jo said.

'The police have been here so much,' Mr Aziz said. 'It is better if we are left alone to grieve now.'

'Of course,' Jo said, getting up awkwardly. 'If you would rather be alone . . .'

'No, no, please don't be offended. We are very grateful to you for coming. It is just that we have been overwhelmed by all the questions—police, reporters, so many questions. There seems to be no end to them. What has Karim been doing since he left school? Who are his friends? So many questions. And we have so few answers, you see.'

'So few answers?' Jo repeated, feeling that she had missed something.

'We do not know what Karim has been doing for the last six months,' Mr Aziz said, his voice dull with pain, glancing helplessly at his wife and the four girls whom, she knew, he would not regard as an unmixed blessing when their dowries had to be taken into account. 'He left home, you see. Karim, my only son, had left us.'

Mrs Aziz, who could clearly follow some of the conversation, broke into a stream of rapid Punjabi at that and her husband responded sharply. Jo turned towards the door, overwhelmed by the sheer weight of emotion in the room which she could not possibly share. She made her farewells awkwardly and Khawar, the oldest of the daughters, shyly followed her through the shop to the door.

'What did your mother say?' Jo asked quietly. The girl looked at her silently for a moment, glancing back at her grandfather who was still deep in conversation in the inner recesses of the shop.

'She said that Karim was a wicked boy,' the child said softly.

'But why? What had he done?'

'He went away, and he lived with a white girl,' Khawar said even more quietly. 'We needed him here.'

CHAPTER 5

Teaching the next day was almost impossible. The school reacted to the escalating attention of the media, local and national, is if an electric current had been run through its collective body. Karim's death had featured in several of the national papers that morning and on breakfast-time television, with much speculation about the motive for the killing and the history of intermittent racial intolerance over twenty years in the town. Jo was not surprised after that to find that many of the Moslem girls in her class failed to turn up for registration.

The Asian boys, on the other hand, were there in force, moving around the school in tight little groups and eyeing

51

their contemporaries of other cultures with ill-concealed hostility. Almost overnight, a harmony which had been carefully nurtured for years had been torn apart and ancient suspicions reasserted themselves. In every class she taught during the morning, Jo found a small group of Asian boys sitting defensively together at the back, their faces sullen and uncooperative, while the rest of the class fidgeted and shuffled nervously, unable to concentrate in the unbearable tension which had been created by the murder itself and by the now widely accepted assumption that the motive for the killing had been racial.

In the staff-room at lunch-time there was an uneasy calm as newspapers were passed round and sandwiches eaten, until Maggie Turner, a young PE teacher with spiky punk-ish hair who was seldom seen out of her black tracksuit, exploded angrily, her colour rising in indignation.

'We can't just carry on as if nothing's happened,' she said. Two dozen pairs of anxious eyes swivelled in her direction.

'What do you suggest?' Peter Masefield asked quietly. 'There's a couple of centuries of racial tension swirling around out there and it's not likely to be dissipated until the police make an arrest. I happened to be reading *Othello* with a fifth-year group this morning and you could have cut the atmosphere with a knife. All of a sudden half the class were rooting for the Moor and the rest were baying for his blood. It was frightening.'

'*Othello* was a bloody silly thing to read with them today,' Maggie retorted sharply.

'Or the best thing,' Peter came back. 'At least it raised the issue that's on all their minds in a way we could handle —just.'

'I gave up trying to teach and just let them talk,' Jo Robertson said.

'And what are they saying?' Maggie came back. 'All I'm getting from what's left of the girls' PE groups is that it wasn't us, miss, and it wasn't our brothers, and we don't see why Karim's friends are behaving as if it was.'

'There's going to be trouble at the end of school if we're

not careful,' broke in another anxious voice from the back of the crowded room. 'Some of the Asian lads are just spoiling for a fight.'

At that moment the staff-room door opened and Margaret Jackson came in. The room fell silent as they waited for her to speak. She stood for a moment, taking in their anxiety, her own face showing signs of ususual tiredness beneath its impeccable make-up. In one of those unexpected flashes of insight, Jo Robertson realized that Margaret was ill, that what they had all always taken as a continuing sinewy toughness, both physical and mental, was in fact imperceptibly turning into a pale and somewhat frightening fragility.

'I'm sorry you're having such a rough day,' Margaret said at last, with a perceptible effort to make herself heard at the back of the room. 'We seem to be learning rather fast about the destructive power of the media. I'm told that there will be at least one television crew at the school gates at four o'clock. I've told them that they are on no account to come on to the school premises, but I'm afraid I can't stop them trying to speak to the students as they leave.'

'I'll stop them,' Maggie Turner muttered belligerently, just loud enough to be heard but not loud enough for Margaret Jackson to have to respond.

'What I think we'll do,' the headmistress said, 'is have them all back in the hall at ten to four for a little pep-talk before they go home. I don't want them chattering to reporters without realizing what they're saying. Nor do I want any mayhem on the way down through the estate between the Asian boys and the rest. So a few volunteers casually driving or walking down with the main crowd might be a good idea—just to keep an eye on things until they are all well dispersed. Yes?'

'Isn't that a job for the police?' asked a voice from the back of the room, to a sharp intake of breath from Maggie Turner and one or two of the other younger staff. Margaret Jackson took the question seriously and paused for a moment's thought before replying.

'I could have a word with the detective chief inspector

who was here yesterday,' she said at last. 'I don't want them to get the impression that we're expecting a riot. I'm not expecting a riot,' she added firmly. 'If what we've been doing here with these children for the past six years means anything at all, a riot should be the last thing that will happen. But a tactful police presence between here and Aysgarth Lane might not be a bad idea today.'

Against her better judgement, Jo went with Peter Masefield, at his insistence, to the school gates to supervise the departure of the pupils. A television crew and several reporters had stationed themselves on the pavement opposite the main entrance, but Margaret Jackson's instruction not to talk to the media, delivered to the whole school at her special assembly, seemed to have been taken to heart. Most of the children looked subdued as they straggled out of the gates, their earlier excitement dissipated as they came to terms with the fact that someone of their own age had died. Some of the groups of girls came out with their arms around each other, one or two of them actually in tears and most of them looking tense. The boys, of all races, made more of a show of bravado as they marched out of the gates, but although the Asian boys stuck unusually close together in defensive groups, they glanced at Jo and Peter placatingly and there was no sign of aggression, verbal or otherwise.

Most of the youngsters deliberately kept away from the Press as they dispersed up the hill to the council estate which effectively surrounded the school or set off downhill in the direction of the town centre. The side-road lined with brick and concrete maisonettes in which the school stood eventually joined Aysgarth Lane, one of the main raods out of Bradfield to the north, a busy and congested artery lined with small shops and workshops converted from Victorian houses. At that point the stream of youngsters leaving school diminished to a trickle of mainly brown faces heading for the side-roads of stone and brick terraces nearer the town centre.

Within ten minutes the flood of children, many of them

hurrying home unusually quickly, had almost dispersed and the disappointed reporters began to drift away to their parked cars, shrugging dispiritedly to each other. A couple of uniformed policemen strolled past, apparently discreetly following the groups of Asian boys who were trudging home down the hill. Obviously Margaret Jackson's quiet word with Chief Inspector Huddleston had had its effect.

Jo shivered and pulled her coat more tightly around her. It was a raw evening and already getting dark.

'Come up to my place,' Peter said quietly as they watched a straggling group of girls dodge the most persistent of the reporters and run off giggling. Jo looked past him for a moment, staring unseeingly at the haze which was gathering around the newly illuminated street-lights. It would be foggy later, she thought. Tears pricked the back of her eyes.

'Just to talk,' Peter said more insistently. 'We must talk, Jo.' She sighed, and nodded.

'Yes, all right,' she said.

Peter Masefield lived alone in a small stone cottage on the very edge of the town where the urban landscape petered out into scrubby countryside which was not quite rural but was at least, as he said, a sort of green. He had been brought up in the hills of Cumbria and still missed, he said, the open country of his boyhood. Jo parked her car close behind his on the verge outside the cottage and followed him in. The single living-room was cold after being unused all day, and Peter lit the fire which was already laid in the stone fireplace and went into the kitchen, where she heard him put the kettle on. She sat down on the edge of a chair near the flames which rapidly took hold of the piled-up fuel in the fireplace, keeping her coat pulled well around her, partly because she still felt chilled by the raw evening and partly because she was determined not to stay long.

It was a comfortable room, with the slightly battered furniture made inviting by a scatter of rugs and cushions in vibrant reds and oranges, and every available inch of wall space filled with books and posters from Stratford and the London theatres. On the mantelpiece, among a clutter of *objets trouvées*, polished pebbles and pieces of rock, and a bleached piece of wood which looked as if it had been picked up on a sun-drenched beach, there were several colour photographs of a boy and a girl of about ten and eleven. Their blue eyes and brown curly hair, even with faces only half-formed, left little doubt that they were Peter's children.

He came back into the room with two mugs of tea which he put down carefully on the coffee table in front of the fire before sitting on the arm of her chair and putting an arm around her.

'Do you love me, Joanna?' he asked lightly, although she knew that his intent was deadly serious.

'I love you,' she said, so softly that he had to strain to hear her.

'And will you marry me?'

She pulled herself free of his arm and reached over to pick up her mug.

'Don't ask, Peter,' she said.

He got up and crossed the room to the window where he pulled the heavy curtains across with a angry gesture. He was a tall man, thin-faced, with a touch of asceticism usually relieved by the ironic amusement with which he looked at the world from those clear blue eyes. But this evening he looked tired as he turned back to Jo, and there was both hurt and anger in his face. He sat down on the opposite side of the fire from her, spreading his hands out wide, palm up, in a gesture of supplication.

'What do you want from me?' he asked.

Jo did not answer immediately. She sipped her tea and avoided his gaze.

'I can't ask anything of you,' she said at last, so quietly that he had to lean forward to catch what she said. 'I can't leave Neil. Or, if you want it your way—I won't leave Neil.'

'That's final, is it?'

She could not bring herself to speak again, and merely nodded as a single tear crept down her cheek. Peter sat looking at her for a moment without speaking. She made a forlorn figure, hunched over her steaming mug of tea in her thick coat, her fair hair falling over her face and veiling

56

her expression. He longed to take her in his arms but the corrosive bile of anger which had been within him for days prevented him from following his instinct. Instead he got to his feet and picked up an educational paper which was lying on the dining table on the other side of the room. He riffled through it impatiently until he found what he wanted and handed a page with a marked section to Jo, who took it unseeingly.

'There's a job advertised in Kendal,' he said coldly. 'I'm going to apply for it. I'll be very surprised if I don't get it.'

He had intended to hurt her and was gratified by the effect of his words. She turned very pale as the shock of what he had said registered, and the single tear which had betrayed her earlier was followed by more, coursing silently down her cheeks. She made no attempt to brush them away and they fell in glistening drops on to the front of her dark coat, to be as silently absorbed and replaced by more. She nodded dumbly and got to her feet, placing her mug with careful precision on the table.

'You must do whatever will make you happy,' she said.

'Happy?' he retorted bitterly. 'What's happy got to do with it?'

'Well, at least you'll be nearer the children,' she said, glancing at the photographs on the mantelpiece. Peter's son and daughter lived with their mother in Lancaster, which was, she knew, one reason why he would consider moving away from Bradfield, which was a long and awkward journey away from his ex-wife's home. Another was his often expressed wish to return to the countryside where he had spent his childhood and which he still loved with a passion which she had never felt for a place, but which she acknowledged could be as real for this quiet man as it had been for his beloved Wordsworth.

But the real motive for Peter's decision, she knew, was neither convenience nor nostalgia, but an urgent desire, if not an absolute need, to escape from a situation which had tormented them both for the best part of a year. She did not doubt for a moment that if the opportunity was offered, Peter would go.

She walked slowly across the room, her shoulders slumped in despair, and unlatched the wooden cottage door. She did not look back and Peter Masefield did not move from the chair by the fire, where he sat with his head thrown back, his face impassive and unyielding. Only when Jo had closed the door and he heard her car start up outside did he relax and cover his face with his hands.

Jo could not remember the drive home. She found Neil closeted with David, totally absorbed by the game they were working on. She tidied up the house mechanically, picking up dirty plates and cups and newspapers which Neil had left around the living-room, and transferred a ready-cooked meal from the deep freeze to the microwave.

She had offered Neil no explanation for her late arrival home and he had not asked for one. It was quite possible he had not even noticed, she thought bitterly. The computer had not really provided him with a means of making a living, which is what they had hoped, but it at least absorbed some of his restless intellectual energy which, before it had been installed, had tended to find its only outlet in storms of ineffectual rage at the malignancy of Fate, rages which tore her apart emotionally as well as him.

She sat down at the kitchen table, dully watching the food rotate in the oven as she tried to come to terms with Peter Masefield's apparent determination to leave. He had been one of the first people she had met in Bradfield. As head of the English department, he had been a member of the interviewing panel which had appointed her to her job. He had denied having been attracted to her from that first meeting when much later she had asked him mischievously whether that had been the reason she had been successful at the interview, but she did not completely believe him.

For her part, she had been so anxious about Neil, and the possibilities of a house specially converted for the disabled offered them in Bradfield, that the interview had passed in a blur and she had been completely unaware of the intensity of Peter Masefield's gaze throughout the half-hour of question and answer.

It was not for months after she started work at Sutton Park that she became aware that his interest was more than that of a senior teacher concerned to help a new member of staff fit in, more, indeed, than a shared but essentially professional love of poetry and drama and of the amazing miscellany of children who rushed or drifted or stormed around the school: the white and brown and black, the enthusiastic and resentful, the clever and the hard-working —by no means always the same—and those sad souls whose eyes wandered away into some other private world of unimaginable misery almost before a teacher could complete a sentence.

Their affair, which had started almost a year ago, had been just as much of her volition as his, she told herself fiercely, fighting back the tears. She had almost imperceptibly fallen in love with him as they bent their heads over piles of set books and timetables and reports on the school's multitudinous 'problem' children. She had not admitted it to herself, but when they found themselves alone one night outside the school, having safely seen home a class they had supervised on a theatre trip, she had felt no surprise when he had taken her arm in a more than comradely grip and asked her to go to the cottage with him for a drink. Nor had she felt any guilt at accepting the invitation, knowing that a neighbour had agreed to check that Neil had got safely to bed.

They had made love that first night, almost without a word, falling into each other's arms as Peter closed the cottage door as if it were the most natural thing in the world. And that is what it had always seemed, during the brief, snatched hours that they could be alone together, the hours which Jo could in effect steal from Neil by arriving home an hour or so later from her out-of-school duties than she might otherwise have done. But if it seemed entirely natural to lie in Peter's arms in his tiny bedroom at the cottage, watching the changing light over the hills behind the town through the window, it had always felt entirely unnatural to lie and cheat to find the time to be with him, and to maintain a façade of comradely normality in school, where no one, not even Maggie Turner, who was her closest friend on the staff, knew about their relationship.

She and Neil ate their evening meal in the sort of preoccupied silence which was becoming the norm between them. She maintained an iron self-control as she served the food and then picked at it, trying to turn her mind in any direction but the threat of Peter's departure, which she knew was all too likely to turn into a promise. He was a gifted teacher and any school to which he applied would, she was sure, jump at the opportunity of employing him.

Neil hurried his meal and instead of turning the television on, as he normally did, he spun his chair away from the table in the direction of his study again.

'I've got a problem with this latest scene,' he said. 'I want the hero to fall down a very deep crater, and it's proving tricky to give the impression of depth without taking up too much memory.'

'I've got marking to do,' Jo said dully. The more preoccupied Neil was this evening, she thought, the more she might be able to hide successfully the desperate pain which she was sure he would soon be able to read in her face. 'I'll bring you some coffee in a while,' she promised.

She settled down to her marking, with *The Marriage of Figaro* playing softly in the background and for some time she was able to concentrate on the third year stories, full of fantasy and bizarre spelling mistakes, in front of her. But gradually her concentration waned, and as the recording moved into the first notes of '*Dove sono*' and the exquisite sorrow of Mozart's betrayed countess, her own self-control broke and she felt tears about to overwhelm her again. She sat for a moment with the heels of her hands pushed against her eyes.

Unexpectedly, the doorbell rang, summoning her abruptly out of her depression and back into the world. Neil, she knew, would not move if she were in the house, so she got to her feet wearily, glancing in the hall mirror to straighten her hair and make sure that neither smudged make-up nor reddened eyes would betray her before she opened the door. There were two girls on the step, both bundled up in winter coats over long blue trousers and with pale silky scarves wrapped, Moslem style, around their hair and half-covering their faces.

'Ayesha?' Jo asked uncertainly. Both girls pulled back their scarves and Jo recognized not just Ayesha but also her friend Farida Arif.

'May we come in?' Farida asked. 'We're sorry to bother you so late, but we need to talk to you.' Jo nodded, almost too surprised at their unexpected arrival to think clearly.

'Do your parents know where you are?' she asked, as the girls took their coats off and followed her into the living-room. She knew that it was highly unusual for girls of the Moslem community to be allowed out alone in the evenings even at seventeen. Farida slung the traditional scarf on top of her coat and gave Jo a small, self-satisfied smile.

'I'm supposed to be at her house doing an essay, and she's supposed to be at mine,' she said. It was an age-old trick for deceiving parents, but even so Jo was concerned for these two.

'I'll run you home in the car later,' she said. 'So what can I do for you.'

The girls glanced at each other in some embarrassment before Farida, by far the more self-confident of the two, decided to speak.

'It's a bit difficult, Mrs Robertson,' she said. 'If we tell you, will you promise not to tell anyone who told you?'

Jo hesitated. It was the sort of open-ended promise which she knew could lead to difficulties. Ayesha turned away and spoke rapidly and angrily in Punjabi to her friend.

'Look,' Jo said. 'If it's really important . . .'

'It is very important,' Ayesha said, her eyes bright with tears.

'She says she must go home now if you won't promise,' Farida said. 'But Ayesha thinks she knows something about Karim that might have something to do with his murder. The trouble is, if it gets out, it's going to annoy the community, his family, the imam, everyone. So she doesn't want to tell the police herself . . . Please, Mrs Robertson. She ought to tell someone.'

61

'All right, Farida, I won't say who told me unless I really have to—if it were interfering with the police investigation, or something like that. Then I'd have to tell. You do understand that, don't you, Ayesha?'

Ayesha nodded glumly, wringing her hands together nervously.

'So what is it?' Jo asked quietly. 'Is it about his girlfriend?' Jo asked. 'His sister told me that he was living with a girl. Is that it?'

Ayesha's eyes widened in surprise at that and Jo realized that was not what the girls wanted to tell her.

'I thought he was living in a squat,' Ayesha said. 'There were a lot of them there. I didn't know about a girl, especially.'

'Do you know where the squat was?' Jo said. 'I don't think the police have any idea where he was living, so you really ought to tell me about that.'

'Khawar says that it is in Commercial Road, down by the canal. She says Karim came home one night and got into the house while his father was at the mosque. He wanted to collect some things from his room. She was too scared to tell anyone about it, but she told me yesterday when I went round there with my mother.' Ayesha spoke quietly with the broad vowels of her adopted home.

'It strikes me that Khawar knows a lot more than she is letting on to her parents,' Jo said. 'But she can't hide things now, Ayesha. The police really do need to know these things.' There was a sort of unspoken freemasonry, she thought, among these children who balanced their lives elegantly between two cultures, a ready acceptance that families were to be protected from some information which would disturb or distress them.

'That's what I told Ayesha about . . . about the other thing we came to tell you,' Farida said. 'It's too important to keep secret, but Ayesha says everyone will be so furious . . . You know how traditional some people in the community are. My mother says it's time Pakistan came to terms with women's rights, but I think it's going to take generations, even over here. I'm one of the lucky ones, because my mother and father are different, they have a more western marriage, and they won't make me do things I don't want to do. I'm going to university like my mother did . . .'

'So am I,' said Ayesha, suddenly and fiercely. 'I've told my parents they can't stop me.'

Jo looked at the two girls, their dark eyes suddenly blazing with fierce determination, and smiled.

'Hey,' she said softly. 'I've told you we'll all help you get there,' she said. 'Mrs Jackson has talked to your parents, Ayesha. They're very proud of you, you know. They're not going to stand in your way.'

Ayesha looked at Jo for a moment and then nodded.

'Perhaps they won't,' she said.

'But that's not why you came?' Jo said. 'What was it you wanted to tell me that's so difficult?'

'We know why Karim was in school,' Farida said flatly.

Jo felt suddenly unaccountably cold. It was as if that simple statement had taken her back to the changing-room and the shock of finding Karim's body, and for a moment she wanted to tell the two girls that she did not want to hear their revelations, that they should go away and telephone the police immediately and leave her out of their calculations. She did not feel strong enough to support them down the dark labyrinthine corridors of a murder investigation.

But the two pairs of eyes watching her anxiously pulled her back from the edge of panic.

'Why was he in school?' she heard herself say, knowing that she would not like the answer.

'You know there's a sort of basement at the back of the school?' Farida said, her voice firm now the decision to reveal all had been taken. 'I don't know it myself, but Ayesha says that when they were in the third form they found a way under the back of the building, behind the cloakrooms. It's not high enough there for there to be rooms or anything, but you can get under. They crawled in and tried to listen to what was going on up above them in the staff-room.'

Ayesha giggled suddenly, slightly hysterically.

'It was really scary,' she said. 'We took torches and food

63

and stayed under there the whole of one lunch-time. But the next time we went to climb in the trapdoor had been nailed up and we couldn't get in. Someone must have found out and fixed it.'

'So what's this to do with Karim?' Jo asked, half guessing.

'Well, you know people always say there's nowhere for young people to go in the evenings?' Farida said. 'Not the Moslem kids so much, but the others? The trapdoor is unlocked now. You can get in. We looked. Well, Karim and his friends from the squat decided to use that place. They were climbing in through a window after the school was shut and meeting there. That's why Karim was in school that night. They called it the Cellar and were using it as a sort of club.'

'But you said your community leaders wouldn't like it?' Jo said.

'Yes, well, some of the Asian boys were going there to meet white girls,' Ayesha said very quietly. 'They're going to be very angry about that.'

'Not just meet,' said Farida flatly. 'They were going there to do—you know—sex. We think.'

'Oh God,' Jo groaned. She could imagine the outrage in the Moslem community if the police arrived on local doorsteps asking young Moslem boys for details of their sexual partners. The entire neighbourhood, including the school, would be thrown into an uproar.

'Are you sure?' she asked the girls. Farida's surface sophistication had deserted her as she too allowed herself to consider the full implications of what she had said. But although there was now deep anxiety in their eyes, both girls nodded determinedly. They were, they said, quite sure.

'Because you've been there yourselves?' Jo suggested quietly.

Ayesha shook her head wildly at the suggestion but Farida hesitated, perhaps flattered by the idea.

'Or you know who has?' Jo persisted gently.

Again Ayesha shook her head, but Farida nodded slowly.

'No, not me,' she said. 'I haven't been. Even my mother

64

would be furious. But I know someone who might have, at least he's been somewhere like it, he told me, and now I think that is probably where it was.'

'Can you tell me who?' Jo persisted. The girl looked down at her hands, which were tightly clasped in her lap. Then she shrugged her slim shoulders and parted her hands in an elegant gesture of surrender.

'It was my brother Sammy,' she said.

'Don't be so bloody stupid, woman,' Neil Robertson said. 'Ring the police now.'

His wife's jaw tightened into an obstinate line which he recognized and on the whole admired, but which on this occasion horrified him.

'In the morning,' she said, not for the first time. 'I want those girls left out of it. In the morning we can look in the basement ourselves and then send for the police—simply tell them we had forgotten about that void under the school, just looked in there out of curiosity. The girls don't know any names, except for Farida's older brother, and even that is very vague. He didn't actually say where he'd been— was just showing off his western sophistication to his little sister and said a bit too much.'

'You're being over-protective, Jo,' Neil said angrily. 'You have to leave that sort of decision to the police. Ring them now and tell them what's happened. I insist.'

Jo shook her head and glanced at the mobile telephone which she had put on the top bookshelf out of Neil's reach. It was a dirty trick, but she was absolutely determined that what she was doing was right.

'In the morning,' she said. 'It may all be a complete fantasy. I want to check it out myself first before I tell any-one else.'

She had taken the two girls home by car and then told Neil exactly what they had told her, to his obvious displeasure. Now he swung his wheelchair right up against her chair and took hold of her arm in a fierce grip.

'Call the police!' he said angrily again.

'You're hurting, Neil,' she said, trying to pull her arm away.

'And you're behaving like an idiot,' he said. She turned away from him, on the edge of tears, all the emotion of the evening's parting from Peter and the anxious interview with the girls overwhelming her at once. If he hit her, she thought, as he had done before in a fit of rage, she would not be able to bear it tonight. But instead his mood swung suddenly and he reached across to take her other arm and pull her closer. He leaned across the arm of his chair and turned her face towards his and kissed her on the lips.

'You are a bloody fool,' he said. 'And I love you. And I want you. Put me to bed.'

Putting Neil to bed with the aid of the bungalow's ingenious system of pulleys which enabled him to swing himself into the bath and into his bed was not the struggle it had been in their London flat. Even so, when Jo finally pulled the bedclothes over him and sat on the edge of his single bed, shivering slightly in her thin nightdress, she felt drained and devoid of feeling. Neil pushed himself awkwardly to the far side of the bed with those powerful arms and pulled her towards him.

'Come in,' he said and she lifted the bedclothes wearily and slid in beside him and perfunctorily satisfied his need. Later, back in her own bed, shivering with exhaustion, she fell asleep on a pillow soaked in tears.

CHAPTER 6

The trapdoor into the under-drawing of the school was concealed behind one of the wooden benches and rows of clothes hooks at the darkest side of the boys' changing-rooms. It was careless, though perhaps understandable, Jo thought, that the police had not noticed it during their examination of the room, although she supposed that the forensic officers had spent most of their efforts on the shower room itself. She had asked Maggie Turner to come with her

66

to check out the girls' story of the night before, telling her simply that she had overheard some youngsters discussing how to get into the closed-off area of the basement the evening before.

'It's probably nothing,' she said as they pulled the heavy wooden fixture away from the wall, though as soon as she saw the trapdoor, its screw fixings obviously loosened and the square wooden door standing slightly proud of the surrounding plaster, she knew that what the girls had told her had some substance.

'These screws are really lose,' Maggie said in surprise, pulling the two at the top of the door away quite easily.

'Here,' Jo said, passing Maggie a small penknife which she always carried in her bag. 'You'll get them all out with that.'

They had borrowed a torch from the school caretaker and once the trapdoor fell towards them they shone a thin beam into the dark interior.

'It's huge,' Maggie said. 'It must go right back to the rear wall, under the gym and the staff-room.' Slowly she swung the beam of the torch around the space they had opened up until finally she gave a low whistle.

'There's been someone in here all right,' she said quietly. 'Give me a hitch up. We'd better have a look.' Jo helped Maggie up into the doorway and then took her hand to haul herself up and follow her into the dark interior of the building. The torch gave an unnervingly small beam of light in so large a space. Up above, the sounds of the school about to start its day echoed resoundingly in the confined space, footsteps booming on the wooden floors and the sounds of children's voices distorted eerily in the claustrophobic darkness.

Maggie shone the light on the floor beneath their feet. It was boarded and dusty but the dust had obviously been recently disturbed and a clear pathway led through the dirt in the direction of the farthest corner of the basement. They followed the pathway without speaking until, Jo guessed, they were roughly beneath the gym which lay at the rear corner of the building, its floor effectively at ground level.

Below, the basement space had reduced in height so that both women had their heads almost touching the floorboards above. This section of the basement was underground, a space where neither light nor sound was likely to penetrate into the outside world at night.

Maggie shone her torch slowly over a raggle-taggle collection of mattresses, rugs and cushions arranged roughly in a circle. To one side, against the wall, was a series of wooden boxes and even a low coffee table on which a not inexpensive record-player and speakers, apparently wired into the ceiling above, and a collection of bottles and glasses.

'A veritable little nightclub,' Maggie said drily. 'Warm, dry and far enough away from anyone else at night to be virtually soundproof. The cunning little brats. They're even plugged into the school's electricity.'

'Do you think this was Karim's brainchild?' Jo wondered.

'Oh, I doubt it,' Maggie said. 'This has a decadent western look to it, don't you think? Just look at all that booze, for heaven's sake. That must have cost a fortune.' She reached out a hand to the nearet bottle of gin but drew back as if stung when Jo said loudly:

'Don't, Maggie! Fingerprints, you idiot! They'll be in here looking for fingerprints.' She just caught Maggie's shamefaced grin in the dim light.

'Too early in the day for me really, anyway,' she said. 'So hadn't we better go and call in the cavalry?'

Chief Inspector Harry Huddleston was not best pleased to be called back to Sutton Park by Margaret Jackson to be told what his scene of crime officers had missed. Having sent Mower to cordon off the relevant part of the school basement again and recall the forensic investigating team, he sat in Mrs Jackson's most comfortable visitor's chair and took out his chagrin on the three women who faced him across the ornate wooden fireplace which graced the head's study.

'But why did no one here remember the bloody underdrawing or whatever you call it?' he growled.

'It seems very few people knew it existed, Chief Inspector,' Margaret Jackson said patiently, not for the first time. 'As I've already said, staff turnover is high. We've had three caretakers in my six years here. None of them ever mentioned to me that you could get underneath the back part of the building. It's not something which crosses your mind as you walk through the cloakrooms themselves. Apparently there are just two entrances, one in each set of changing-rooms, and the one at the girls' end is almost completely hidden by a large mirror. Whoever has been using the space—and I'm sure it can't be children currently at the school—must have discovered the entrance by chance and gone exploring.'

'But you remembered, Mrs Robertson?' Huddleston said heavily, switching his gaze to Jo. She nodded.

'As I said, I remember hearing some youngsters discussing how they'd climbed under the staff-room—oh, months ago, and that set me wondering last night.' It was not exactly what she had told Maggie that morning and she could feel, rather than see, her friend's glance of faint puzzlement as she repeated what she had already told the Chief Inspector.

'But you can't remember who you heard?'

'No, I can't,' she said firmly. 'I'm sorry, but it was just a snatch of conversation in the corridor. It hardly registered at the time. I expect I had other things on my mind.'

'Aye, well, I think I'll go and have a look at this little nightclub now, if you don't mind, Mrs Jackson,' Huddleston said, getting to his feet heavily. 'I'll be wanting another statement from you, Mrs Robertson, later on, and you Miz Turner.' The emphasis was clumsy and made Maggie laugh delightedly as the policeman closed the door behind him.

'Maggie, you only do it to annoy,' Margaret said with an asperity which was belied by the look of affection she directed at her head of girls' PE. 'Don't you have a few hockey teams to go and whack into shape now?'

Maggie looked at her watch and sighed dramatically, although the glance she gave Jo and Margaret was concerned not amused.

'I know when I'm not wanted,' she said as she went out, closing the door quietly behind her.

Margaret Jackson sat down behind her desk and looked at Jo consideringly.

'So, are you going to tell me what all that was about?' she asked at last.

'I can't,' Jo said, not even trying to prevaricate with Margaret because she knew it would be a waste of time. 'I was told in confidence.'

'And you're not impeding the police inquiry with your little white lies?'

Jo shook her head. 'I don't think so,' she said. Margaret looked at her colleague for another long moment and then nodded, apparently satisfied.

'So, what is our deeply embarrassed policeman going to want next, do you think,' Margaret asked, a hint of weariness on her voice. 'I suppose he'll want to know if any of our youngsters have been using this illicit den, or whether it's been confined to outsiders. Will he interview them all, do you think? I don't envy him that prospect. It'll take weeks! It'll be next term before we're back to normal at this rate.'

'The kids have already seen the police come back and are jumping up and down in their seats again,' Jo said. Like most of the staff, she had hoped that the third day after the murder would see something like a return to normality as the school came to terms with what had happened.

'I don't think any of them can have known what was going on in that basement,' she continued slowly. 'I'm sure someone would have dropped a hint. You know what they're like, some of them, only too ready to ingratiate themselves by telling tales if there's anything to tell.'

'Even so, a few firm words at registration this afternoon, reminding them of their duty to help the police . . . ?'

'Not a duty many of them take very seriously,' Jo said grimly. 'Even so, something might emerge, with a little encouragement.' That settled, the two women sat for a moment in a slightly strained silence which Margaret Jackson eventually broke with some evident reluctance.

'How are you coping, Joanna?' she asked quietly. 'You look tired. Is there anything you want to talk about?'

It would be comforting, Jo thought, to unburden herself to a sympathetic ear. The temptation was very great but with an effort she resisted it and got to her feet with a faint smile.

'We all need a holiday,' she said. 'Roll on, Christmas.'

'Let's get out of here for a bit,' Maggie Turner said to Jo, waylaying her as she pushed her way into the crowded staff-room that lunch-time with her arms full of exercise books. Jo glanced quickly across the room at Peter Masefield who was deep in conversation with a colleague. He caught her eye briefly and very deliberately looked away again, an exchange which Maggie marked silently but did not acknowledge.

'Right, Maggie, you're on,' Jo said. 'I've just put three of 4P in detention. If I don't get out of here there may well be another murder before the day's out. Your car or mine?'

They chose Maggie's red MG, her pride and joy.

'Where to?' she asked as she waited at the school entrance for the passing traffic to clear.

'Commercial Road,' Jo said suddenly. Her friend looked at her curiously but turned towards Aysgarth Lane and the steep hill which led towards the centre of the town. Waiting at traffic lights, Maggie looked at Jo Robertson again.

'You look terrible,' she said flatly. 'What the hell's going on?' Where Margaret Jackson's sympathetic approach had failed, Maggie's bulldozing concern cut through Jo's defences like so much soft sand and she told her about Ayesha and Farida's visit the night before. Maggie listened intently as she drove fast and skilfully through the lunch-time traffic.

'Hence Commercial Road?' she asked as she turned out of Bradfield's bustling main shopping mall into a gloomy side-street which led towards the canal. Jo nodded.

'Just to look,' she said. Maggie glanced at her again quizzically.

'And then there's the rest,' she said. 'Has Neil found out about Peter?'

Jo looked at her friend in astonishment, her stomach lurching uncomfortably as her world took on a new perspective. Maggie's eyes danced with a glee which was by no means without sympathy.

'Maybe only someone who knows you as well as I do could see when things were going right there,' she said gently. 'But any fool can see that something's gone very wrong now. You're avoiding each other as if you both suspected the other of harbouring a social disease. Come on, Jo, share it! What are friends for?'

Maggie pulled the car up with a jerk on the corner of a dilapidated street which boasted no official sign. Instead someone had used a red spray-can to scrawl Commercial Road on the half-demolished brick wall which was all that was left of what looked as though it had been a factory on the corner. Opposite stood a pub, left abandoned like a single tooth in a mouthful of decay, as the terraced houses to which it had clearly once been attached had been pulled down and their sites abandoned to piles of rubble now overgrown with weeds.

'Hardly looks like quiche and white wine country,' Maggie said ruefully. 'But if a half and a pork pie will do? You did insist on this neighbourhood.' Jo managed a half-smile.

'Let's go for it,' she said. The two women, Maggie still in her black tracksuit and Jo in her unobtrusive teacher's uniform of sweater and matching skirt under a dark coat, attracted curious glances from the pub's handful of male customers as they settled themselves with their lunch in a corner of the lounge bar, a room which seemed to distinguish itself from the public bar merely by providing its clients with a square of muddy carpet on which to dribble their beer. Sipping her lager and picking at an unattractive-looking sandwich, Jo told Maggie about Peter's decision to leave Sutton Park. The younger woman sat silently for a moment staring into her glass of Guinness with sombre eyes, her free hand twisting a wayward strand of dark hair on her forehead as she considered what Jo had just told her.

'Go with him,' she said at last, with a challenge in her voice. 'Just because Neil's in a wheelchair doesn't mean he's not a slob. Leave him.'

'That's easy to say,' Jo said angrily, flushing slightly.

'He needs you, I suppose!' Maggie said, attempting a not very convincing sneer. 'How many women are going to crucify themselves with that excuse before men learn to stand on their own two feet? Sorry, that's not the most appropriate phrase in the circs, but you know what I mean. He may be entitled to your loyalty as a wife, but if that's finished between you, he's not entitled to use you as a bloody nursemaid for the rest of his life.'

'It's not as simple as that, Maggie,' Jo said. 'I loved him.'

'But you don't love him now?' The question hung unanswered in the air between them while Jo sought the strength to put into words something which she knew to be true but had avoided admitting even to herself for months.

'No,' she said very quietly at last. 'No, I don't love him now.'

'And he thumps you,' Maggie said triumphantly, as though that concluded the argument. Months before she had persuaded Jo to admit that the bruises on her arm were not as accidental as she had at first claimed.

'Oh, not for ages,' Jo said quickly. 'He's been much better lately, much less frustrated since we came to live here. I really think he's beginning to adapt. I can't walk out on him now. I couldn't live with myself.'

Maggie shook her dark, close-cropped head angrily.

'Can you really go on with it if Peter leaves?' she asked. 'I know you're tough, but are you that tough?'

'I don't know,' Jo said hopelessly. 'I really don't know.'

Maggie finished her drink quickly and glanced at her watch. Half their lunch-hour was gone.

'We'd better have a look at this squat, then. That's why we came.'

They walked quickly the length of Commercial Road, most of which had been demolished and roughly fenced off obviously in anticipation of some major redevelopment.

'Isn't this where they were going to build some amazing new sports and shopping centre?' Maggie asked. 'It fell through when the bottom dropped out of the property market?'

'There are a few houses left down at the bottom,' Jo said, quickening her pace. The road ended in a dead-end for traffic, although a narrow muddy track led off to the left towards the canal, whose oily black water could be seen intermittently between the broken fencing of old doors and corrugated iron which separated the road from the towpath. But as they approached they could see that the remaining terraced houses were all boarded up, with heavy demolition machinery parked nearby.

'They're all coming down,' Jo said dully. 'There can't be anyone living here now.'

'If they ever were,' Maggie said. 'Perhaps the girls got it wrong. It was only gossip, after all.'

Just to be sure they walked to the very end of the street, where a faded hoarding announced that the site had been acquired by a local company for the construction of a shopping and leisure development. Maggie snorted.

'Leisure,' she said dismissively. 'Squash courts and a health club, as far as I can remember. Fat chance any of our kids'll have of using that sort of facility. What this town needs is a proper sports centre that ordinary people can afford.'

'Come on down off your soap-box,' Jo said affectionately. She had heard Maggie's passionate arguments in favour of healthy living many times before. They turned away from the row of houses, with their blind wooden windows and doorways. Some of the men who had been in the pub were approaching down the street and the first among them clambered on to a heavy bulldozer and started the machine up with a roar. By mid-afternoon, Jo guessed, not a house would remain standing in Commercial Road.

As they walked back to Maggie's car parked on the

corner, Jo became conscious of an elderly woman standing on the opposite side of the street watching them. She was bundled up in a worn tweed overcoat much too large for her, several scarves of indeterminate colour, her skinny bare legs rising from an incongruous pair of red and white training shoes. She clutched a bulging plastic carrier bag in her arms which gave every appearance of holding her entire worldly possessions.

'Do you think the old bag lady lives down here?' Jo muttered to Maggie.

'Let's ask her,' Maggie replied and together they crossed the road. The woman watched them suspiciously, her eyes rheumy but sharp and hostile. She put her carrier bag down on the ground, where an indescribable torrent of dirty rags spilled from it on to the pavement, and the stale, sharp smell of unwashed body and dirty knickers made the two women draw back sharply in involuntary distaste.

'You social workers?' she asked querulously. 'I ain't goin' in no 'ome.'

Reassured that they were not about to do her good violently, the old woman softened slightly. She had been living in one of the empty houses at the end of the street, she told them, until workmen came the previous day and threw her out, boarding up the windows and doors firmly behind her.

'Was there anyone else living down there?' Jo asked.

'There was kids,' the old woman muttered. 'Noisy kids. They've gone now, any road. Went yesterday, day before yesterday, I don't remember when.'

'How many of them?' Jo persisted, but the old woman shook her head vaguely. Six or seven, she thought, but she could not be sure.

'Boys or girls? Black or white?' Maggie asked.

'Lads and lasses,' the bag lady admitted. 'There were a dark lad, a Paki lad, the others were white. Give us a bob for a cup o' tea, will yer?'

Jo took a pound coin out of her purse and put it into the old woman's grubby outstretched hand.

'Where are you going to sleep tonight?' she asked. 'Isn't there a hostel or something.'

'Nah,' the old woman replied scornfully. 'I'm not going to one o' them places. Full o' vermin, they are. I'll manage. I always manage.'

'We'll be late,' Maggie said anxiously, looking at her watch again. 'I've got the fifth year for netball and if I'm not on time they'll all slope off and not be seen again for the rest of the day.'

As they walked back to the car, Jo looked increasingly thoughtful.

'I think I'd better go to the police,' she said at last. Maggie nodded.

'I think you better had,' she said.

Quickly they retraced their steps and drove back into the town. They did not notice a black Mercedes sports car which had been parked out of sight round the corner of the pub pull in behind them as they passed with a very thoughtful Sammy Arif at the wheel. As Maggie's red MG turned back into the school car park Sammy pulled to the side of the road again and dialled a local number on his car phone.

CHAPTER 7

Police work is ninety-five per cent routine, four per cent logic, and a bare one per cent intuition, Harry Huddleston had never tired of telling his junior officers. But with Christmas coming, his wife urging him to put in shorter hours in honour of various social arrangements she had made, and his retirement edging ever closer, Huddleston was becoming impatient with the innumerable routine interviews that Karim Aziz's death entailed.

He had set up inquiries in Bradfield and in Manchester where, as he suspected, Geoff Regan had been seen at the football match by other supporters and even by an officer of the Manchester force who, as the group had been leaving Maine Road peaceably enough after Bradfield United's unexpected win, had not bothered to take any action about the youths' illicit presence. Even worse, Regan had come to the notice of the Manchester police again that evening on the fringes of a pub brawl. If the pathologist's estimate of the time of death, which now stood between ten o'clock and midnight the night before the body was found, were correct there was no way Regan could have been back in Bradfield in time to be involved.

Inquiries in Bradfield itself had not proved much more fruitful. A handful of Sutton Park pupils had volunteered information about the secret meeting place under the school, but when each was exhaustively interviewed at home with their parents present it turned out that they had heard little more than rumours about a club. None would admit to having ever ventured underneath the school, nor could they come up with the names of any likely habitués who had. Huddleston suspected that they had volunteered more in a spirit of curiosity than helpfulness.

Inquiries among the town's floating population of young homeless, who flitted like ghosts from squat to squat and occasionally in and out of the bleakly Christian night shelter which the Methodist Church ran in its basement, came up with no one who admitted to knowing Karim or where he might have been living during the six months he had been away from home.

Worse, as far as Huddleston could discover as a result of time-consuming interviews with a young Asian woman constable as interpreter at his side, the boy had dropped out of sight and out of mind once he had left the close embrace of his own community, where his family, right down to second cousins, and former schoolfriends, were equally unforthcoming about his likely movements.

Huddleston had been unimpressed too by a visit from Jo Robertson. She had come into the police station the day before looking pale and guilty and told Kevin Mower, in the Chief Inspector's absence, about her trip to the supposed squat in Commercial Road. But when officers had been dispatched to find the old woman Maggie and Jo had spoken to they had been unable to locate her. Nor had the demolition gang who were still working there admitted to even noticing the bag lady that day or any day. Huddleston had been left with a dissatisfied feeling both that Jo Robertson had told Mower less than the full truth about the incident, and that the Sergeant had not pressed her half hard enough about her reasons for going to Commercial Road in the first place.

'She picks up far too much information by hearsay, that one,' he grumbled to Mower later. 'I'll get back to her in a day or so, any road. I reckon she knows more than she's saying about a lot of those youngsters at the school. You should have pushed her harder. Fancy her, do you? A pretty face and a good pair o' legs and you're all over the place.'

'Not my type, guv,' Mower said dismissively, though he allowed himself a small smile at the lie.

They had spent a fruitless hour and a half at the Sergeant's computer terminal seeking some significant fact which had so far escaped them.

'You're going to finish up getting a result on your own at this rate, lad,' Huddleston grumbled to Mower, screwing his eyes up impatiently at the glare from the screen. A note of inconclusion was not what he had anticipated leaving the force on. 'I'll be long gone by the time you get a nibble. There's nowt there.'

He turned away from the computer in disgust. It was the sort of police work to which he had adjusted only grudgingly and now his freedom was approaching he was less circumspect about voicing his doubts about high technology. Mower had no such reservations: he searched through the electronic files expertly, though to little effect.

'Maybe we should be looking for the dog that didn't bark,' he said at last, ignoring Huddleston's look of mock disgust at the allusion. 'Why didn't Arif report Karim missing when he first went, for instance? Surely any normal family would have come to us if a lad of that age had bunked off. But they did nothing. And why can't we find any trace of where he'd been living? Assuming he stayed in Bradfield—and if he was killed here that must be a reasonable assumption—where the hell was he all that time? It's almost as if someone's deliberately wiped the slate clean. No one can vanish as completely as he seems to have done.'

'Look up squats on that machine of yours,' Huddleston said suddenly. Mower ran through the files again and brought up on the screen a list of addresses that had been accumulated during their investigations among the town's homeless young. None of the current residents of the series of derelict and semi-derelict houses that the murder team officers had visited had admitted knowing Karim.

'There,' said Huddleston, pointing at the bottom line on the screen. 'Commercial Road—demolished. We couldn't interview anyone who'd been living there because it was nowt but a heap of rubble, right?'

'That's right. Several of the kids mentioned a squat down there, guv, but the whole row was pulled down this week. They didn't seem to know Karim, though—or didn't want to, maybe. It's that site where they were planning a super-market and a leisure centre. I read about it in the local rag. If there'd been anyone living there, they were gone by the time we went looking. But we didn't even find anyone who admitted ever being there. Which is a bit odd, considering the way those kids flit about from gaff to gaff. It's as if no one wants to talk about that particular house. They've either clammed up or left town. But why?'

'They weren't bad houses down there when I were a lad,' Huddleston grunted. 'Half the time they pull things down out of sheer wanton destructiveness as far as I can see. Any road, never mind that. What I thought I remembered reading somewhere was that that development had run into trouble. It wasn't going ahead because of the property situ-ation or summat like that. So why bother to pull down the rest of those derelict houses all of a sudden. Is that the coincidence we should be looking for? Find out just who owns that site, will you, lad, and when the decision was made to demolish and why. If that's where our boy was living there just might be a connection.'

The winter afternoon was already fading into misty evening, with a threat of rain in the air, when the last truck of the day ground into Commercial Road to collect a final load of rubble from the building site. Fred Halliday, the demolition company's foreman, was well pleased. Another half day, he reckoned, should have cleared the site, leaving only a last stretch of fencing to be erected before the contract was completed at least a day ahead of schedule. After helping the truck-driver to reverse on to the brick-littered mud that was all which now remained of the back gardens of the Commercial Road terraces, Fred took off his hard hat, went into the dilapidated site hut and put the kettle on.

He had taken no more than the first drag on his cigarette when a shout from outside brought him to the door of the hut. The truck-driver waved him urgently towards the pile of rubble which was being gradually shifted by bulldozer into the tipper. Even as he watched irritably, aware of the kettle coming to the boil behind him and the *Sun* still almost unread on the table beside it, the bulldozer-driver clambered stiffly down from his cab, leaving the engine stuttering. The two men stood a yard or so from the scoop of rubble. As Fred approached, his work boots squelching through thick, dark mud, the truck-driver turned away, a look of disgust on his face.

'What's up?' the foreman asked. 'I reckoned we could get shot o' this lot tonight.'

'You'll not get shot o' that in a hurry,' the driver said, spitting emphatically on to a pile of broken bricks. 'That's a police job.'

Halliday followed the other men's eyes to where what looked at first glance like a bundle of rags lay crumpled among the tangle of bricks, slates and broken timber which the scoop had scraped up from the heap of rubble to which the houses had been reduced. His eyes fastened on the sole sign that his first impression was mistaken, a gnarled and filthy hand which protruded from the rags, still clutching a bulging plastic carrier bag. Close beside the hand a muddy red and white training shoe lay half concealed in the rubble.

'Christ, you can smell it,' Halliday said in disgust. 'That must be the bag lady the Bill were going on about t'other day. She were there all t'time. Teck your truck up to t'phone

80

by t'pub, Jack, will you, and dial 999. I've got t'kettle on for a sup o'tea while we wait.'

'Well, if you're sure there's a connection, Harry,' Detective-Superintendent Jack Longley, head of Bradfield's CID, said slowly. He and Harry Huddleston were sitting, sunk deep into leather armchairs, in a discreet alcove in the bar of the Clarendon Hotel, a favourite haunt of the community's pillars of the distinctly middle-aged and corpulent variety. The Clarendon had been one of those gothic Victorian hotels sinking slowly and without complaint into a delapidated old age in the 1970s, only to be dragged dramatically out of its decline by the property boom. Refurbishment or —as Huddleston, who had relished its previous tatty splendour, preferred to put it—tarting up had restored it to something of its former glory. With its gothic arches unveiled from behind panels of hardboard and its cornices picked out anew in red and gold, the Clarendon was enjoying a second youth as a centre for that strata of the town which prided itself on demanding something a little more solidly classy than anything the plate-glass and concrete air-conditioned upstarts which had attempted to push the old lady into the gutter could offer.

Longley had been on the way out of the police headquarters in search of his regular after-work refreshment when Huddleston had waylaid him, anxious to update him on the body which had been found on a building site earlier in the afternoon. Instead of going back to his office, Longley had insisted that Huddleston join him for a drink.

'It's a coincidence,' Huddleston conceded, sipping his half-pint with exaggerated daintiness. Pints were not served.

'Could be natural causes or an accident. She'd been buried in rubble so it was difficult to settle on a cause of death. We'll need the PM results f that. All I'm saying is, leave it with me for a few days while I check it out. We were looking for her, after all. As far as I can tell, she was the only person who'd admit to seeing Aziz after he left home. If her death is just coincidence it's a bloody unfortunate one.'

'You're talking to the site workers, I take it?'

'I've got the lads checking up on everyone who's working there now, and anyone who worked there during the first phase of the demolition. Asking about the old woman and the kids who were allegedly squatting there. Someone must have seen them,' Huddleston said. 'They're not all buried under the bloody rubble.'

'I'll leave it with you, then,' Longley said. 'For the time being. How's your London lad shaping up, by the way? Young Mower?'

'He'll do,' Huddleston conceded half-heartedly. 'He's sharp enough when he's not admiring the scenery.'

'Scenery?' Longley said. 'An eye for the ladies, has he? You'd better see it's only an eye, not a hand, else he'll be on his travels again, that one.'

'That was it, was it?' Huddleston said, almost to himself.

'So I'm told, strictly off the record,' Longley said. 'A DCI's wife.'

'Silly young sod. Doesn't he know better than to mess on his own doorstep? Any road, if brains are owt to go by, he'll do. End up a bloody chief constable, like as not, with his degree and his computers. You'd better find him a wife to keep his mind on the job.'

'Like yours does, I suppose,' Longley snorted in disbelief. The small amount of time that Huddleston spent at home was legend in the force. 'You might do better to introduce him to the joys of county cricket.'

'Nay, you haven't got the subtlety for that, you southerners,' Huddleston said, contentedly ploughing old furrows. Longley hailed from a village a few miles south of the Yorkshire border and was not allowed to forget this seriously disabling disadvantage of birth when cricket was under discussion.

Huddleston sipped his drink reflectively and glanced around the deliberately dimly lit bar, where a few tasteful Christmas decorations swirled slightly disconsolately in the draught from the heavy mahogany and glass swing doors.

It was not his favourite watering-hole: he much preferred the noisy lounge of the Woolpack where one 'quick half' with the boys from CID tended to lead to another pint of Tetley's and then another. That would be what he would miss most, he thought gloomily, when he left his office for the last time at the end of the month and became the prisoner of a world of domesticity with which he was almost totally unfamiliar.

His wife, he knew, had plans for what she called 'their' retirement, but they bore little relationship to his own determination to spend as much time as possible at Headingley, Park Avenue, Abbeydale Park and points east, south, west and occasionally north, wherever the Yorkshire team might find itself over a summer season. It was the prospect of the months between October and April which filled him with real despondency.

His attention snapped back to the present as across the room, among a group of middle-aged men at the bar, he spotted someone he knew and his eyes hardened.

'You know I'm not sure how many folk I've put away in thirty years,' he said quietly to Longley. 'But the ones that'll rankle when I pack it in are the ones that got away.'

Longley followed the direction of the Chief Inspector's gaze and nodded contemplatively.

'You never had anything on him, Harry. And it wasn't for want of trying.' As if he had overheard them, which was certainly impossible above the steady hum of conversation in the bar and the muted Christmas carols which were being piped all round the hotel, the object of their attention turned and looked directly at them. For a moment his eyes met Huddleston's in an overt and slightly mocking challenge, before he turned to his companions and made a comment which clearly amused them.

'He's coming over, dammit,' Huddleston said.

'He's an honest citizen as far as we're concerned,' Longley said warningly. 'Don't get demob happy, Harry. He's Rotary, of course. He'll be at your do next week.'

Terry Hardcastle strolled across the thick carpet of the bar, a smile on his face which did not extend to his eyes.

He was a tall man and as heavily built as Huddleston himself, his bull neck straining against the collar of a pale silk shirt and a pastel striped tie in which Huddleston himself would not have been seen dead, his hands far too large for the cut glass in which the Clarendon served its gin and tonic. In spite of his expensively fashionable clothes, there was nothing effeminate about Hardcastle. He had the muscular solidity of a heavy-weight boxer and sharp, watchful eyes to match.

'I have to dash now, Harry,' Hardcastle said, nodding to Longley. 'Else I'd buy you a glass to celebrate your retirement.' The choice of phrase was ambiguous, and deliberately so, Huddleston was sure.

'But I'll be at your Rotary do next week,' Hardcastle went on without waiting for a response. 'I'll be glad to get them in then. There can't be many coppers as have done as much for charity as you have. You'll be greatly missed.'

Huddleston nodded almost imperceptibly, not trusting himself to speak.

'We'll all miss Harry,' Longley said without irony. 'The villains most of all.'

'Aye, I'm sure,' Hardcastle said. 'Especially them.' He inclined his head almost graciously to the two seated policemen before going back to his friends at the bar.

'Cheeky sod,' Huddleston growled. 'I were so close to nailing him a couple of times . . .'

'But not close enough,' Longley said warningly. 'And it's all a long time ago, Harry. He's hardly involved in the betting shops now. He's gone legit. Diversified. You'd not get anything on him now.'

'Mebbe not, but I'd give a couple of season tickets at Headingley for another try.'

CHAPTER 8

The school hall was quiet, the calm before the storm, Jo Robertson thought as she stood on the edge of the stage with Peter Masefield surveying the ranks of chairs set out for the concert. The decaying state of the hall made her angry, as it often did. How many generations of hopeful young voices had been raised here, she wondered, and how many hundreds of shining faces had gazed at their future with all the optimism of youth, unaware of the often harsh disappointments which awaited them beyond the school gates.

Certainly the fathers and grandfathers of some of this evening's performers would have clattered in and out of this very room when the paintwork had been new, the windows shining and the ceiling unmarked by years of damp and grime, and its clientele exclusively male. Others, boys and girls whose families had come from much further afield, undoubtedly regarded the dilapidation of parts of Sutton Park as a marked improvement on their own remote village schools or, in some cases, no school at all. Even so, the place was an insult to young people, she thought, an insult which generations of politicians had calculated, accurately enough as it turned out, that they could get away with indefinitely just so long as Sutton Park continued to serve a part of the town which more often than not lacked any effective voice in the scheme of things.

Tonight, the school was, as usual, making the best of it. With the curtains drawn and the fifth year's best efforts at festive decoration with colourful paper chains and balloons hiding the worst of the stains on the walls and ceiling, the room had taken on an almost cheerful appearance. Even Jo felt her spirits lift slightly as she and Peter took a last-minute look at the preparations some half-hour before the audience was due to arrive.

Behind them the five members of the rock group were

still together on the night in spite of a near terminal fit of temperament by the tempestuous Vinny Barnes at the dress rehearsal the day before. They were plugging up their amplifiers which occasionally filled the room with a resonant shriek which drowned all coherent conversation. Freed from school regulations now, the five black boys wore an equally distinctive uniform of monumental training shoes, bright baseball caps, carefully turned up jeans and baggy T-shirts adorned with slogans which were just sufficiently inoffensive to have passed muster with Mrs Jackson and no more.

Even allowing for the noises behind them, the two teachers were not making much effort to speak, except in monosyllables. They had gone through the motions of working together on the final preparations for the concert performance in a state of silent and painful tension. Jo had learned on the staff-room grapevine that Peter Masefield had definitely applied for the job in Cumbria and nursed within herself a bitter sense of grievance that he had not felt able to tell her so himself.

For his part, Peter maintained his normal air of calm competence in public, avoiding Jo whenever possible, and when it was not possible and they were thrown together by the concert, adopting a chilly remoteness which was belied by the anger which very occasionally showed in his eyes.

'I think that's it, then,' Jo said, pushing her hair away from her face wearily. 'Just so long as we don't get too many people coming in without tickets, like we did last year. It only needs the fire-officer to drop in . . .'

She shrugged, with a rueful half-smile. Sutton Park's parents were not the best organized and very often turned up for school events on the spur of the moment, throwing carefully made plans for seating, catering and public safety into disarray. For a moment their eyes met and Jo thought that at last Peter was about to breach the wall of reserve which had come between them. But he hesitated, his jaw tightening, and eventually turned away towards the boys on the stage behind them.

'Come on, lads,' he said. 'If you don't get yourselves

organized you're still going to be wiring those amps up when the audience arrives. Let's have you out of here in five minutes, right?'

Jo walked slowly down the wooden steps into the body of the hall, the moment of optimism evaporating as quickly as it had arrived. Sod you then, she thought, blinking hard and taking several deep breaths to steady herself as she noticed a small group of people entering the hall by its rear doors. She forced herself to smile a welcome as she recognized Farida Arif and her two friends, carrying their instruments, closely following a young Asian man, elegantly dressed in dark slacks and a light blue sweater which she guessed must be cashmere.

'I brought the young ladies up by car,' Sami Arif said easily as he approached. 'My parents will be coming along very shortly.' He glanced lazily around the empty hall, taking in the packed rows of chairs and the preparations still going on above them on the stage.

'You're expecting a good turn-out, I see,' he said, his dark eyes bright with a half-mocking good humour. 'Going away to school, I missed out on all this worthy community stuff, you know? I'm afraid all I got at my alma mater was the Festival of Nine Lessons and Carols, and if you didn't happen to be a fully paid-up Christian, then jolly bad luck.'

'Your parents do know that Mrs Jackson is expecting them for refreshments in her room, don't they?' Jo asked, trying to inject some warmth into her voice. How was it, she wondered, that Sami Arif, for all his charm, exhibited all the most objectionable attributes the English public school system bestowed on its alumni while his sister had apparently avoided them at her equally exclusive girls' school? Perhaps it was Farida's failure or possibly her determination not to conform which lay behind her decision to move to a new school when she was sixteen. Sami nodded absently in response to Jo's question, his eyes roaming again and fixing briefly and with obvious condescension on the rock group descending noisily from the stage.

'Something for everyone, I see,' he said. 'The parents won't be long. They're bringing Ayesha and Safia's families up with them. Doing their bit for the community, and all that.'

Jo turned to the three girls in irritation which dissolved into pure delight as they took off their outdoor coats. She was not unaware that they were all attractive girls, even in school uniform, but tonight they looked stunning. Each was in traditional dress, satin trousers in jewel colours of turquoise, deep red and emerald, with a tunic of the same colour patterned in gold or silver. They wore filmy scarves over their dark hair and ear-rings and necklaces which she guessed were of gold, and just enough make-up to emphasize the fact that they were, in fact, young women, not children any more.

'You look wonderful,' she said.

Farida, always the most confident, acknowledged the compliment with a gentle inclination of the head and a slightly mischievous smile.

'And carefully chaperoned,' she said, with a glance at her brother. 'Though I'm not quite sure who is chaperoning who.' Sami Arif's face darkened for a second and then he too smiled, although Jo wondered how genuine his amusement really was.

'Whom, Farida, who is chaperoning whom. You won't get your place at Oxford if you can't master English grammar, will she, Mrs Robertson?'

'Oh, I think Farida's grammar will pass muster, Mr Arif,' Jo returned sharply, stung into schoolmistress mode by the young man's patronizing tone to his sister. But she bit back her question about where he had learned his own manners. Antagonizing the son of a school governor was perhaps not a wise course, she told herself, while despising her own caution even as she bit her tongue.

'Girls, Ms Turner is expecting you in the gym,' she said. 'You can leave your outdoor clothes in there and use it as a dressing-room if you need to. Will you be joining your parents, Mr Arif?' Sammy looked at her with a hint of mockery in his eyes.

'Oh, I think I'll avoid the bunfight. Not really my scene,'

88

he said airily. 'I'll just see the girls to their dressing-room and then wait for the show to begin.'

The elegant quartet made their way out of the hall, closely followed by the five members of the pop group who had at last finished their elaborate preparations on the stage. Jo watched them go, the brown and the black, jostling their way amiably out of the swing doors together, and wondered how long they would continue to be protected, as protected they undoubtedly were in school, from the bitter currents which swirled around in the adult world outside. Peter Masefield came up quietly to stand behind her and almost without thinking she turned to him as though nothing had come between them.

'Are we over-protecting them?' she asked.

'No, we're giving them space to grow, that's all,' he said, understanding her question at once. 'Just because it's nasty and brutish out there doesn't mean the school has to be the same. Heaven forbid.'

'It was nasty and brutish for Karim,' she said quietly.

'That's still bothering you?'

'It's not something you forget very easily . . .' Her voice trailed off as Peter put his hand on her shoulder and she felt the familiar electricity strike at the very core of her being.

'We need . . .'

'We must . . .'

They spoke in unison and broke off, laughing.

'Please, Peter,' she said, lifting his hand off her arm and keeping hold of it for a second before drawing away and glancing round the empty hall guiltily. 'Please, let's talk. Later? Why don't you give me a lift home? I haven't got the car. The damn thing wouldn't start this morning.'

'It's a date,' he said lightly, turning away as the first tentative group of Asian parents and young children came into the hall by the rear door. 'Here come the punters.'

By nine-thirty the school had begun to quieten down again. The wildly keyed-up performers who had flocked back to the gym to take off their make-up and change back into

89

street clothes had begun to straggle out to find their parents. The last beaming family group were making their way out of the hall and back towards the front entrance of the school, dragging over-excited younger children by the hand, to wait for the performers to emerge. Margaret Jackson had reassembled her party of school governors in her office with an offer of a final cup of coffee, and this time, Jo Robertson noticed, the elegant figure of Sami Arif had gone along with the group which included his parents.

In the gym, Maggie Turner, dressed in honour of the occasion in a long Paisley skirt and cowl-necked black sweater, was stuffing discarded cotton wool balls and other debris into a large black plastic bin-bag when Jo joined her, having made sure the hall was almost empty.

'Hey, man, did you get that applause, Mrs Robertson?' said Vinny Barnes, the pop group's lead singer, whose dreadlocks stood up in a dark glistening aureole of triumph.

'You were tremendous, Vinny, if a bit loud for my taste,' Jo said, meaning it.

The boy grinned delightedly. 'You should hear 240 watts, if you think that's loud, ma'am,' he said. 'A hundred ain't nuthing!'

'I should save anything louder for a pop festival,' Maggie Turner said tartly, picking up a broken drumstick from the bench where the group were sprawled in an exhaustion which was only partly simulated. 'Is this any use any more?'

The drummer, a small, very dark boy whose face was still wet with sweat, shook his head. 'That's had it,' he confirmed. 'Knackered, like me.'

'Home, then, boys,' Jo urged. 'You'll need your sleep if you're going be fit for school again tomorrow.'

'Sleep, what's that?' Vinny asked the room in general, flinging his arms wide. 'Hendrix never slept.'

'Hendrix is dead,' Maggie said dismissively, 'and maybe that's because he never slept. Don't forget you lot've got PE first thing in the morning, if I'm not mistaken. Mr Hackett won't want you on the football pitch with your eyes shut.' All five boys groaned melodramatically at the thought, but gradually began to pick up their belongings and move themselves in the general direction of the door.

Jo glanced across at the only other group left in the gym: the three Asian musicians who were huddled in a corner, deep in conversation. As she approached they all glanced in her direction and she was surprised to see that they had lost the obvious elation with which they had left the stage a quarter of an hour earlier and were looking at her with troubled eyes. Farida pulled up her headscarf, which had fallen back over her shoulders, to cover her hair in what Jo suspected was deference not to her own family as much as some of the other Asian parents who were still in the school.

'Sammy's going to take us home,' she said and glancing at the other girls: 'Are you ready?' Ayesha and Safia nodded and pulled on their coats, extinguishing the luminous beauty of their costumes as the light in their eyes had also, Jo thought, already been puzzlingly extinguished.

'Did you enjoy it in the end?' Jo asked, knowing that Safia had, in particular, been very nervous before the performance. The girls nodded again, in that same unnerving silence and Ayesha and Safia picked up their instruments and walked slowly towards the door. Farida hesitated and Jo waited for the girl to summon up the courage to speak. Instead she reached into her coat pocket and held out a small plastic package to Jo.

'We found this on the floor,' she said dully.

Jo knew instantly what the package was, and felt herself go very cold.

'Where?' she asked quietly, and Farida pointed to the corner of the room where she and her friends had left their coats and instrument cases while the concert had been in progress. Jo looked at the white powder inside the plastic wrapping. She knew enough about drugs to know that this was not cannabis, a substance which cropped up occasionally in almost every school, but something a whole lot more dangerous.

'Vinny, do you think?' she asked, instantly despising herself for the ease with which the question came. But she was surprised at the vehemence with which Farida shook her head.

'I don't think so,' she said.

'So who?' Jo asked. 'If you have any idea, Farida, you must tell me. Did you see who dropped it? Was it Ayesha or Safia?' Again Farida shook her head with total conviction.

'No, of course not,' she said. 'They wouldn't be so stupid as to take that stuff.' For a moment they both stood silently, their eyes fixed on the tiny packet of white granules, both aware of the enormity of the consequences which would inevitably follow from its discovery. At last Farida shrugged slightly, suddenly looking much older than her seventeen years, and very tired under the carefully applied make-up.

'It's not fair if anyone in school gets the blame,' she said so quietly that Jo had to strain to catch what she was saying. 'I think it's cocaine,' she said. 'And I think my brother probably dropped it. If the others hadn't seen it I would have put it in my pocket and taken it home. Please, please don't tell anyone.'

'No way,' Peter Masefield said flatly. He and Jo Robertson were sitting in his car, parked just around the corner from Jo's house in the shadow of a large tree. 'You can't do that,' he said. 'You'll have to tell Margaret in the morning, and get the police in.'

Jo nodded in reluctant assent.

'Of course, you're right,' she said. 'I don't know what I was thinking about. I'm just tired, I suppose.' She glanced down at her lap where the small plastic packet of some still undefined substance, which she had thought for one self-deluding half-hour that she might 'lose', lay like an accusation between them.

After she had left the school gym she had hung around for a while in the entrance hall waiting for Margaret Jackson to emerge from her office. Gradually the school had emptied, but there was still no sign of the head and her guests when Peter himself had brought his car round to the front of the building and flashed his lights to attract her attention. On the spur of the moment she had put on her coat, with the packet still in the pocket, and left the building. On the short drive home she had broken the tense silence in the car and told Peter what had happened.

'It was just the thought of the police tramping round the school again asking questions,' she said, her voice hoarse with fatigue. 'When this time it's nothing to do with the school, if Farida's right.'

'*If* Farida is right,' Peter said tersely. 'You're very trusting all of a sudden. You should know better.'

'It couldn't be anything to do with the girls,' Jo said fiercely. 'They were very—oh, I don't know—very shocked, I suppose. Very upset.'

'You can't protect Farida, anyway. If it really was her brother who dropped it, the whole family is going to be upset,' Peter said. 'You have to tell the police. See Margaret in the morning and take it from there.' Jo nodded again.

'I think,' she said, 'I'm losing my grip.'

Peter laughed but it was an empty sound, without mirth. 'I think I've lost mine.'

He put his arm around her and kissed her gently, without passion, and gradually some of the tension which gripped them both ebbed away. Jo let herself relax against him and her eyes wandered down the long street of suburban houses, where the lights of Christmas trees were beginning to appear in front windows. She had never felt less like celebrating Christmas, she thought. Even the usually infectious enthusiasm of the children at school, of all religions, for the coming celebrations had not communicated itself this year when she faced, for the first time, the prospect of the holiday season entirely on her own with Neil, he having refused all offers to visit his parents' home in London or to invite anyone to join them at the bungalow.

The two weeks of the school holidays, when Peter would be spending some of the time with his children and even the briefest meeting would be almost impossible to arrange, stretched ahead like a prison sentence. How much worse it was going to be if Peter really did move away, she thought.

'I know you think I'm trying to hurt you by leaving Sutton Park,' Peter said quietly, as if reading her thoughts. 'But in the end, I think it's best for both of us. We can't go

93

on tearing each other apart like we have been doing. I think you're wrong to feel so tied to Neil, but if you can't change, then let's leave it at that . . .' He gave an almost imperceptible and dispirited shrug.

'Leave me to that?' Jo came back bitterly, pulling herself away from him with a sharp gesture in the direction of her home where they knew Neil would be waiting for her. 'What you don't realize is just how like a tomb that place has become. All the life has gone out of it. It's all crumbled away into dust. You want to abandon me to that? How can you say you love me and then walk out and leave me?'

It was the age-old cry of the abandoned lover and Peter groaned and buried his head in his hands against the steering-wheel.

'I love you so much,' he said, his voice muffled. 'So much that I can't bear not to be with you all the time. I just can't bear it. I have to go because knowing you are with him hurts too much.'

Jo did not answer, and eventually Peter turned to see that her face was wet with tears, just visible in the dim light from outside the car. They were conscious of the shadow of a passer-by on the pavement outside and the faint sound of footfalls.

'That's David,' Jo said, wiping her eyes. 'He must have been with Neil all this time. I'll have to go.'

Peter shrugged dispiritedly.

'Of course,' he said. 'He needs you.'

If irony was intended she did not respond. Her whole body cried out for the comfort of his arms but she turned away and opened the door, letting in a blast of night air as cold as the charity she knew she could expect if she ever did leave Neil. Few would forgive her, she thought, and she doubted that she would ever forgive herself.

'I'll see Margaret in the morning about the other thing,' she said. 'More anger and telegrams.' Her voice was flat and devoid of emotion now and he could see even in the dim, flickering light from the street lamps that her face was cold and set. As she slammed the door behind her, Peter

94

saw vividly the tomb she had conjured up, and he banged his clenched fists against the steering-wheel in frustration.

The trouble with the drugs squad, Harry Huddleston always said, was not that they enjoyed merging into the local scene Miami vice style—although that was true enough he thought as he surveyed Detective-Inspector Ray Watson's jeans and garish white and purple and undoubtedly expensive training shoes with profound distaste. The real trouble with the drug squad was that they were so bloody young. It was an area of duty which attracted the smart new breed of well-educated copper he so disliked. Indeed, he more than half suspected that Kevin Mower, not that long arrived from the Met as a result of his mysterious personal career move, fancied his chances with the trendy lads who were based not at Bradfield's central police station but five miles away at the county headquarters, surrounded by their computers and their intelligence officers planning their glamorous undercover operations.

Still on this occasion even Huddleston had to concede, albeit grudgingly, that Watson had had the grace to consult him before rushing on to his patch and conceivably into his case after a call from Margaret Jackson at Sutton Park School.

'There was nowt,' Huddleston said again. 'Plenty of booze, plenty of space for a kiss and a cuddle, but if they'd been doing owt else in their little den there was no trace of it. And it wasn't for want of looking, was it, lad?' He consulted Mower, who was propped against the office window-sill, pale yellow shirtsleeves rolled up and elegantly trousered legs crossed, with a sharp and speculative look in his eyes.

'Well, there's something up there now, it seems,' Watson said, tossing his longish hair back with what Huddleston found an intensely irritating gesture. 'Though just what it is, they claim not to know. "White powder in a plastic packet," and they thought we ought to know about it.' He mimicked, unfairly Mower thought, a rather refined female voice.

'Aye, well, they wouldn't know, would they?' Huddleston said heavily. 'The place is run by a gang of women—don't know their arse from their elbow, as far as I can see. Completely amazed by what was going on in their under-drawing and a body in their showers.'

'Are you getting anywhere on that?' Watson asked, knowing very well how anxious Huddleston would be to wrap his last murder inquiry up before his departure at the end of the year. The older man shrugged his broad shoulders and scowled, unwilling to admit how completely the inquiry had run into the sand but anxious to squeeze as much information as possible from Watson on his return from the school.

'No weapon, no motive, no witnesses,' he grunted. 'All we've got is an old bag lady found rotting under a demolished squat who allegedly knew the victim. Wearing ruddy kid's training shoes, which may mean something, I suppose, though I'm damned if I know what. Mower here tells me they cost sixty quid new and've been out of fashion for six months or more. Which reminds me, I haven't had a path report on her yet, damn it. It could have been natural causes, for all I know, though I somehow doubt it.'

Huddleston glanced at his sergeant with an unexpected gleam in his eye.

'I tell you what, lad,' he said. 'Why don't you go up to the school with Inspector Watson here and have a word with our Mrs Robertson while I chase up our forensic friends. Take her over that visit to Commercial Street again —and this time push her on just why she went down there, will you? A bit of pressure's what's needed with that one. I know you'll enjoy that. And catch that gym mistress as well, though I don't think there's much there for you— either of you. Looked ever so slightly bent to me, our Maggie did. That's it. Go and give the ladies a going-over.'

Mower shuffled himself upright with just the slightest hint of discomfiture but Watson ignored Huddleston's undisguised leer.

'Robertson?' he asked sharply. 'She's the one who found the packet of coke, or whatever it is.'

'Did she now,' Huddleston said heavily. 'She's in all the right places at all the right times, that one, isn't she, Mower?'

'Sir,' the sergeant said non-committally.

The pain which Margaret Jackson had been successfully concealing for months had reached an almost unbearable pitch that morning. She had swallowed several analgesics with her coffee and now lit a rare cigarette with hands that were shaking slightly. Jo Robertson, who was perched in her favourite spot on the office's window-seat, watched with growing concern. She was looking unusually pale herself this morning but was as reluctant to discuss the reasons for that as Margaret evidently was to admit that she was unwell.

'Did the governors enjoy the performance last night?' Jo asked, as much for something to say as because she really cared.

'Mr and Mrs Arif were really thrilled by Farida and her friends,' Margaret said. 'And delighted with the reception they got. Mrs Arif is very keen on traditional music, apparently, although it's not highly regarded in Pakistan because of its Indian connections. She encouraged the girls. They were good, weren't they?' Jo nodded, pleased. She had put some effort into persuading the girls to perform in the face of their claims that they were only beginners.

'What did you make of Farida's brother?' she asked, returning to the subject which in fact obsessed her. Margaret looked at her for a moment without speaking.

'A very smooth young man,' she said. 'Did you know he played cricket for Cambridge University? But there's a chip on that elegant shoulder, I think. I asked him if he still played and he went into a long diatribe about the Yorkshire County Cricket Club not giving trials to young Asian players.'

'But they'll only take people who were born here, won't they?' Jo asked. 'Or have they changed that rule now?'

'Yes, they have, but I don't think it was his own talent that he felt was being ignored, anyway, but all the young

Asian boys who were born here in Bradfield and are playing in the Asian league. I think he was genuinely concerned for them, but there was something else, a bitterness of his own there, somehow. Anyway, I asked him if he would like to come and help coach a team here. Some of the boys are very keen and it's not really Mike Hackett's game. He's an athletics man at heart.'

'Did he say he would?' Jo asked curiously. She had not envisaged community service as one of Sami Arif's priorities in life.

Margaret laughed wryly. 'He suddenly claimed to be leading an enormously busy life, if that's what you're thinking,' she said. 'And especially busy on Wednesday afternoons when Mike runs cricket practice.'

'Here comes the force of law and order again,' Jo said quietly, glancing out of the window to where she could see Sergeant Mower and another man she did not know, tall, with longish hair and casually dressed, getting out of an unmarked car.

'We could have done without this,' Margaret said, the look of strain returning to her face. 'Our reputation is taking more of a hammering than I suspect it can stand. Our numbers will be down next year at this rate, without a doubt.'

'I did think of just pocketing the evidence and not telling anyone,' Jo admitted grimly. 'Peter persuaded me that my duty as a citizen lay elsewhere.'

Margaret looked at her sharply, unsure how seriously the admission was meant to be taken, but not surprised to hear Jo mention Peter Masefield's name in a less than professional context. She prided herself on knowing what went on in her staff-room and she had not missed the pain two valued members of staff had been causing each other for the past few weeks, although she regarded it as no part of her job to interfere.

'You've no idea who could have dropped it?' she asked, not for the first time, and not for the first time Jo shook her head emphatically.

'Absolutely no idea,' she said.

If Margaret Jackson had looked at her sceptically after that denial, it was as nothing to the scepticism with which Detective-Inspector Ray Watson regarded her across the headmistress's desk half an hour later. Mrs Jackson was due to teach that period and had left the police to talk to Jo in her office. Jo had retained her seat by the window, her back to the pale intermittent sunshine, her face therefore in shadow. That must have been deliberate, Sergeant Mower thought as he took up a watching brief, his notebook out, on the opposite side of the room where he, completely incidentally he assured himself, had a good view of Jo Robertson's legs, decorously crossed at the ankle but none the less attractive for all that.

Jo Robertson was lying to the police, as she had tried to lie to Peter Masefield and successfully done to Margaret Jackson, by omission. She held no brief for Sami Arif, who was a young man she had felt no warmth towards on their brief acquaintance, but she was determined not to break Farida's confidence and pass on her suspicions about her brother. The police would have to work that out for themselves, she had decided, knowing very well that her loyalty was at the least perverse and at worst criminal. She comforted herself with the knowledge that working it out would not be likely to take the police very long.

Meeting Inspector Ray Watson for the first time, who in spite of the longish hair which flopped boyishly across his forehead and his street-wise appearance, had a rather unnerving sombre stillness about his eyes which Jo suspected concealed a ruthless intelligence, she was even more sure that if Sami Arif was on drugs the police would either know about it already or would soon find out.

'I've made you a list of people who were in or around the gym last night,' Jo said.

'All pupils here, or staff?' Watson asked.

'No, not all of them. There were a few people—family or friends—who helped youngsters in with equipment, that sort of thing.' She passed him the list of names which had been lying on Margaret's desk and watched while he scanned it quickly.

'Right, we'll start with the people in school,' Watson said. 'The kids first and then you and Ms Turner.' He used the abbreviation without irony, Mower noted approvingly, and he flashed an amused glance at Jo Robertson which she was too preoccupied to notice.

'It will take time to get the studentss' parents in,' Jo said. 'Some of them won't be available in the daytime . . .' Watson waved an impatient hand.

'We're not under any obligation, Mrs Robertson,' he said. 'We're only asking preliminary questions. If you want to sit in on the interviews, fine, that's up to you. That's all that's required.'

He glanced at the plastic packet which still lay on Margaret Jackson's desk like an unexploded bomb, open now and quickly indentified as cocaine when Watson arrived by the simple expedient of his tasting it.

'We're not talking pot, here, Mrs Robertson,' Watson went on, his voice hardening. 'This is serious stuff and if it's being hawked around behind your bike sheds, you need to know about it as quickly as we do.' Jo nodded sombrely.

'I'll sit in,' she said. 'That's what Mrs Jackson wants.'

'Right.' Watson's eye travelled down the list of names again. 'We'll start with this lot,' he said. 'The rock group —and before you accuse me of being prejudiced, I'll plead guilty. It's prejudice based on pretty solid evidence, and you'll just have to believe it. In my experience, long hair, loud music and illegal substances go together.'

It was not an argument sixteen-year-old Vinny Barnes took kindly to. He drooped, rather than sat, on the hard chair that the police had positioned in front of Margaret Jackson's desk, his dreadlocks limp this morning and his eyes heavy with tiredness, but none the less belligerent for that, every inch of his body oozing lazy defiance.

'It ain't mine, man. No way,' he said with force. 'You think I'd be stupid enough to do that sort of shit?'

Jo allowed herself the faintest of smiles. She knew, though the police would not, that Vinny was exaggerating his West Indian accent, not normally very noticeable. He was, to his own satisfaction at least, gently sending the police up.

'What sort of shit is it, Vinny?' Watson came back quickly. 'Do you know?' Vinny glanced at the packet in Watson's hand and shrugged.

'How do I know?' he said. 'Coke? Crack? Heroin? How do I know, man?'

'But not pot, not cannabis, not ganja? You know that?'

The boy looked at the policeman with an expression of contempt.

'You mean do I know what cannabis looks like? C'mon, man, what d'you take me for? Is knowing what it looks like going to incriminate me, or what? Any ten-year-old around here knows what it looks like. Isn't that a fact, Mrs Robertson?' He appealed to Jo, who was holding her watching brief on the window-seat again, with an extravagant wave of the arm and a mischievous gleam in his eye. She was deeply unhappy with the turn events had taken, wishing that she had insisted in talking to the Inspector alone before he had started his interviews with pupils.

'I think that's about right, Vinny,' Jo said. She had asked Vinny and the rest of the rock group if they wanted their parents called to the school to be with them while they were questioned by the police, only to be scornfully refused. 'We're questioned by the police on the street almost every Friday night,' Vinny had said without rancour, and Jo believed him.

'And does ''everybody'' know where to get cannabis?' Watson persisted, ignoring Jo's intervention. 'Does every ten-year-old know where to get it?' Vinny shrugged.

'Maybe,' he said. 'You'll have to ask the kids in the first year. I can't speak for them.'

'But *you* know where to get cannabis?'

'So if I do? There's a difference, man,' Vinny said, glancing at the packet of cocaine on the desk.

'Possibly,' Watson conceded. 'But not much. And my guess is that if you know where to get that, you know where to get this too.' He held the packet of cocaine up towards the boy. 'Isn't that a fact, Vinny?' The boy shrugged again and did not reply.

'Come on, Vinny,' Watson said, his tone harder. 'I want

101

answers. I want to know where this came from. I want to know if this is just a one-off or if someone's dealing around here. And my guess is that you know the answer to those questions.'

'No way, man, no way,' Vinny said again, angrily this time. 'That's not mine, and I know nothing about coke around here, nothing at all. It's not my scene.'

'You mean it's not around the music scene? Come on, I know better.'

'Mrs Robertson, do I have to put up with this?' Vinny said, turning to Jo, but before she could reply, Inspector Watson had thumped his fist on the desk angrily.

'If you'd rather answer questions down at the nick, lad, that's fine by me. So far we've done it softly, softly. But believe me, I'm looking for some answers from you and your mates. You're into hard rock and I'm into hard drugs and if there's any connection, take my word for it, I'm going to find it.'

'I think, Inspector, Vinny needs legal advice or his parents here if you're going to pursue this any further,' Jo broke in. Watson looked at her, his dark eyes hostile, but then he nodded and glanced at Mower, who was watching the confrontation with studied impassivity.

'All right,' he said more quietly. 'You're saying this is not yours, right?'

Vinny nodded.

'So did you see anyone else with it, anyone drop it?'

Vinny shook his head this time. 'I've never seen that before,' he said flatly. 'Nor anything like it. I'm clean, man.'

'I may need to talk to you again, Barnes,' Watson said. 'Will you give the sergeant your home address and phone number? You are on the phone?' The boy nodded again with a slight smile now, which seemed to Jo to mix relief with an element of triumph. He left the room with Sergeant Mower and Jo glanced at the Detective-Inspector non-committally. He stretched back in Margaret Jackson's chair and ran his hand through his long hair, pushing it away from his face, and looked at her speculatively.

'I suppose you think I harassed him,' he said. 'If you'd

102

seen as many kids screwed up on heroin as I have, you might not be so worried about it. And it's kids Vinny's age who are out on the streets dealing the stuff. Some of them start buying when they're ten and selling by the time they're twelve.'

Jo shrugged almost imperceptibly. The policeman was not telling her anything she did not know by heart. These were the facts of life against which the school battled, in its own way, daily.

'By rights you should interview Vinny with his father,' she said. 'Dr Barnes wouldn't stand for any harassment.'

'Dr Barnes?'

'Vinny's father is one of our local GPs.' She searched his face for any sign of surprise but found none. Watson just watched her impassively for a moment and then grinned boyishly.

'*Touché*,' he said. 'So I wasn't expecting that.'

'And Vinny is hoping to go to medical school too. He's a very bright boy, one of our brightest, as well as a talented musician. You really must watch who you are stereotyping, Inspector, it could get you into all sorts of trouble.'

Watson nodded.

'Good homes don't necessarily produce lily-white kids,' he said. 'That's a stereotype too. But perhaps you'd like to fill me in with a little background on these kids before I talk to them.'

'If you hadn't been in such a hurry earlier on I would have done that,' Jo said.

'Obviously you don't think Barnes brought that packet into school.'

'No, I don't,' Jo said. 'I don't think any of the students brought it into school.'

Watson looked at her reflectively for a moment.

'You sound very confident about that.'

'I know them all. I know them very well. We've been working on last night's concert for the past two months. If I didn't know them before that, I certainly do now. None of them is a likely cocaine-user, let alone a dealer. I'm absolutely certain of that.'

Inspector Watson glanced at the list of names which Jo had given him.

'Are you saying that it's more likely to have been someone who came in from outside? Mrs Barnes? Who's that, Vinny's mother? The respectable doctor's wife? Or who's this, Sami Arif? Who's he? Farida's father, brother, or what?'

'Brother,' Jo said neutrally. 'And by the way, their father is a governor here—used to be mayor, you remember?—though I think he's resigned as a councillor now . . . I'm sorry,' she said as Watson threw a glance of mock despair at Sergeant Mower, who had been standing in the doorway listening to their exchange.

'Proper citadel of respectability we've got here, guv,' Mower said, with a grin at Jo. 'Whiter than bleedin' white.'

'The fact remains that one of these eminently respectable citizens—or rather more likely their offspring, if I may say so in spite of your reservations, Mrs Robertson—brought a packet of coke on to these premises last night. And I'm not kidding when I say I intend to find out who that was, your ethnic yuppies notwithstanding. Right?' Watson concluded uncompromisingly.

Jo uncrossed her legs, aware of Kevin Mower's intense interest in the manœuvre and wishing she had worn trousers instead of a rather short skirt that morning.

'So you want me to wheel the students in as planned?' she asked quietly.

'Just as planned, please, Mrs Robertson, but before you bring them in you can fill me in on any background details that you think might be relevant. Outsiders we'll deal with later.'

CHAPTER 9

'Buggeration,' Chief Inspector Huddleston said feelingly as he faced DI Watson and DS Mower across his cluttered desk. The information that the two younger officers had brought him after their morning at Sutton Park was not what he wanted to hear, although he was still professional enough, even with barely more than a fortnight of his career left, to concede that his theory that Karim Aziz had been the victim of a random racist killing was becoming increasingly untenable.

'Did we ask forensic to look for signs of drugs?' he asked Mower accusingly. 'It was the first thing I asked Amos Atherton to look at, and there was no trace of puncture marks. Not a sign he said and he confirmed it in his report, didn't he?' He glanced irritably at Mower again.

'He confirmed it,' Mower said. 'But I don't recall whether or not they did a blood analysis.'

'Cocaine leaves no traces, not with a lad that age,' Watson said. 'Not externally. But it will show up on a blood test if he'd been using it recently.'

'I'll talk to the pathologist again, sir,' Mower said hastily, annoyed at his own failure to notice the omission and anxious not to bear the brunt of any more of Huddleston's irritation, especially in front of the drugs squad officer.

When the sergeant had left the room, Huddleston sighed heavily again and picked up the phone, but did not dial.

'It's the sort of situation where we'll have bloody community liaison down on our necks if we're not right careful,' he said heavily. 'Mohammed Arif, ex-councillor, ex-mayor, chairman of the Asian Community Council, school governor, respectable businessman, reputedly a millionaire, unless that bank collapse has ruined him: let's just see if we can find out if anyone knows anything we should know before we go blundering in there, lad.'

'It's the son I'm interested in, sir, not the old man,' Watson said mildly. 'I don't imagine the father's doing cocaine.'

'But the lad has previous?'

'He was done for possession while he was at Cambridge. For his own use, he told the magistrates, and got off with a fine and a lecture on the error of his ways from the bench. But it's a hard habit to break. You know that.'

'And the sister let on?'

'No, she didn't. She's a very self-possessed young lady is our Farida. Not what you'd expect to meet up there at Sutton Park, by a long chalk. Ran away from boarding-school or something, the Robertson woman said, and decided she wanted to go to a comp. Some kids don't know which side their bread's buttered, do they? Anyway she was quite adamant that she had no idea who had dropped the packet of stuff.'

'But you don't believe her? Why's that, then?'

Watson did not reply immediately. He had spoken to Farida Arif ahead of her two friends, who were much more hesitant and uncertain in their protestations that they had no idea where the packet of cocaine had come from. It was, in fact, Farida's certainty which had convinced him that she was lying, that and the unmistakable tension which had gripped Jo Robertson as soon as the girl had walked into the room to be questioned.

He had been unsurprised later when the police computer came up with the information that Sami Arif had a record of cocaine abuse, a fact which confirmed that his sister had in all probability been knowingly covering up for him earlier. But as to whether or why Jo Robertson might have been a party to that deception he remained mystified, even after he had taken a formal statement from her about the previous evening's events. She had no idea, she had assured him, her eyes unclouded now, who might have dropped the packet in the school gymnasium. No idea at all.

'What do you make of Jo Robertson?' he asked Huddleston thoughtfully. The Chief Inspector settled himself more comfortably in his chair and snorted.

'Bloody feminist,' he said scornfully. 'Anti-racist, anti-sexist, anti-men. About as much use in bed as a praying mantis, I shouldn't wonder. But intelligent. Nobody's fool.'

'You talking about the beautiful Joanna, guv, the light of my life?' asked Kevin Mower, coming back into the room with a sheaf of reports in his hand.

'You want to watch her and her do-gooding friends,' Huddleston snapped. 'You're a sight too ready to make excuses for all and sundry yourself.'

106

'I've just found a reason to go and have another heart-to-heart with her, guv,' Mower said mildly. 'That little old lady she said she saw down Commercial Road didn't die of natural causes after all. According to the PM, there's what looks suspiciously like a knife wound in among all the other cuts and bruises. She was dead before she was buried in the rubble. And there's more.' He waved the reports in the air for a moment before dropping them with a flourish on Huddleston's desk.

'Young Karim was doing coke. The results of the blood test have just come through.'

Mohammed Arif drummed his fingers on his vast mahogany partners' desk impatiently. He was a tall man, the black hair only slightly grey at the temples, the lips thin and unsmiling and the dark eyes unfriendly in a narrow, distinguished face.

'I'm sorry I cannot help you, Chief Inspector,' Arif said again to Harry Huddleston, who perched rather than sat in the rather spindly visitor's chair opposite him. Across an expanse of richly patterned oriental rug, Detective-Inspector Watson sat, equally ill at ease, his trainers tucked under his chair as if to keep them out of sight. Arif straightened his military-looking striped tie with long brown fingers and shrugged beneath his well-cut grey suiting.

'What my son does is his concern, but I can assure you that the incident in Cambridge was a youthful indiscretion which has certainly not been repeated to my knowledge. But you will have to speak to him yourself when he returns from London.'

'And that will be when, Mr Arif?' Huddleston asked.

'Tomorrow afternoon at the latest. I expect him to telephone me this evening to discuss the meetings he has had today. I will mention your visit to him then. I am sure you will find him most cooperative.'

'An unexpected trip, was it, sir?'

'Unexpected?' Arif said, surprised. 'Not at all unexpected, Chief Inspector. His appointments in London have been arranged for weeks.' Arif flicked over the pages of his desk diary as if to confirm the facts to his own satisfaction.

'As you know,' he went on, 'Sami joined the business when he came down from Cambridge. His legal knowledge —and his energy—have been invaluable to the company, and he had contacts in the City which I cannot match. One of the advantages of a British education.'

'A private education,' Watson intervened with unexpected aggression, to the evident surprise of both older men. 'Is that where he picked up his habit? At his expensive school?'

Arif looked at Watson with an expression bordering on contempt, but he evidently thought better of his first instinct, which had been to ignore the interruption and return his attention to Huddleston as the one of the pair deserving of his attention.

'His former habit, Inspector Watson,' Arif said with distaste. 'His former habit was acquired at one of your older universities. It was, I believe, quite rife in certain circles there at the time—until the unfortunate death from an overdose of the son of minor royalty which you will recall, I am sure.

'There are self-evident advantages to a British education, as I am sure you know. But there are disadvantages too. One is the racism which my daughter encountered at her expensive girls' school—subtle, snobbish, spiteful racism from which I was pleased to remove her for the healthier atmosphere of Sutton Park. The second is an inevitable exposure to a morality which is not mine, nor that of my community. My son, as you observe, has to some extent suffered from that. You must not make the mistake, gentlemen, of assuming that everyone shares your obvious conviction that all that is Western is inevitably superior to all that is Eastern. It is not a view I share.'

Huddleston swallowed hard at the end of this assault while Watson allowed himself a glimmer of a smile.

'Tell me, Mr Arif, as a prominent member of your community,' Huddleston began at last in a half-strangulated tone. 'Tell me to what extent you are aware of drug abuse among your young people, youngsters like Karim Aziz, for instance.'

Arif sat for a moment unmoving, his features as gaunt and unyielding as an Aztec statue and his eyes deep pools of darkness. Finally he brushed an infinitesimal speck of dust off the single buff file which lay on the desk in front of him with an impatient gesture.

'Among my young people,' he said coldly, 'by which I suppose you mean young people from families with roots in the sub-continent, among my young people I am not aware of much drug abuse at all. It may happen, but I would say it is not rife. If on the other hand you asked the same question of my wife, who teaches at the college of higher education, you might get a different answer about your young people and those with roots in the Caribbean.'

'So you would say your son—at the time of his indiscretion—and young Karim, who we know was using cocaine, are exceptions,' Watson came back quietly enough to prevent Huddleston from responding to the deliberate insult.

'Quite so, Inspector,' Arif said. 'As I suspect you very well know. And now, if you will excuse me, I have a great deal of work to be getting on with. I will tell my son at the earliest opportunity that you wish to speak to him.'

The trouble which Sutton Park school had been half-expecting ever since the discovery of Karim Aziz's body came that afternoon and the catalyst was a brief paragraph in the local evening paper to the effect that the police had been called back to the school to investigate the discovery of drugs on the premises. Margaret Jackson was aghast at the implications of the paragraph when an anxious parent brought an early edition to her at lunch-time.

Any school was vulnerable to damage to its reputation at a time when pupils were scarce and the money to run schools followed them inexorably. A 'down-town' school, like Sutton Park, fighting against all the disadvantages some children brought with them from run-down homes and disintegrating families, lived on a permanent knife-

109

edge, always aware that the withdrawal of children in a parental panic could deal it a fatal blow. Margaret put the paper on one side and wearily began to compose a reassuring letter to parents, the second she had written that week.

By the mid-afternoon break teachers were coming into the staff-room seriously worried. Jo Robertson, tired after an hour spent fruitlessly trying to interest a fourth-year class in war poetry, took a cup of tea from the bar and sought out Maggie Turner in the crush.

'Vinny Barnes and friends are absolutely furious with the police,' she said.

'I'm not surprised. Dr Barnes won't be too happy when he sees that it's got into the local rag,' Maggie said. 'I had Vinny's sister in my netball group just now and she and her friends were very angry. They're absolutely convinced the rock group was picked on because they're black.'

'It wasn't like that, it really wasn't,' Jo said helplessly. 'The stuff was found in the gym and they were there. The police had no choice but to question them. You know that.'

'Well, that's not the way the black kids see it,' Maggie said flatly. 'I've never known them so twitchy.'

'I know. I had to separate a couple of lads just now—Jackie Ledger for one, d'you know him? Not a boy I've ever known get physical before. He actually called me something quite rude before be backed off. Normally I'd have had him in detention before his feet could touch the ground, but this afternoon I thought it was better to let it ride.'

'I know what you mean,' Maggie said ruefully. 'This is one day I'll be glad to see the end of. By the way, did you see the local paper yesterday?' When Jo, with a mouthful of biscuit, shook her head, Maggie nodded grimly.

'I didn't think you could have done,' she said. 'You remember the old bag lady we saw when we went looking for the squat down in town, the one who said she'd seen Karim Aziz down there? They've only found her dead under the last of those demolished houses.'

'Dead?' Jo said foolishly. 'You mean killed? Murdered?'

'No, it didn't say that. Just that her body had been found and the police didn't suspect foul play at this stage—which

I suppose means they think she may have died of old age or something.'

'It's odd, though, isn't it?' Jo said thoughtfully. 'A coincidence?'

'I think this drug thing may be more than a coincidence,' Maggie said, finishing her tea with a gulp. 'First a murder and now drugs—it's too much, isn't it? There has to be some connection.'

'Well, if there is, the police don't seem to have found it yet,' Jo said. 'That nice Sergeant Mower seems quite mystified.'

'Fancies you, does he?'

'He couldn't take his eyes off my legs this morning,' Jo laughed.

'I always knew there was something to be said for trousers,' Maggie said, smoothing her tracksuit affection-ately. 'It gives the fifth-year lads less to think about, too.'

'Don't,' Jo groaned. 'I've got a fifth-year group next—and there's the bell. If we get through today without a riot we'll be lucky.'

Maggie Turner recalled those words as she walked wearily back from the hockey pitch at the end of the day to be confronted by a group of about twenty black youths storm-ing out of school angrily. Alarmed by the barely contained aggression with which they swept round her and the strag-gling band of younger girls she had been teaching, she stood for a moment watching as they made their way towards the main gates.

She was puzzled to see the group stumbling and jostling to a sudden halt at the school entrance, where the pavement was bordered by a metal railing intended to prevent chil-dren running out of school and into the roadway. Instead of turning left or right to make their way home, as Maggie had expected, the boys stayed where they were, effectively blocking the main exit for the children who were beginning to straggle down the pathway behind them.

Curious, Maggie joined the quickening exodus to the gates until she could see clearly what was beginning to

111

agitate the small crowd which was building up. Across the road from the school another group had assembled. These were too old to be pupils at Sutton Park or any other school. They were young men in their early twenties, big, burly, crop-headed and white, and wearing tight jeans and high laced boots which were the trademark of a particular sort of political extremist.

Taking in the scene at a glance, Maggie turned on her heel and ran back into school and along the corridor to the main office where she burst in on Jean Phillips, who was placidly photocopying a sheaf of documents with her back to the window.

'Get the police, Jean,' Maggie said sharply. 'We've got the makings of a full-scale riot out there.' She waved at the still fast-gathering crowd outside and burst without ceremony into Margaret Jackson's office.

Margaret Jackson did not anger easily, but now she was very angry indeed. White-faced and determined, having shrugged aside suggestions from her staff that she remain in her office, she led a small group of teachers down the pathway to the school gate, shouldering her way through the younger children on the edge of the crowd to the road itself where the two opposing groups of men and boys, one white and one black, were facing each other like two opposing packs of wild animals. The grunting noises and obscene gestures with which the white men were taunting the black youths were fast building up a tension which could only eventually explode.

Geoff Regan and his mates greeted the arrival of the teachers with derisive cat-calls and obscenities and from somewhere in the press of Sutton Park pupils a stone was thrown, bouncing harmlessly off the wall behind the opposition. Flanked by Maggie, still clutching her hockey stick, John Davis, the deputy head, and Peter Masefield, Margaret very deliberately turned her back on Regan and his friends and faced the boys at the front of the angry crowd in the school gateway, and held her hand up for silence.

Very gradually the shouts and jeers subsided and she could make herself heard.

'I want you all to go back into school,' she said with complete conviction. 'And I mean all. We have sent for the police, and when this—this—obstruction has been moved, you will all be able to go home as usual.'

The chorus of jeers from behind her reached a new intensity at that.

'Need the pigs to take you home, monkeys?' Came Regan's voice, raised above the rest. 'P'raps if you ask them nicely they'll take you all the way back to the jungle where you belong.'

Somewhat along the front row from Vinny Barnes and his friends, this was too much for one small dark boy, who gave an inarticulate shout of rage and dodging outstretched staff arms hurled himself across the road straight at Regan who welcomed the assault with a delighted leer.

'Stay there!' Margaret shouted with all the power of her lungs at the rest of the hesitant front row of the crowd. 'Do not move!' Sheer force of personality kept the front rank of teenagers in line while behind her the other three staff moved fast to separate Regan and the schoolboy, though not before Regan had smashed his fist with deliberation and horrific force into the younger boy's face, to raucous cheers from his friends.

'You bastard!' Maggie said, as they struggled to extricate from the mêlée the only half-conscious boy, blood streaming from a cut eye. With equal deliberation, and considerable malice aforethought, she gave Regan a hefty crack on the ankle with her hockey stick which sent him reeling into the arms of the crowd behind him with a howl which raised an answering cheer of delight from the intense crowd opposite.

To the relief of the adults in the roadway, the sound of police sirens could now be clearly heard.

'I'll get you, cow!' Regan screamed as his friends helped him to his feet. 'And I'll get all you effing black bastards, see if I don't! We'll be back!'

'Go back into school now,' Margaret Jackson said again with total authority, and slowly and reluctantly the crowd began to do as she asked, even as Regan and his friends turned and began to run down the hill and into the side roads of the council estate where they were soon lost from sight.

Shaking with nervous tension, Maggie and Margaret helped the injured boy back into school while Peter Mase-field and John Davis stayed at the gate to greet the police, who arrived with a single squad car and a squeal of brakes, and to keep the excited crowds of pupils within the gates until all threat of further violence seemed to have passed. Willing and anxious assistance met them inside school where Margaret Jackson passed a hand wearily over her forehead before going back into her office. She looked deathly pale, and rather diffidently Maggie Turner followed her.

'Are you all right?' she asked. Margaret half turned and smiled faintly but she did not reply before she collapsed in a heap on the floor.

'She has cancer,' Jo said dully as she handed Neil his scotch and water. 'I knew there was something wrong, but not that. It's so unfair. She's only fifty. It's the bloody job, you know. There's so much stress now that I actually think it's beginning to kill people.'

'She's had longer than I had,' Neil said dismissively. He was sitting at the living-room table surrounded by sheets of paper working out a problem with one of his computer programs. Jo had arrived home late and guiltily, having promised Neil that morning that she would be home on time now the pressing demands of the Christmas concert were over. He had greeted her sulkily and appeared to be only half listening as she told him what had happened after school and the equally shattering news which Maggie had relayed to the staff-room after she and Jean Phillips had brought Margaret Jackson round from her faint and left her sitting defiantly at her desk again, insistent that she was now perfectly recovered.

Jo sat down at the other side of the table and looked at her husband. He was, she thought, still an attractive man,

114

his dark hair, a little longer than he had worn it for work, framing a broad face with a strong jaw and prominent cheekbones. His eyes were fixed now in concentration on the task in hand. Only his mouth, which had developed a slightly petulant droop where there used only to be determination, hinted at the anguish within; that and the enormous physical tension of the man betrayed by his sharp, stabbing attacks on his paper with his pencil. It was, she thought, a cruel imprisonment which he suffered and as she watched him silently she wanted to reach out and tell him that she would not, could not, willingly make it worse. But the moment passed.

'It sounds to me as though that bloody school is falling apart, one way and another,' Neil offered at length. 'You need a sick headmistress like you need a hole in the head.'

'She says she's not dying,' Jo said quietly. 'Or not imminently. At least that's what she told Maggie. Whatever that means. There are remissions that can last a long time, but not much hope in the long run.' She shrugged dispiritedly. The events of the afternoon had shaken her more than she had admitted to herself and she felt drained of energy and, more unusually, of her normal optimism.

'Yes, well, there's not much hope for anyone in the long run, is there?' Neil said. 'Nor for some of us in the short run. So what's new?'

Jo felt a sudden surge of outrage which quickly turned to pity for Neil and looked quickly away so that he would not read it in her eyes. There was nothing which angered him more than pity and it was, she knew, a fragile basis for a marriage, although she suspected it was now the only one they had.

'So, have the police sniffed out your cocaine freak?'

'Not as far as I know,' Jo said. 'But they still had the visitors to interview after they'd finished at school. They got nothing out of any of the kids, as far as I could see. But they don't give much away.'

'Coke's an unusual thing for kids to get hold of anyway,' Neil said. 'It's not your usual street drug in this country.

Much more a yuppie habit—or was when the yuppies had money to burn. You remember Rod Calloway?'

Jo nodded. She remembered Rod, a colleague of Neil's to whom she had been introduced once at a party: a tall, blond young man with all the charm and confidence an expensive education could bestow and less human warmth than you would meet in the average bus queue. She remembered his cold blue eyes and wandering hands, which she had brushed away irritably, hands which had wandered not long afterwards into the firm's computerized accounting system in what was apparently a last-ditch attempt to sustain his habit.

Rod had vanished from Neil's firm and her social life overnight, with little comment and less fuss, just as Neil himself had been similarly discarded when he too became, for quite different reasons, unfit to pursue his trade. Time and the markets wait for no man, she remembered him saying on Rod's departure. Within six months a new face had taken over his desk too and he was, no doubt, as quickly forgotten.

She could imagine colleagues, even now, in the wine bar the company's young executives had adopted as their own, looking blearily at each other over their G and Ts as someone recalled Neil's name and failed to put a face to it. 'Was he the one with the habit who went to gaol?' they would ask each other. 'Or was he the one who caught the bug in Hong Kong or somewhere? Was it AIDs, by the way? Did we ever know?'

'No one has ever been in touch since we came up here, have they?' she said.

'Did you really expect them to?' Neil said harshly. 'You know London. We could as well be on the far side of the moon as far as they're concerned. They might have heard of Yorkshire as a jolly good place for a weekend's shooting, or a nice line in economical country cottages, but not much else. Otherwise, from down there it looks like a place to avoid. A few million grouse surrounded by all those revolting coal miners and dark Satanic mills. Sick visiting won't be on the agenda.'

He bent his head over his work again, effectively closing the subject, and within minutes wheeled himself back into his study. He did not like to be reminded of their former existence or the way it had abruptly ended. Jo sighed and turned her attention to a pile of exercise books she had brought home with her, the last marking of the term, she hoped.

She was deep into a sixth-former's assessment of Keats's 'Ode to a Nightingale', modern realism head-to-head with nineteenth-century romanticism, when a sharp peal on the doorbell brought her back to reality with a start. Neil had gone back to his computer and she knew that he would not willingly be distracted. She got wearily to her feet. It had been a traumatic day and she was looking forward to a long soak in the bath and an early night. As soon as she saw Farida and Ayesha on the doorstep outside again, their headscarves pulled well over their faces, she knew from the panic-stricken look in both their eyes that there was no longer any chance of that.

'Come in,' she said quickly. 'Whatever's the matter?'

Farida marched into the living-room with a self-confidence belied by the fear in her eyes and took her coat off to reveal a smart western trouser suit, the compromise between fashion and tradition many of the Asian girls settled for when outside their own families. She flung her coat angrily on to the settee, while Ayesha stood more timidly in the doorway, a look of deep apprehension on her face.

'They want to send us back to Pakistan,' Farida burst out furiously. 'I won't go. I simply won't go. They can't make me.'

At this Ayesha's precarious self-control gave way and she burst into heartbroken sobs as Jo took her helplessly into her arms.

'My family,' she said, 'my family . . .' But could get no further.

'Calm down,' Jo said quietly. 'Calm down and tell me what's happened—from the beginning.' It was not an instruction that Ayesha was going to be able to follow, but Farida took a deep breath and began to explain.

'I got home late,' she said. 'We all did, after the trouble at school. Everyone was late. I didn't think anything of it, but later on I heard my father having an argument with my mother and Sammy. Sammy had been in London but he came back early. My father seemed surprised to see him. I was working in my room and didn't take much notice, but eventually my mother came up and said that after all the trouble at school—today with the yobbos at the gates, and the drugs and everything, Father thought that it would be a good idea if she took me home for the holidays—to Lahore, I mean.'

'Just for the holidays?' Jo asked.

'So they said,' Farida went on bitterly. 'But then I rang Safia and Ayesha, and I found out that Safia's family had already sent her to an uncle in London and she was flying to Pakistan tomorrow, and Ayesha said . . .' She looked at her friend who was still sobbing quietly.

'Ayesha said that her family was insisting that she should go too, but they wanted her to stay out there, go back to the village and live with her aunt.'

'Oh, Ayesha,' Jo said, putting an arm around the sobbing girl and thinking of her often expressed determination to go to university.

'I won't go, I won't go,' the girl said, burying her face in her crumpled headscarf.

Jo looked at Farida, puzzled.

'Surely you don't think your parents want you to stay there, too, do you?' She had met Mrs Arif on several occasions and had always gained the impression that both she and her husband were delighted with Farida's ambition to go to Oxford. She could not reconcile her impression of a charming, self-confident fellow-teacher with what Farida was now saying.

'I don't know,' Farida said, a break in her voice. 'They are all behaving very oddly. My mother was talking about a holiday, but when it came to discussing the packing she seemed to want to take everything with us, absolutely everything, as if we were going to stay. I saw Sammy briefly and he was all evasive and odd. When Ayesha said she was going to run away I decided to go with her. I don't understand what's going on. I really don't. But I'm not getting on that plane. I don't think they want me to come back.'

'Farida, I'm sure you must be making a mistake. Your mother wouldn't do that to you,' Jo said quickly.

'No, but I think my father might,' Farida said fiercely. 'He seems to be in some sort of panic about what's been going on at school. You know Moslem men. Some of them pay lip-service to women's emancipation but when it comes to the crunch they'd much rather stick to traditional values. It won't be some backward village for me, just some second-rate women's college. Instead of Oxford! I won't go, I simply won't.'

Jo looked at the two girls helplessly. Ayesha had stopped sobbing now and a look of equal determination was creeping into her eyes.

'One of my cousins,' she said very quietly, 'has three children. She is only one year older than I am. I am not going back to live in Pakistan. I would rather die. I've lived here for almost the whole of my life, and I am never, never going back.'

Jo sighed.

'I don't know what I can do to help you,' she said. 'I don't even know if I ought to help you. It's not part of my job to encourage you to run away from home, for goodness' sake. In fact, your families could well argue that it's part of my job to persuade you not to. Anyway, I don't know where you can go. I can't let you stay here. We don't have room . . .'

'No, of course, no, Mrs Robertson,' Farida said quickly, regaining some of her normal self-confidence. 'We didn't expect anything like that. Of course not. But isn't it true that if we are seventeen our families can't make us live at home?'

Jo nodded. She had occasionally had to advise pupils who had been thrown out of the family home by irate parents or who had decided themselves that life at home had become intolerable. There was, she knew, no legal obligation on parents to house teenagers of this age—or on teenagers to live in the family home if they did not wish to. But it was not a legal point which she anticipated being greeted with any enthusiasm by the parents of these two girls, and she hoped it did not fall to her to have to explain it to them.

'We know there's a sort of refuge place for women, isn't that right?' Farida went on. 'There was a girl I knew who was married very young and ran away there last year. It caused a great commotion at the mosque. What we wondered was if you knew where it was?'

'Farida,' Jo said desperately. 'Don't you think what you two are doing is going to cause a great commotion at the mosque too? And for your parents? Your whole community is going to be absolutely furious if you do this. And what about your reputations? You are young unmarried Moslem girls and you know very well what people will think if you take off like this. You may not think it's important now, but if later on either of you wants to marry in your own community, then it might matter a great deal.'

'Yes, yes, we've thought of all that,' Farida said impatiently. 'That's why the refuge is the ideal place to go. It's all women. They don't even let men over the threshold. We'll be perfectly safe there—almost like a nunnery, I should say. A touch of the Ophelias.' She grinned briefly, but her eyes were pleading.

'Come on, Mrs Robertson,' she said. 'Please help. It's only until all this blows over. I'm sure when our parents see just how serious we are about staying, they'll give the whole idea up. We'll be back at school next term as if nothing had happened.'

Jo ran a hand through her hair, desperately trying to decide what to do. She was torn between her first instinct, which was simply to help anyone who sought her aid, and a caution born of certain knowledge that her interference would lead to complications which would almost certainly be unpleasant.

'Please, Mrs Robertson,' Ayesha said. 'I won't go home and there's nowhere else I can stay.'

'All right,' Jo said at last, reluctantly. 'But you must telephone your parents to let them know you're both safe. Do you understand?'

The two girls nodded reluctantly.

'I don't know where the refuge is myself, but Maggie . . . Ms Turner does, I think,' Jo went on. 'I'll phone her and ask her if she will take you there. At least you'll be safe for tonight. When we've all slept on it we can talk again tomorrow.'

CHAPTER 10

'I can't be one hundred per cent sure, Harry, you know that,' Amos Atherton, Bradfield's portly forensic pathologist, said testily. 'The old woman's body was in a hell of a state after several days under a couple of tons of rubble. You saw it yourself. You're bloody lucky we found the knife wound at all, if you want to know. It was difficult to spot under all those abrasions and bruises. All I can say is that it could be the same knife. I can't rule it out. But as to going into the box and swearing that it was the same knife —not on your nelly. More than my reputation's worth. D'you want another?'

Atherton and Huddleston were standing at the bar in the Woolpack with empty pint glasses in front of them. It was, the doctor had said, by way of a farewell drink because he would be on holiday when the Chief Inspector's more formal farewells were being made at the end of the month. All right for some, Huddleston had muttered testily, nevertheless accepting the invitation to an early lunch, partly because he never refused the offer of a pint of Tetley's and partly because he never missed the chance of pressing anyone—subordinate, witness, suspect or professional adviser—to expand on whatever limited information they had deigned to record in their statements or reports.

It was not that he did not trust the written word, merely that he regarded it only as a starting point. Even so,

121

Atherton was proving recalcitrant over the possibility of confirming verbally what Huddleston suspected—that the knife which had killed Karim Aziz was the same one which had despatched the so far unidentified, and probably unidentifiable, old woman whose battered body and pathetic bundle of belongings had been found on the site of Karim's squat.

'I've not had two stabbings in a week in twenty years,' Huddleston said lugubriously, after taking a deep draught of his second pint. 'Not without it being the same knife and the same bloke as did the knifing.'

'Could well be this time,' Atherton agreed. 'But damn tricky to prove on the forensic evidence. How about some steak and kidney pie? She's not a bad cook, the lass they've got here. Knows how to make pastry.' The Woolpack, tucked away down a back street which had so far escaped the depredations of the developers who were slowly and inexorably turning Bradfield's idiosyncratic Victorian stone heart into a late twentieth-century brick and concrete clone of every other town in the country, made few concessions to fashion, least of all in the matter of food. It remained a quiche-free zone, and was accordingly much appreciated by the likes of Huddleston and Atherton.

'Aye, we might as well,' Huddleston conceded.

'You're getting nowhere with the Paki lad, then?' Atherton asked curiously as they carried plates laden with huge unhealthy-looking portions of pie, peas and chips, swimming in dark brown gravy, to an empty table.

'Nowhere as you'd notice,' Huddleston admitted. Atherton sat looking at his lunch for a moment with an expression of comic distaste on his face.

'I should know better than this, being a doctor,' he said half-heartedly, before loading his fork with a mammoth mouthful and shovelling it between his lips appreciatively. 'I don't suppose it's any good wishing you a healthy as well as a happy retirement, is it?'

'I'll not get either if Yorkshire don't buck their ideas up next season,' Huddleston said between mouthfuls of beer and pie. 'Young Halliday's doing nowt useful in Australia.

Might as well not be out there for all the games he's getting.'
The two men shared a dogged enthusiasm for the apparently permanently ailing county cricket team, which many of their acquaintances thought went beyond the bounds of common sense and even Yorkshire loyalty.

'You'll be getting a season ticket this summer, then?'

'Aye, well, I will if Susan gives up all these daft ideas she's got for tripping off to Majorca and Corfu and God knows where,' Huddleston grumbled.

'The beer in Corfu's bloody disgusting,' Atherton said. 'Gnats' piss. I was conned into a holiday there a few years back. Never again.' The two men ploughed through their meal in companionable silence. It was not yet one o'clock and the bar was still comfortably empty when Huddleston spotted Sergeant Mower standing in the doorway and obviously searching for someone. The Chief Inspector raised his arm in greeting and when the younger man approached thrust two pint glasses and a ten-pound note into his hand.

'Fill 'em up, lad, and get one for yourself,' he said expansively. Mower opened his mouth as if to argue, but then, seeing the steely glint in his superior's eye, obviously thought better of it and moved away to the bar.

'A likely lad, is he, that one?' Atherton asked, watching as the Sergeant put a bomber-jacketed shoulder effectively into the thickening lunch-time crush around the bar.

'He'll do,' Huddleston conceded cautiously. 'For a southerner.'

Mower came back to the table with the drinks and a look of suppressed excitement in his eyes.

'Summat new?' Huddleston asked. He had left the Sergeant to find out more about the building site where the old woman's body had been found, without much expectation that his inquiries would take him any further forward. The Sergeant nodded but glanced sideways at Atherton.

'Get on with it, lad,' Huddleston said. 'Amos has been involved in more sudden deaths in this town than you've had hot dinners.'

'It's the development company,' Mower said quietly,

123

although in the increasingly crowded bar there was little risk that anyone more than a yard away could overhear him. 'I got details of who's involved from the Town Hall because I wanted to ask them why they'd suddenly begun demolition again after leaving it alone for months. One of the directors is Terry Hardcastle. I thought you'd be interested in him. Another is Mr Mohammed Arif.'

'Well, well,' Huddleston said, scooping up the last of his gravy with a forkful of pastry and chips. 'And what do the commercial boys have to say about that? You've asked them, of course?'

'Right,' Mower came back sharply. 'They say there's nothing known about the company. They seem to have cashflow problems, like everyone else in development and construction just now, which explains the delay on the scheme. But nothing more than that. But they did come up with one other useful item. Arif's import/export company is in trouble too, had money in that bank that went bust, and guess who's a director there these days?'

A beatific smile spread over Huddleston's usually lugubrious features.

'Don't tell me, lad,' he said. 'Let me guess. It has to be my old friend Hardcastle again. Now what, I wonder, is he getting out of importing and exporting, do you think? You can bet your life it's something pretty substantial because our Terry is not in anything for charity, whatever line he may sell the Rotary Club. Charitable Terry Hardcastle is not.'

Sutton Park was subdued that day. It was as if the near-explosion at the school gates the previous afternoon had drained away all the nervous energy which had been fizzing around the classrooms ever since the discovery of Karim Aziz's body. The hum and clatter in the corridors was muted as the pupils surged out for their lunch-time break and Jo came out of her classroom dispirited after an A-level class which had been notable for Ayesha's absence and for a general desultoriness of response from a group which though small usually tackled its work with enthusiasm.

Jo walked back to the staff-room, still affected by the deep depression which had seized her the previous night after Maggie had arrived at the house and agreed to deliver the two tearful Asian girls to the women's refuge on the far side of the town. That they had been right to help she did not doubt: that there would be a happy outcome for the girls she doubted very much. They had already defied convention by running away and their families would be furious. They were both able and ambitious girls but she could see no way in which they could fulfil their ambitions without their parents' help and support.

She had explained all this to them the previous night, and had extracted promises that they would telephone their parents to let them know they were safe. But both girls had insisted that for the time being they wanted to remain at the refuge and that on no account should their families be told precisely where the safe house was. It was a location which was a jealously kept secret among Bradfield's women's groups and Jo herself remained unsure of the exact address after Maggie had driven the girls away at speed.

'I hear Ayesha and friends have gone missing,' said Peter Masefield, catching up with her at the staff-room door. She had hardly spoken to him since the concert, and even now his mood was remote and his eyes carefully neutral. He looked tired, she thought, as tired as she felt herself.

'So I hear,' she said. The fewer people who knew exactly where the girls were the better, she thought, and although she would normally have confided in Peter, the distance which now seemed to have opened up between them encouraged her to count him out of this particular confidence.

'Old Councillor Arif won't be too pleased,' Peter said.

'Fathers are never pleased when their daughters grow up,' she said sourly, knowing that this was an inadequate explanation for the cultural and emotional upheaval which was no doubt at that very moment going on in Farida and Ayesha's homes.

'Well, I hope it doesn't muck up Ayesha's chance of going

125

to university,' Peter said, an edge to his voice. 'That girl has real potential.'

'I know,' Jo said, pushing her way ahead of him into the staff-room and effectively ending the conversation. Maggie Turner, who had been watching the exchange, caught her arm as she dropped her bag on to her desk.

'I'm on playground duty,' she said. 'Do you fancy a stroll round the hockey pitch?' Jo glanced round the crowded room where colleagues were eating sandwiches or deep in conversation in clusters which broke and reformed as the gossip ebbed and flowed. Peter was now on the opposite side of the room, his back turned deliberately, she thought, and she was seized with a sense of desolation.

'Let's get out,' she muttered and followed Maggie through the door.

Sutton Park's sports field sloped perceptibly on the edge of the steep escarpment above the valley in which Bradfield had grown and flourished as a textile and engineering centre for almost two hundred years. The slope was a perpetual source of irritation to Maggie and her colleagues who had constantly to apologize to visiting schools for the fact that, left to itself, a hockey or football would roll gently in a southerly direction for some considerable time. In a high wind footballs had been known to fly over the chain-link boundary fence and bounce haphazardly down the scrubby slope beyond to land in the yard of a dustbin manufacturer a hundred feet below.

Maggie leaned against the fence so that she was facing the field and the school and could keep at least one eye on the impromptu games of soccer which were going on around each of the four sets of goal-posts. Her short dark hair was tossed around her face by the sharp breeze which whipped across the valley bringing a hint of rain. Jo pulled her coat around her.

'There's going to be recriminations,' Maggie said.

'How do you know?'

'I saw Mr Arif arrive with Sami and another man as I was coming in from hockey. They looked furious.'

'They can't know that we had anything to do with the girls' disappearance,' Jo said, without conviction.

'If the girls made those phone calls we asked them to they could have told them,' Maggie said. 'We didn't really expect to keep it quiet, did we? We're never going to win with these patriarchal religions if we don't come out into the open and fight. These people can't bundle young women of that age around the world like so many parcels.'

'I'm not sure the girls have quite such a crusading attitude,' Jo said drily. 'All they think they've got is a temporary difficulty with their parents.'

'They must see the wider implications,' Maggie said angrily.

'It may look very different from their side of the fence,' Jo said mildly. 'For all we know they're devout Moslems. They're certainly proud of their culture. That was why they agreed to perform at the concert. They've never given me the impression that they're particularly militant feminists. Just keen to get a decent education—till now with a lot of encouragement from home.'

'All women are feminists under the skin,' Maggie said, but Jo only laughed.

'You should meet my mother,' she said. 'She's pure unreconstructed ''*Kirche, Kuche, Kinder*'', and there's plenty more where she came from. When Neil was taken ill she suggested that I give up work to look after him. She'd no conception of how little his pay-off would leave us to live on. No idea at all. My father looked after the family finances completely for the whole of their married life, as far as I can work out. It's positively Victorian.'

'So is packing two non-consenting seventeen-year-olds off to Pakistan at a moment's notice,' Maggie said, swinging back to her current preoccupation. 'So what do we tell the boss if they bring out the thumbscrews?'

'What we did, I suppose,' Jo said slowly. 'And why.'

'But not where the girls are?'

'No, not where the girls are.' She looked at Maggie, tall and slim in her tracksuit, her eyes sparkling, her look cheerfully determined.

'You know they're going to put a lot of pressure on, don't you?' she said, thinking how young her colleague still looked, little more than a student although she knew she had been at Sutton Park for more than five years.

'I can cope,' Maggie said flatly. 'I won't be bullied by a gang of men.'

When it came to the point, it was not the men who exerted the greatest pressure but Margaret Jackson. Jo had been summoned to her office after lunch and went in to find the school governor, Mohammed Arif, sitting in the head's most comfortable chair and flanked by his son, Sami, and a third man whom Margaret introduced as Mr Aziz, Ayesha's father, Karim's uncle. All three greeted her gravely but said nothing. Margaret herself was at her desk, looking pale but in perfect control in a dark green suit and cream shirt which were so far disguising the fact, apparent around her gaunt cheeks, that she was rapidly losing weight. She motioned Jo into a chair.

'Mrs Robertson,' she said formally, 'I think you already know that Farida and Ayesha ran away from home last night. From something which Farida let slip when she telephoned home, Mr Arif and Mr Aziz believe that you may know where the girls are. I told them that I felt sure that if you had that information you would have told me about it, but I think they would like to hear that from you.'

That sounds as though it lets Maggie out, Jo thought thankfully. She looked down at her hands which she realized she was clasping in her lap like a guilty schoolgirl. She untwined her fingers and rested them on the arms of her chair and swallowed hard. Her voice, when she spoke, sounded to her to be quite remote from her body.

'They came to my house last night asking for help,' she said. She felt rather than saw the three men bristle but they said nothing. She flashed a look of appeal at Margaret but she did not respond, clearly waiting for her to continue.

'They said they didn't want to go on this visit, holiday, to Pakistan, that you were insisting on,' she continued, addressing herself to Mohammed Arif. 'Something had

128

happened to make them think that you wanted them to stay there. Neither of them wanted that. So they asked me to find them somewhere safe to stay.'

Arif looked at her impassively, the anger only visible in his eyes, which were burning, and in the tension which was making a nerve on his temple throb. He still did not speak.

'So you know where they are now?' Margaret said coldly. Jo nodded.

'So you will be only too happy to tell their families where that is so that they can arrange for them to come home.'

It was not a question, much more an instruction, and one which filled Jo with an anger which took her by surprise.

'No,' she said more firmly. 'Farida and Ayesha asked me not to do that. They are perfectly safe in an all-women's house—no men,' she emphasized, flashing a quick look at the two fathers. 'But they want to stay there until the whole business has been sorted out.'

For a moment there was silence. Then Mr Aziz broke into rapid and obviously angry Punjabi. Mohammed Arif listened courteously and then turned back to Jo.

'I wonder, Mrs Robertson, if you quite realize the implications of what you are doing. What my friend Mr Aziz was just saying was that his daughter's reputation stands in great jeopardy. That may strike you from a western standpoint as an outmoded concept, perhaps, but believe me, in my community, even among educated families, it still has real force. I myself tried to explain this to Farida when I spoke to her this morning, clearly without effect. I must insist that you tell us where the girls are so that we can arrange to bring them home before any more damage is done. Believe me, it is in the best interests of the girls themselves.'

'I'm sorry,' Jo said. 'You must persuade the girls themselves, not me. I have no right to break their confidence. I will get a message to them and ask them to telephone you again, if you like.'

'Jo, that isn't good enough,' Margaret broke in firmly. 'We have no right to interfere in this way. It is not the school's function: advice is one thing, this—this, com-

129

plicity, is something else. You must let the families resolve the problem.'

Jo shook her head angrily.

'These are intelligent young women, not children,' she said. 'They are not obliged to live at home if they don't want to. You know that, Margaret. It's come up often enough before with children from other families. The girls have a real fear that their education is going to be disrupted by this trip to Pakistan and that would be a tragedy for them.'

'You talk as though Pakistan was incapable of training a doctor or a teacher for itself,' Sami Arif broke in, his voice full of contempt. 'A typical reaction, I suppose. Though one would expect you lily-white liberals to know better.'

Jo flushed.

'You know that's not what I mean,' she said. 'It was the girls themselves who were alarmed last night. They came to me. I knew nothing about all this until they knocked on my door. Ayesha thinks she is going to be sent back to her aunt in a remote village . . . They are frightened, Margaret, genuinely frightened.' She appealed to the head for support, but Margaret remained impassive, refusing to meet her eyes.

'They do not need to be frightened,' Mohammed Arif broke in impatiently. 'Tell me where they are and we can sort out all this nonsense in ten minutes.'

'I'm sorry,' Jo said quietly. 'I can't.' There was a moment of silence while the three men took in this point blank refusal before Mr Aziz broke into an angry torrent of Punjabi again and Mohammed Arif rose to his feet magisterially and faced Jo.

'Is this your last word, Mrs Robertson?' he asked, his voice hoarse with suppressed anger. Jo nodded, her mouth dry. She tried to guess what would happen next, but could not.

'Jo, will you please wait outside for a minute,' Margaret Jackson broke in before any of the men could respond again. 'I'd like to talk to these gentlemen in private, please.

She sat in Jean Phillips's office for a good ten minutes,

feeling more and more like a naughty schoolgirl, as Jean continued to work at her word-processor, only looking away from the screen and pausing in her rapid tapping at the keyboard to give Jo an occasional glance of old-fashioned disapproval.

At last she heard Margaret's outer office door open and the head take her farewells of her visitors. The red engaged light over the door changed to green and she was summoned back into the office over the intercom. The headmistress was standing with her back to the door looking out of the window with one hand holding the window-edge as if for support. She turned slowly, with the movements of a much older woman, and Jo was moved almost to tears by the sight of her making her way slowly back to her desk.

'I'm sorry,' Jo said again. 'I didn't mean to put you in this situation. But I can't let Farida and Ayesha down. You understand that.'

It was a statement of belief in Margaret, made with a certain knowledge of where her sympathies would always lie in a conflict between the girls' ambitions and the restrictions of tradition. But Margaret did not respond. She sat looking at Jo for moment without speaking, her expression a mixture of sadness and grim determination.

'Sorry isn't good enough,' she said at last. 'Mohammed Arif can close Sutton Park down. He knows that. He as good as threatened it.'

'What do you mean?' Jo asked desperately.

'Think about it,' Margaret said, an edge to her voice now. 'A third of our students are Moslems. If it gets about that we are helping Moslem girls to defy their parents, as it surely will get about, if the Aziz family take their younger children away, as they say they will, if the community leaders and the imam let it be known that this is not a good place for devout Moslems to send their children, as they surely will, if a respected man like Mr Arif lets his displeasure be known, as he surely will . . . what do you think will happen to our numbers? Where will our next intake of pupils come from? How long will we survive when there are empty places at Highgrove and St Mark's? Without our Asian pupils we'll be closed within a year.'

'That's blackmail,' Jo whispered, her mouth dry.

'Mohammed Arif is not so crude,' Margaret said. 'His son spelt it out.'

'What do they want you to do?' Jo asked.

'They want me to persuade you to cooperate with them, or ask for your resignation.'

'Margaret, you can't,' Jo said, as horrified as if Margaret had reached across the desk and struck her across the face. She searched Margaret's face for any sign of sympathy, but found none.

'You can't,' she whispered again, but she already knew she could.

'If it comes to the crunch, I have no real choice,' the head said. 'I will not sacrifice my school and everything I've worked for here for all these years for you and your principles.'

Chief Inspector Huddleston and Sergeant Mower did not catch up with Sami Arif until half way through the afternoon. When the two men arrived at Arif and Son's offices at two-thirty for their appointment with the younger man they discovered, to Huddleston's bluntly expressed annoyance, that neither Sami nor his father were there. Fifteen minutes later, minutes Huddleston spent fuming around the tiny waiting-room, picking up periodicals which discussed at length the commodities market and export credits and flinging them down again unread, the younger Arif appeared looking distinctly more frayed than normal and without any apology for his late arrival. He waved them into his office, a smaller and rather less opulently furnished version of his father's, but with a bank of high tech equipment on the L-shaped desk.

'What can I do for you, gentlemen?' he asked. 'We have some family problems today, I'm afraid, and I need to get home again as soon as I can.' He listened without apparent alarm as Huddleston explained why they were there, and responded angrily when the Chief Inspector asked him point blank whether he had been in possession of cocaine at the school on the night of the concert.

'You never let go, do you?' he asked, by way of reply. 'A friend at Cambridge warned me, you know, when I was involved in that little difficulty, that it would go on to the computers and never be forgotten. Particularly as I am—what would you call it, Inspector?—black? Asian? Paki? Which label do you prefer? Whatever it is, it goes with drugs, am I right? So if there are drugs around and I am within miles of the incident, then I get a visit from the boys in blue.'

'Mr Arif,' Huddleston broke in dismissively, 'I've asked you a simple question. You may feel as aggrieved as you like but it doesn't alter the fact that I have a right to ask it of everyone who was in the school that night and I must have an answer. Did you or did you not take cocaine into Sutton Park on the night of the concert? That's all. Yes or no.'

'No, Chief Inspector,' Arif came back quickly. 'That is your answer. I did not take it there, drop it there, or indeed use it there, or anywhere else. I do not use cocaine, Chief Inspector. I did briefly experiment with it when I was an undergraduate, as you know, and I regret it—but I have not touched it since. Is that all you want to know?'

Huddleston sat bull-like in his chair for a moment gazing at the slim young man who drummed his fingers impatiently on the desk as he waited for his answer. The mutual dislike, Mower thought, was palpable.

'Aye,' Huddleston said at last. 'I'll pass that on to the drug squad, who are otherwise engaged this afternoon, else they'd have been here themselves. If there's owt else I dare say they'll be in touch.'

He lumbered to his feet. Arif did not get up from his desk, turning away with studied unconcern to begin typing on his computer keyboard as the two policemen made their way to the door.

'I hear you've got my old friend Terry Hardcastle from the Rotary Club on your board here now,' Huddleston said unexpectedly, a hand on the door handle.

Arif stiffened perceptibly but his face remained impassive as the two policemen watched his reaction.

'A fine man,' he said. 'A mutually agreeable business arrangement. I think it is best for firms like this to integrate with the more long-established local companies, don't you?'

'Oh aye, I'm all for integration,' Huddleston said, the irony overtly insulting. 'Give Terry my regards when you see him, won't you? He's a good lad, is Terry. A good lad.'

'You'll have the race relations people on your back if you don't watch it,' Mower said tentatively as he drove Huddleston back to police HQ.

'Rubbish,' Huddleston said. 'That lad's as bent as a seven pound note. If he thinks Terry Hardcastle's a fine upstanding local businessman, he has to be bent. What's his colour got to do with it?'

'You think he's still using cocaine, or dealing?'

'What I think and what I can prove are two different things,' Huddleston said heavily. 'But we'll get there, lad, don't you worry. We'll get there. In the meantime, you go and report back on young Sammy to Ray Watson and see if he's got any bright ideas on that front. I've got some paperwork to get on with.' Which was another way of intimating, Mower knew, that Harry Huddleston required some time to snooze off the effects of the Woolpack's bitter and their steak and kidney pie.

'You stupid cow,' Neil said, his face a suffused purple and his hands gripping the arms of his wheelchair as though he was about to rise up out of it in righteous wrath like some Old Testament prophet and strike Jo to the floor. 'You effing stupid cow.' He spun the chair round towards the living-room door where the boy, David, was standing watching the scene, pale-faced and wary.

'Get home, now, boy,' Neil said angrily. 'We'll have to leave that program till tomorrow.' The boy swallowed nervously and nodded.

'Right,' he said, and spun on his heel. A moment later they heard the front door slam and Neil turned back towards his wife, who was standing defensively with her back to the kitchen door. Neil's outburst had been provoked, and understandably provoked, she admitted, when she had told him what had happened at school that afternoon. She had left Margaret's office in a mood of defiant despair, having conceded only that she would consider her position overnight. Neil had greeted her hesitant explanation of what had happened with one of the sudden rages to which he had been terrifyingly prone in the immediate aftermath of his illness, but which had recently become more rare.

'I'll telephone the girls later and ask them to phone their families again,' she said, with only a slight hope that this concession would defuse Neil's anger. The hope was soon dashed.

'Do what you like tonight,' he said, wheeling himself across the room and parking his chair directly in front of her so that she could not easily move away from the door, which was tightly closed behind her. 'But tomorrow you tell Margaret Jackson where they are. I insist. You've no effing right to put your job at risk. No right at all, with me in this bloody chair. What the hell do you think you're playing at?'

'I'll talk to them,' Jo said again. 'I'll persuade them to go home.'

'And Maggie? What does she think?'

'She thinks the same as I do—more so, I think. But I expect she'll try to persuade them too, when she knows what Margaret wants.'

'And if you can't? Then what?'

'It's their decision,' Jo said. 'I can't make it for them.'

'But if they say no, you'll tell Margaret Jackson in the morning? You'll tell her where they are? You'll get her off your back, you stupid cow?' he insisted, his voice rising to a shout again.

'I'll think about it,' she said.

'Stop playing games, Jo. Stop effing me about. Stop this bloody stupid ego-trip. Who do you think you are? Sylvia bloody Pankhurst or something? Get down off your white

135

horse and get real. This is my life you're putting on the line, as well as your own. And that's not on.'

'I'll think about it,' Jo said again. There was a moment of total silence, long enough for Jo to recognize the inevitability of what was coming next but not long enough for her to escape it. With a vicious twist of his hands Neil rammed the wheelchair hard against the lower part of her legs and as she stumbled in agony towards him he hit her hard about the face, three, four times, until in a welter of thrashing limbs and spinning wheels she succeeded in pushing him away and reaching blindly behind her for the door into the kitchen through which she fell.

For a moment she lay on the floor, head, face and legs throbbing until she realized that it was only the weight of her own body which was preventing Neil from pushing the door open and following her. She reached out and pulled the room's single chair towards her, jamming it under the door handle so that it could not be opened.

Neil hammered on the door in frustration while Jo looked quickly around her. She had come home to find him in the kitchen making himself a cup of tea and had quite fortuitously dropped her outdoor coat and handbag down on the work-bench as she had taken over the filling of the kettle which had, as she had walked through the door, suddenly become a tremendous struggle for him. Almost without thinking, she put her coat on again, picked up the bag and left the house by the back door. As she walked down the path and out of the gate, she could hear Neil's anguished shout of rage behind her.

With the car out of action, she took a bus out of town, up the steep hill behind Sutton Park to a stop which left her a ten-minute walk from Peter Masefield's cottage. With her mind in a confused whirl, she hardly noticed the journey, or the icy, buffeting wind which swept down towards her from the high moors beyond the town as she struggled up the hill.

He answered her knock with a look of surprise which gave no hint of welcome, though he held the door open slightly to allow her to enter. She stepped from the dark into the warm yellow glow of light in his living-room and only then, when he saw the darkening red bruises on her face and the cuts and raw scrapes on her legs where her tights had been torn into gaping holes, revealing the blood beneath, did he react with a sharp intake of breath.

'What happened?' he asked quietly, taking her arm gently and leading her to the chair where he had obviously been sitting himself, close to the smouldering fire and with an open copy of a novel on the arm. The shock seized her now and she began to shiver uncontrollably, quite unable to speak. She looked at Peter mutely, a single tear sliding down her cheek. He handed her a tissue, without comment, though his eyes were full of concern, and went over to a cupboard from which he took a bottle of brandy. He handed her a glass.

'Drink it,' he said. 'Take it slowly. Take your time.' He sat on the arm of the chair and put an arm around her, letting her sip her drink, saying nothing until gradually the shaking which racked her subsided. When at last she seemed calmer he reached out and turned her face towards his and kissed her.

'Tell me what happened?' he said. Haltingly she told him, hesitating most over the row with Neil. Peter listened, prompting her gently when something seemed unclear. When she had finished, he turned away from her, his face grim, not daring to give vent to the anger which almost overwhelmed him.

'OK,' he said, his voice strained. 'Let's leave that for a moment. Come and let me see to that cut on your leg.'

Acquiescent now, as content as a child to let someone else take control, she followed him into the bedroom and obediently slipped off her ruined tights and sat quietly on the edge of the bed while he knelt at her feet and cleaned the cuts and abrasions with warm water and disinfectant and put plasters over the worst of the injuries.

'You'll live,' he said, with a lightness he did not feel. She attempted a smile, only half successfully, and reached out to touch his face gently.

'Thank you,' she said. Peter sat back on his heels and looked up at her appraisingly.

'It can't go on like this, can it?' he asked. 'It seems to me that you've got some decisions to make.'

She nodded, running a finger over the bruises on her face.

'I think they've been made for me,' she said so quietly that he had to strain to hear.

'Meaning?'

'Meaning? Meaning I'm out of a marriage and quite probably out of a job. A dead loss, in fact. Down and out, and nowhere to lay my head.'

He nodded.

'I thought that's what you meant,' he said.

The very act of putting her situation into words seemed to release her pent-up emotion within her and she cried properly then, great racking sobs which Peter shared, taking her into his arms and tilting her backwards on to the bed where they lay locked in each other's arms until eventually she shuddered into a trembling silence, exhausted.

Peter propped himself up on one elbow and looked down at her bruised and battered face, reddened even more now by her tumultuous tears.

'God, you look a sight,' he said, with an attempt at a grin. She punched him gently and touched his face again.

'Do you mind?' she asked.

'Frankly, I don't give a damn,' he said, kissing her on the mouth this time with a slow sensuality which brought an immediate response and answered his half-formed query as to whether she felt up to it.

'With the light out I shouldn't think I'll even notice,' he added, pulling the switch above the bed and plunging the room into darkness just as Jo pulled off her sweater and bra and began to unzip her skirt.

'Oh God, where have you been,' Peter groaned, as they slid between the sheets and their bodies touched. 'I've missed you so.'

CHAPTER 11

Huddleston had been deterred from rushing headlong into Terry Hardcastle's backyard, literally as well as figuratively, by Superintendent Jack Longley. An exchange of directorships between two perfectly legitimate local businesses was not a sufficient basis upon which to launch any sort of criminal investigation, Longley had pointed out with some asperity. But if the word was that Hardcastle's small empire, based on property and construction since he had sold out the burgeoning family chain of betting shops in which he had begun his career, and Arif's import-export business were hard hit by the recession, then Longley was prepared to turn a blind eye to a few discreet inquiries, he said. Just so long as they were discreet.

'I'm as keen as you are, Harry, to see Hardcastle get his come-uppance, but you'll be lucky if you pull it off in the time you've got left. And there's absolutely nothing to suggest that it's connected with these murders. You might be best advised to clear them up and go out in a blaze of glory in the local rag rather than getting snarled up in the higher echelons of Rotary and the square. Chances are you'll get nowhere and cause a lot of bad feeling in the process.'

Huddleston grunted.

'I've always known that bugger's bent,' he muttered. 'No evidence, no proof, just a pricking of the thumbs. He's been laughing at us for years, ever since that time I actually charged him and the witnesses went mysteriously missing before we got to court.'

'Yes, well, you can't win 'em all,' Longley said.

'No, but you can have a bloody good try,' Huddleston had said later to Kevin Mower. The young sergeant's eyes lit up.

'Big fish, is he, this Hardcastle?'

'Big enough. So's Mohammed Arif, of course, in his own way, even though he has resigned from the council.

Community leader and all that. D'you fancy trying to reel him in then, our Terry?'

'What do you think?' Mower asked cautiously. Huddleston laughed. In spite of his distrusted southern speech and manners, the Sergeant reminded him of himself at the same age—keen and openly eager to make his way. He would have to watch out, though, he thought, as he had had to watch out, for those who would be equally as eager to trip him on his way up the promotion escalator.

'I tell you what we'll do, lad,' Huddleston said, with unwonted kindness in his look. 'You see if you can find out from Hardcastle's lads just how deep he's in the mire financially. The workers always have a good idea how the boss is doing. You don't want to believe those newspaper tales that say sackings have come out of the clear blue sky. On the whole you'll find half the work force have got their next job lined up the day before the redundancy notices arrive.

'In the meantime, I'll see what Bradfield's toffs are saying about our Terry these days. You go pubbing and Labour clubbing, lad, and I think I'll pop into the Clarendon tonight to see what's going off at this Rotary do they're laying on for me at year's end. That'll give us a chance to ask a few pertinent questions.'

'You won't talk to Hardcastle himself, then?' Mower asked.

Huddleston shook his head with an expression of pain on his face.

'No, lad, no,' he said impatiently. 'Jack Longley said be discreet, so we'll be discreet. But tomorrow you can pop round to his house to do a bit of crime prevention work— look at the window locks and that sort of stuff, and have a shufti at how his wife's coping. She's a bonny lass, is Brenda Hardcastle. You'll like her, though she's old enough to be your mother, I know for a fact. A bit more to get hold of than that Robertson woman you've been making cow eyes at all week. But she'll not like it if Terry can't keep her wardrobe up to scratch and the gin bottle topped up.'

An hour later Huddleston was standing contemplatively

in the arched doorway of the Clarendon bar for the second time that week. He scanned the close-pressed throng of suits round the bar, and the groups more discreetly arranged round the scattered tables for a moment before coming to a decision. Then he strolled across the soft, yielding carpet to the farthest corner of the room where two men of much his own age, pinstriped, greying and definitely no advertisement for a low-fat diet, were deep in conversation over glasses of scotch. They looked up as he approached and nodded a cautious welcome.

'Harry,' said Councillor Peter Strong. 'Take a seat. You remember my brother Frank, don't you?'

Huddleston hesitated. 'Can I get you both another?' he offered expansively, but the two men shook their heads and Strong gestured to the white-shirted barman who was clearing glasses from a neighbouring table.

'Another scotch here, Bob, would you,' he called. Huddleston accepted the hospitality and sank into the third of the armchairs grouped around the table. He had known the two men for more years than he cared to count now, had in fact been at grammar school with Frank Strong, although their paths had seldom crossed since Peter and his brother had gone into the family textile business and local politics.

'I hear you're retiring, Harry? I didn't think you were old enough for that.'

'Aye, well, they let us out early in the police force,' Huddleston said contentedly. 'Remission for good behaviour, just like the villains.'

'More time for cricket?'

'If there's owt worth watching,' Huddleston conceded glumly. 'That new lad Oakley shows a bit of promise. If they don't lose him to bloody Worcestershire or somewhere. Will you be at the do on the thirtieth, then?' He knew the two men were infrequent attenders at Rotary functions and was slightly surprised when they both said that they would be there. The conversation drifted desultorily for a while around the arrangements he was making for his new life, until he began to glance around the bar cautiously as if

141

looking for someone. Peter Strong raised an eyebrow.

'Lost someone?' he asked, as Huddleston had intended that he should.

'Hardcastle,' he said. 'Terry Hardcastle. I saw him in here the other night, and there was summat I wanted to ask him.' He just caught the almost imperceptible look which the two brothers exchanged.

'Professional, is it?' Frank Strong asked, without quite as much surprise in his voice as Huddleston would have expected.

'No, no,' he said quickly. 'Just social, just social. About the do. Though we have had some contact with him recently, or his firm, I should say. This old dear we found dead on the building site down by the canal. That was a Hardcastle site, as it happens. Contractors doing the demolition, of course, but Hardcastle's development. Coincidence, really.'

He did not seriously expect the Strongs to be fooled by this disingenuousness. It was little more than convention to nudge them into the sort of speculation he wanted to provoke and which he guessed they would not be too unwilling to supply. It was a myth, he thought, that women were the sex more prone to gossip. In the right circumstances and given the right subject, there was nothing that delighted men more than a bit of gentle character assassination. And he guessed, correctly, that the subject and the circumstances were right.

'I'll be surprised if that leisure centre ever gets built, the way things are going,' Frank Strong offered, on cue. His brother nodded sagely.

'Construction's not much cop with interest rates the way they are.'

'And the way Hardcastle's mortgaged up to the hilt,' Frank concluded gloomily.

'Going to come a cropper, is he?' Huddleston prompted.

'Well, he's got this new deal with the Asian fellow, Arif,' Peter offered. 'And that's where the money is these days, you know. With the Pakistanis. Import-export. Though you sometimes wonder what the hell they're importing and exporting. A few of their compatriots, I shouldn't wonder.' He glanced at Huddleston and smiled thinly.

'Only joking, Harry, only joking.'

'Arif's clean, isn't he?' Huddleston inquired, with mild interest.

'Oh yes, indeed, as far as I know,' Peter Strong assured him quickly. 'Pure as the driven snow, as far as I know. A nice bloke, actually. I got to know him quite well while he was on the council, in spite of the party difference. He had a good year as Mayor. A lot of us had reservations when they put him up for it, but he did well. My lot had no complaints there.'

'But it makes you wonder,' his brother added. 'Him getting mixed up with Hardcastle. Now I wouldn't trust him with my grandmother's nest-egg, and that's a fact.'

'And you reckon the cashflow's not so good? Brenda won't like that. Do you remember Brenda at school, Frank? She was a buxom lass even then.'

'I remember Brenda Cartwright behind the bike sheds,' Frank Strong said fondly, a dreamy look coming into his eyes. 'Part of my sex education, she was. I'm not sure she wasn't the best part.' Frank had been married for thirty year to another schoolmate, a thin angular woman called Gwen who was as unlike Brenda Hardcastle now as she had been as a teenager.

'She was part of most people's sex education, Brenda was,' Huddleston said contentedly. 'She did all right for herself in the end, though, didn't she? Or at least, I thought she did. She's never wanted for owt so far. That house of theirs must have cost half a million.'

'Mortgaged. I told you,' Frank said sharply, and Huddleston wondered if he had laboured for thirty years under the delusion that he was the only boy Brenda had offered favours to behind the bike sheds. 'From what I hear it'll be on the market before long.'

'It's common knowledge he's over-extended,' Peter confirmed contentedly. 'The recession's hit him for six. He'll be back on the race-course where he started before long, I shouldn't wonder.'

'Will he now,' Huddleston said quietly, almost to himself.

Jo woke up with a start and for a panicky moment could not be sure exactly where she was. Gradually the events of the early evening came flooding back and she tentatively felt the bruises on her face and flexed the muscles of her legs, where a throbbing pain centred just above her left ankle. She turned her head to discover Peter Masefield fast asleep on his back in the other half of the double bed. She had, she remembered, fallen asleep in his arm, but sleep and time—and she glanced at her watch to find to her surprise that no more than an hour had elapsed—had thrown them apart. Perhaps that was fair enough, she thought sadly, and wearily rolled out of bed and collected up her clothes which were lying discarded in a heap on the floor.

In the bathroom she examined her bruised face critically in the mirror. One red weal already encircled her eye and would, she thought, be quite purple by the morning. Another was confined mainly to her forehead and if she brushed her hair slightly forward could be quite effectively concealed. If she wore trousers instead of a skirt only the black eye would be a readily visible legacy of Neil's assault if she decided to go into school the next day.

But would she, she asked herself. She turned on the shower and let the warm water wash over her hair and face as well as her weary body as if it could take away the tangled thoughts and emotions which tormented her as easily it washed away the stickiness of the day. But while it refreshed her physically, she stepped out of the shower, wrapped in Peter's towel, with nothing of her near-desperate self-questioning resolved.

She was already dressed and combing her hair into some semblance of order when she caught sight of Peter's reflection in the mirror. He stood for a moment watching her, without speaking, his face impassive. She avoided his eyes and kept on combing in an effort to persuade her hair to fall across her face and hide the worst of the bruises.

144

'You're going back.' It was a statement rather than a question and when she failed to answer his face took on the closed watchfulness with which she had become familiar over the last few weeks, the hurt carefully hidden at the back of his eyes.

'Is there anything Neil could do which would change your mind?' Peter went on. 'I realize there's nothing I can do—or say.' Satisfied with her hair, Jo turned towards him and shrugged imperceptibly.

'I don't know,' she said. 'All I know is that I have to go back. I can't leave him.'

'Not now? Not ever?'

'Not now. I'm not sure about ever.'

'And all that,' Peter said, with an angry gesture at the tumbled bed behind him. 'All that meant nothing?'

'You know it meant something. You know I love you. And there's no future in it,' Jo said, as if repeating some mantra in a dull monotone. 'I can't leave him.'

Peter stood looking at her for a moment before turning away, his shoulders slumped, to hide the look of despair which overwhelmed him.

'I'll take you home,' he muttered almost inaudibly as he went back into the bedroom and closed the door behind him.

In the car on the brief and silent journey back into town, Jo sat with her hands tightly clasped on her lap, choked with an emotion which she felt threatened to break through her self-control if she so much as glanced at Peter. She would, she feared, soon break in two and she almost began to wish that if Peter was to leave Bradfield, the deed should be done quickly. Perhaps if she no longer saw him every day the pain of loving him and not being able to fulfil that love would begin to diminish, though that too was something she both hoped for and dreaded at the same time.

Turning off the main road into the tree-lined avenue where Jo lived, Peter slowed down suddenly as he found the way blocked by vehicles. Two fire-engines, their blue lights revolving urgently, an ambulance and a couple of police cars blocked the road completely while dark uniformed figures moved about determinedly in the semi-darkness between them and the row of bungalows on the far side of the road. It took Jo a moment to register what was happening, but as she took in the confused scene outside her heart suddenly lurched.

'Where's the fire?' she said urgently.

'Let's go and see,' Peter said, pulling in to the side of the road behind the nearest of the police cars. A small crowd had gathered and they pushed their way to the front where they realized that the fear which had seized them both had an all too terrible foundation. The Robertsons' bungalow was wreathed in choking black smoke, into which dark, clumsy figures in masks and helmets came and went with almost slow-motion deliberation.

Jo broke free from Peter's restraining arm and pushed her way roughly past two policemen who were rather boredly keeping the onlookers away from the fire-fighters' scene of operations. With a despairing scream she stumbled over hoses and between startled firemen until at the garden gate she was grabbed unceremoniously by a burly policeman who spun her away from the house back towards the side of the nearest fire-engine, where she leaned limply for a moment, her knees weak and her breath coming in small shallow gasps which made speech impossible.

'Now just where do you think you're going?' he asked, not unkindly. Peter, who had followed her, and been followed in his turn by another police officer, took Jo by the shoulders and turned her towards him and held her close against his chest.

'This is Mrs Robertson,' he said to the police. 'It's her house. Do you know where her husband is?'

The policeman's eyes met Peter's for a moment over Jo's head and he knew from the sudden look of compassion which he found there that the news of Neil would not be good.

'Perhaps she'd better come and have a word with the chief fire officer,' the policeman said quietly. 'His men have brought someone out.'

Whenever Jo found the courage later to think about

146

that night again, it was always the blackness of it she remembered: the blackness of the smoke which was still swirling out of the front door and windows of the bungalow, no flames, not even a touch of smouldering red now, to indicate the fierceness of the inferno which had caused the smoke, just a drifting, foul-smelling, choking haze of darkness, blacker than the night air itself. Then there was the blackness of the ambulance into which she tried to clamber when they told her that Neil's body was still there, and from which she was urged away by kindly hands, intent on sparing her feelings. In fact it was Peter who was allowed to go inside to identify the body, to see the red blanket pulled briefly back to reveal a face which had been roughly wiped clean of encrusting smoke so that the features, surprisingly peaceful for one who had met so horrific an end, were revealed. He was not burned, Peter had to reassure Jo over and over again later. He had, as the fire officer gently explained, not burned to death, but died in the lethal smoke. It was very common, and not a painful way to go.

'But how?' she had screamed at him, distraught. How had the fire started? How could it have started? He didn't smoke. There was no open fire. She had only been out for a little time, a very little time. And when he had explained that there was a burnt-out chip pan on the stove she had laughed hysterically.

'Neil never cooked,' she cried. 'He wouldn't cook. Couldn't cook. He would never, never make chips. Never, never, never.'

'The house is not habitable,' the fire officer said to Peter over Jo's head again. 'Can you make arrangements for her to stay with friends or relations tonight? There's nothing more to be done here. Just clearing up, which will take some time.'

Peter had half guided, half carried her back to the car, where she slumped in the passenger seat, gazing with unseeing eyes out of the window at the ambulance, which was just pulling away, its emergency light switched off now that the need for haste was over.

'Jo,' he said gently, but she took no notice. He sighed,

and ran his hands across his face wearily, trying to scrub the shock out of his own mind. Jo had no family in Bradfield, he knew, but he also knew with absolute certainty that this was not the time to take her back to his own house. If and when she wanted to come to the cottage again, he thought, then it should be her decision, not his. Thoughtfully he started the car and reversed away from the scene of tragedy and turned towards the town centre.

Maggie Turner lived on the top floor of a tall gothic Victorian house which had been converted into flats. As Peter stood supporting Jo on the broad stone doorstep waiting for an answer to his ring he glanced up to the gable windows three storeys above them and saw with some relief that although the curtains were drawn he could see light behind them. Maggie answered the intercom and unlocked the front door for them without question. She was waiting on the top landing, dressed, unusually for her, in a long oriental patterned skirt and a dark red shirt.

'So this is how you keep fit, is it?' Peter asked ironically, when they slightly breathlessly reached the top of the last flight of stairs. Maggie did not reply. Horrified, she looked at Jo, who was clinging to Peter's arm, her face ashen beneath the steadily darkening bruises, before she took her other arm and helped her across the threshold and into the flat's small and cluttered living-room.

'What on earth's happened?' she asked as she guided Jo into a comfortable armchair by the gas fire, where she slumped back with a look of infinite weariness before closing her eyes tightly as if to blot out not just the light but the whole world.

Maggie took Peter into the flat's tiny kitchen where, tersely, he told her exactly how the events of the evening had unfolded.

'She can stay here, and welcome,' Maggie said quickly. 'She can sleep in my room and I'll kip down on the settee here. No problem. Then in the morning we can contact whoever we need to contact. She has a mother somewhere, Bournemouth, or Eastbourne, isn't it?'

'The police will want to talk to her. The fire officer said

there's bound to be an inquest,' Peter said grimly. 'There always is, for a sudden death, he said. Even an accident.'

'And she was with you when it happened? It's all going to be very messy.' Maggie could already see the unwanted headlines in the local paper if Jo's relationship with Peter became public in the aftermath of Neil's death.

'Dear God, don't I know it,' Peter groaned. 'My first instinct was to put her in the car and drive as far and as fast as I could.'

'Running away isn't going to help,' Maggie said quietly.

'And you heard about the trouble at school?'

'Yes, they don't seem to realize that I'm the one who knows where the girls are. Jo doesn't actually know where the refuge is. I took them down there. Jo didn't come anywhere near the place.'

'And you're not telling, I suppose?'

'You're bloody right I'm not,' Maggie said firmly. 'They treat those kids like chattels, those Moslem men. They're young women, not children. In this country they have a perfect right to decide what they want to do and where they want to go. You know that, Peter.'

'So you'll let them sack Jo?' he came back sharply.

'No, I won't,' Maggie said, equally firmly. 'If it comes to that, I'll get the girls to move—somewhere not even I know about—and then tell Margaret where I took them in the first place. If they want a witch hunt, they can have me, not Jo. Anyway, after tonight no one is going to pursue Jo on that issue any more. They can't, can they? They wouldn't have the brass neck?' She looked at Peter with an appeal in her dark eyes which he did not fully understand. He pulled open the kitchen door slightly and glanced at where Jo was still sitting, totally immobile, by the fire.

'We'd better put her to bed,' Maggie said softly. 'She's in shock. Don't worry, Peter, my dear. I'll look after her for you. I promise. I love her too, you know.'

CHAPTER 12

'There can't be any mistake?' Harry Huddleston said to Amos Atherton sharply. The pathologist, rubber apron smeared with blood, took off his operating gloves with an expression of disdain on his face.

'Do you know what the human lung looks like when it's been filled with oily smoke?' he asked. He waved a hand at his operating table where the mortal remains of Neil Robertson lay under a sheet which had been so hastily pulled up that one hand, curled into a blackened claw, lay upturned as if in supplication to an uncaring world.

'His lungs are pink as a baby's bum. He was not a smoker, like you, you old bugger, and his lungs are a credit to him.'

'So he was dead before the fire started?'

'He was dead before the fire started. He did not burn to death, though one side of his body had third degree burns. He did not asphyxiate, although there are traces of smoke in every orifice. As you will see in my report—although I know damn well you're never patient enough to wait for something as formal as a piece of paper, Harry—as you will see in my report, the cause of death was a fractured skull. The deceased was hit a very heavy blow on the back of his head before that fire started.' Atherton took off his apron and handed it to his assistant who was hovering anxiously at his side.

'You know you're due at the infirmary, sir,' the young man offered tentatively.

'Of course I bloody know,' Atherton snapped, before turning his attention back to Huddleston, who was looking very thoughtful.

'The fire department says the wheelchair had overturned in the kitchen and he was on the floor close by. Could he have fallen and cracked his skull on the floor?' Huddleston asked.

Atherton shook his head emphatically. 'Not unless the floor was poker-shaped and came up and hit him,' he said. 'Do you want to see the fracture?' He turned to the table as if to pull back the sheeting but Huddleston shook his head sharply as Atherton had known he would.

'No thanks,' he said quickly. 'I'll take your word for it. The trouble with fire is that even if it doesn't destroy the body, it'll have destroyed a lot else.'

'You can take my word for it that you're looking for the proverbial blunt instrument, tubular, an inch or so in diameter, and heavy. Very heavy. An iron bar, a poker, something of that sort. The fire's unlikely to have destroyed that.'

'So it was murder?' Huddleston said, almost to himself.

'Well done, Harry. You're getting there,' Atherton said as he led the way out of the laboratory into the corridor outside. 'I can't spell it out much more clearly. Laddo in there was hit on the head and then the house was set on fire to make it look like an accident, I'd say. Only the boys with the turntable ladders got there a bit too quickly for the evidence to be all burnt up. One of those plans that sounds all right in theory but isn't very likely to work out in practice. It's surprising just how long it takes for a body to be burnt out of all recognition, you know. I remember a case in Liverpool when I was a student—'

'Aye, not now, Amos,' Huddleston stopped him. 'Not now. I'll see you in the Woolpack for a jar about six if you like, and you can tell me then. I'm a bit pressed just now.'

Sergeant Kevin Mower was well pleased with himself as he strode purposefully back into police headquarters that lunch-time. He had spent the morning pleasantly and, he hoped, fruitfully, at the home of Mr Terry Hardcastle in the leafy suburb of Southwaite on the northern edge of the town. And Mrs Brenda Hardcastle had been as welcoming and hospitable as Harry Huddleston had suggested she might be.

The house was long and low and modern, built in the local stone, or a reconstituted version of it that must have satisfied the planning committee of its authenticity, but in a style which would not have appeared out of place in Beverly Hills. The doors of a triple garage stood open to reveal one empty space and comfortable room for the soft-topped black Ford Escort with almost as many letters and figures after its name as there were in its TAH 03 registration number, and a gleaming four-wheel-drive Land-Rover, TAH 02, which were parked there. The number plates alone would have cost him a year's salary, Mower thought ruefully as he paused beside his own car which he had parked at the end of the broad gravelled drive.

The house spread out from an elaborate portico, offering only high blank windows screened by louvred blinds on to the immaculate lawns and flowerbeds between the house and the road. Mrs Hardcastle opened the door herself. She was not a tall woman, and not young, although it was difficult to estimate her age exactly, so professional was the attention she had given to her ash-blonde hair and peach and white complexion. She was dressed in a very short black leather skirt and a soft sweater loose enough round the waist to conceal any extra inches the years might have added and low enough at the neck to offer a hint of that ample bosom which was still remembered so appreciatively by her schoolmates in the bar of the Clarendon Hotel.

By rights, Mower thought, she ought not to be able to get away with it at her age. The skirt was too short, the hairstyle too girlish, the whole effect too absurdly sexy: and yet get away with it she undoubtedly did, in spades, by dint of completing the ensemble with a knowing but quite genuine smile which invited the onlooker to join with her in enjoying her bit of fun.

'Come in, Inspector,' she said, glancing at Mower's warrant card. 'Oh, sorry, Sergeant. Sergeant Mower, come in. My husband's out, of course, and he's the expert on security, but I'll show you what we've got.'

Her lip twitched imperceptibly as she waved Mower past her into the spacious carpeted hallway, giving a glance of frank appraisal to his own dark good looks and his well-fitting slacks and casual jacket. Then, with immense

152

seriousness, she had showed him round the house, explaining where the video cameras and security lights were fitted, where there were pressure pads in the drive and on the broad terrace which spanned the rear of the house overlooking a couple of acres of immaculate garden and a heated swimming pool, and where infra-red sensors in all the downstairs rooms would trap an unwary intruder.

'Of course, we don't keep my jewellery here,' she said airily, as she finally led him into the vast sitting-room where huge picture windows overlooked the terrace and waved him into a purple velour armchair so deep that he thought he would never finish his descent into its depths.

'Terry doesn't think that's safe. That's all in the bank. But I suppose there's enough here to tempt a thief, with all Terry's electronic equipment—he's a bit of a hi-fi buff, you know—and my porcelain collection.' She waved towards a wall of glass-fronted shelves which housed an array of painted and gilded plates and small statuettes which Mower recognized must be valuable although quite how valuable he could not guess.

'That lot's insured for £25,000,' Mrs Hardcastle said dismissively, as if reading his thoughts. 'Would you like a drink, Sergeant? Something before you go?' She opened the doors of a large wall bar to reveal an array of glasses and bottles.

'Coffee?' said Mower tentatively. 'It's a bit early for anything stronger.'

'Oh, come off it, Mr Mower. Don't you have another name, by the way?' Mower told her his other name and she pulled two glasses out of the cupboard with a bottle of malt whisky. 'A small one, Kevin, a small one for the road.'

Mower sank back into his enveloping chair and sipped his malt appreciatively, deciding that he might as well be hung for a sheep as a lamb, especially if the sheep stood a better chance, to mix an animal metaphor, of coming home with the bacon. Brenda Hardcastle chose a seat close to his, but not so close as to constitute an open invitation to impropriety, more an encouragement to confidences.

'So is it adequate then, Kevin?' she asked, leaning

153

towards him with her glass held between her palms just at the point where her sweater rolled far enough forward for him to get a good view of her swelling breasts beneath. He swallowed his scotch too quickly and choked slightly.

'More than adequate, Mrs Hardcastle,' he said with a grin. She looked at him with sharp-eyed amusement before leaning back in her chair, removing him, as it were, from temptation.

'The security systems,' she said drily. 'Do you reckon they'll do? I like to know because it's all in my name, of course. For business reasons, Terry says. The house, the cars, everything.' She made a small purring noise of satisfaction at the back of her throat which almost had Mower choking again.

'You seem to be very well protected, Mrs Hardcastle,' he said feelingly.

'Aye, well, I'm surprised you're wasting your time with us, to be honest,' she said. 'We had another young crime prevention officer up here less than six months ago. Mind you, it's much appreciated, you know. Much appreciated.' She gave him another knowing smile of complicity which said as clearly as necessary that she knew that whatever reason Mower had for his visit it was certainly not to inspect the security systems.

'All part of the service,' Mower muttered into his whisky, as close as he ever came to embarrassment. 'Do you let us know when you go on holiday?'

The question had sprung into his mind unbidden and he could not guess why it caused an unexpected tightening of Mrs Hardcastle's lips and a coldness to cloud her previously ingenuous blue gaze.

'Yes, we let the local bobby know, of course we do,' she said sharply. 'In fact I did let him know about our Christmas trip to Madeira but now that's off I suppose you'd better tell him we'll be here after all.'

'Madeira's supposed to be very nice,' Mower said thoughtfully. 'I've got an auntie in Essex who went a year or so ago . . .'

'Reid's Hotel,' Mrs Hardcastle snapped unexpectedly.

154

'We were supposed to be staying at Reid's Hotel. Something a bit special, that were supposed to be.'

'Family problems, is it?' Mower suggested tentatively, the sympathetic tone belied by his eyes which were cold and sharp now.

'Bloody business problems more like,' his hostess came back. 'Can't afford the time, he says.' She shrugged, causing an upheaval under the sweater which caused Mower to take a deep breath.

'Well, I'll tell the local man anyway. You don't want him clumping about in his size twelves if you're in residence, do you?'

'No, I do not,' Brenda Hardcastle said emphatically. 'I'm not at my best cooking a bloody turkey and all the trimmings, I can tell you. Christmas at home? You can stuff that for a lark. Well, I've told him, I'm not having his mother here, whatever she thinks about it. Common as muck, she is, wandering round in her slippers all day. Still thinks she's running that scruffy little betting shop down at Five Lane Ends they had when Terry was a lad. Another?' she asked, waving the bottle of malt in Mower's direction. He shook his head regretfully and wondered if he were in the wrong job. There were other occupations, he thought, in which he might be able to combine his intellectual talents with others which at present, he felt, were being allowed to atrophy.

He took his leave reluctantly and walked slowly back to his car. On his way back into town he pulled into a side-street and drew up outside a shopfront discreetly classy in dark wood and brass, with a hefty wire grille still half drawn across the plate glass. Inside he steered the proprietor, whom he had made it his business to get to know when he had arrived in Bradfield, towards a glass-fronted case of porcelain *objets*, similar in size and opulence to those displayed in Mrs Brenda Hardcastle's sitting-room.

'Get much call for this sort of stuff?' he asked casually.

'Not a lot,' the proprietor said. 'It's mainly one-off items for anniversary presents and such. We did have a big collector up in Southwaite, but she's been unloading lately. It's

155

this recession, you know. The cash simply isn't there any more, even up there.'

'I saw a lot of stuff like this in Southwaite—Mrs Hardcastle's place. Is she your collector?' Mower asked with studied casualness. His informant looked dubious, before deciding his best interests lay in confidence.

'She was my mainstay, she was,' he said slightly bitterly. 'But she's been swapping the real thing for cheap copies recently. Raising a bit of the ready, I'd say, without wanting to let on.'

'Ah,' Mower breathed happily. 'I wondered why a hi-fi buff boasted a CD player and amps a damn sight cheaper than mine.'

Mower's sunny mood was rudely shattered as soon as he reported back to Harry Huddleston's office. He found his superior waiting impatiently for him, fingers drumming on his desk and the ashtray full of half-smoked butts.

'You'd better read those before I tell you owt else,' Huddleston said, slapping two buff files on to the Sergeant's desk. Mower flicked them open quickly. One was the pathologist's report on Neil Robertson's post-mortem, the other the fire officer's report on the causes of the fire which had ostensibly killed him. Mower was appalled by what he read and knew that his reaction was not a professional one. He felt Huddleston's eyes on him and did not look up until he had read and re-read the conclusions of each report more than once. He swallowed hard before he looked across at Huddleston.

'He was murdered,' he said flatly.

'I've had the house sealed,' Huddleston said. 'The fire officer says there was no sign of a break-in, but I've got a couple of scene of crime boys going over the place just in case. Any road, they say the kitchen door was unlocked, so there wouldn't have to be a break-in, would there? Anyone could walk in.'

'Where's Mrs Robertson?' Mower asked, his face impassive.

'She stayed the night with her friend Mizz Turner, I'm

told. Her colleagues seem to be rallying round to look after her and her mother is on her way from the South Coast somewhere. What is it about that woman that has you all in such a tizzy? She's a mousy little thing to my mind. I can't see owt in her.'

Mower looked at Huddleston speculatively for a moment before replying, wondering if he could get away with ignoring the question but concluding from the belligerence in the Chief Inspector's eyes that an answer of some sort was expected. He shrugged.

'She's not sexy in an obvious way,' he said. 'She just makes you very curious about what she'd be like in bed.'

Huddleston snorted in disbelief.

'Aye, well, you'd best restrain your curiosity in that direction,' he said. 'I was waiting for you to come back. It's time we had a chat with Mrs Robertson, I think, don't you?'

'You don't think she . . . ?' Mower could not quite conceal the look of concern in his eyes and Huddleston reacted angrily.

'I don't know what to think, lad. Nor do you. We start murder investigations with open minds, Sergeant, so just you think on.' At that moment, to Mower's relief, a uniformed officer came in.

'Superintendent Longley would like to see you straight away, sir,' he said to Huddleston.

'I dare say he would,' Huddleston muttered grimly as he got to his feet. 'We've got more unexplained bodies littering the town this week than we've had the last three years. You get your act together on this one, young Mower, or I'll have you back in the Smoke before you even notice you're travelling down the M1. Some bugger's hit a crippled man on the head with a blunt instrument and left him to burn in a fire, and if you think the press won't have a field day with that you're dafter than I think you are. So fettle yourself, as they say up here. We've got work to do.'

Huddleston swept out of the room, slamming the door behind him and fluttering the clutter of papers on desks and shelves. Mower sat motionless at his desk gazing at Amos Atherton's clinical description of Neil Robertson's

157

fatal head injury. Huddleston's tirade had had its effect and his brain felt cold and clear. He had no doubt, deep down, that he would do whatever the job demanded of him.

He had within him, he knew and slightly feared, a ruthlessness which might have been bred by the job but he suspected went back much further than that to the time when most city boys face the choice between taking dangerous mischief the extra step into crime or not. Egged on by his gang of mates to break into his own school, he had not only turned his back on them, but betrayed them to the police.

He had had few friends after that and a coldness had entered his soul, which he carefully disguised most of the time beneath a sharp urban wit, more than a little charm and a genuine—and usually, he found, mutual—attraction to the opposite sex. But for Kevin Mower the job came first and if the demands of the job meant arresting Jo Robertson for murder, then that was what he would do.

Jo Robertson spent her first day as a widow in a state of emotionally frozen dispassion. Her brain felt supernaturally clear. She remembered the events of the previous evening in minute but unfelt detail, right down to the moment when a fireman had put his arm round her to prevent her entering the ambulance which stood among the chaos of hose reels and vehicles outside her home and told her that Neil had been brought out of the fire dead.

The whole sequence of events had a remote, dreamlike quality as if they had happened to someone else. She had as yet no sense of loss or grief, had not wept, had simply gone into some sort of emotional hibernation except in one crucial respect. She had wakened in the night and decided, quite coldly, that she was to blame for Neil's death, that by leaving him alone in the house after their row she had been the cause of the terrible accident which had killed him.

She had allowed her friends to spend the morning making arrangements on her behalf. Maggie had telephoned her mother and broken the news and Mrs Bailey had announced her intention of driving to Bradfield immediately. The fire brigade and the police had been contacted. The former told them that the house was sealed for the time being and in any case uninhabitable. The latter that they would wish to interview Mrs Robertson later in the day. Margaret Jackson had called at the flat and offered Jo an annexe to her own house, a 'granny flat' which she frequently loaned to young members of staff who had just moved to the town and which happened to be empty, for the use of herself and her mother until it was possible to return to her own home—if she ever felt that she could do that. Maggie had fussed about, finding some clothes which fitted her guest and going out to buy a toothbrush and toiletries.

At lunch-time Peter Masefield had come round to the flat from school, looking gaunt and exhausted, with dark circles under his eyes. He searched Jo's bruised face anxiously and took her, unresisting, into his arms and held her close without speaking. At length she pulled away and sat carefully in her chair by the fire, as if any sudden movement would shatter her equilibrium.

'I killed him,' Jo said. 'It was my fault. I should have been there.'

Peter groaned. 'No, that's nonsense, Jo,' he said.

Jo shrugged almost imperceptibly and said no more, turning her head away to gaze unseeingly at the flickering flames of the gas fire. Peter turned to Maggie who was standing by the kitchen door watching them. She beckoned him into the kitchen and shut the door behind them so that Jo would not overhear.

'She won't talk,' she said quietly. 'She's still in shock, I think. I can't get through to her at all. It would be better if she cried, or screamed, or something, to let it all out, but she won't. All she says occasionally is that she blames herself.'

'But she's never hesitated to leave him alone,' Peter said. 'He wasn't that helpless, was he? He could cope?'

'Of course he could bloody cope,' Maggie said scornfully. 'Better than he wanted to let on, I think. He could drive the car, go to the shops, cook if he felt like it, which appar-

159

ently he never did . . .' She shrugged. 'Shock does funny things to people,' she said.

'She obviously doesn't want me anywhere near her,' Peter said wearily, making no attempt to hide his own distress. Maggie touched his arm gently.

'It'll be all right, Peter,' she said. 'She'll get over it in time. People do, you know.'

At two o'clock Peter went back to school, after sitting silently with Jo for half an hour. An hour later Sergeant Mower rang the doorbell and followed Chief Inspector Huddleston up the long flights of stairs to the top floor. Maggie Turner met them at her front door.

'Mrs Robertson is still very shocked,' she said in an unfriendly tone to Huddleston. 'Do you really need to bother her now?'

'I'm afraid so,' Huddleston said curtly, brushing past Maggie and stepping into the living-room, where Jo still sat silently by the fire, huddled into a borrowed black sweater which was several sizes too large for her. Her face was very pale, and the bruises inflicted the previous night had swollen, almost closing her left eye and darkening across her cheek and brow. She had brushed her hair away from her face almost as if she wanted to expose her scars to public view. Mower drew a sharp breath when he saw her, but Huddleston remained completely impassive, merely nodding in Jo's direction and taking the chair opposite her across the fireplace.

'You look as though you've been in the wars, Mrs Robertson,' the Chief Inspector said at last. 'How did that happen?' Jo looked up and met his gaze directly.

'My husband hit me,' she said quietly, but in a clear firm voice. 'He did that every now and again.'

'Did he now,' Huddleston said thoughtfully. He glanced at Mower who took his notebook out of his pocket and sat down at the dining table in front of the window, turning his chair so that he could watch the duel which was about to commence. Maggie crossed the room determinedly and sat down on the settee between Jo and the Chief Inspector.

'You won't mind if I stay,' she said flatly. Huddleston

160

ignored her. He had not taken his eyes off Jo, who returned his gaze.

'You will understand that we have to ask you some questions about last night, Mrs Robertson?' he said. Jo nodded.

'Of course,' she said. She clasped her hands tightly in her lap. Mower glanced at her and marvelled at how completely she was keeping the emotions which must surely be beneath the surface under control. He was expecting Huddleston to explain the new developments over Neil Robertson's death to his wife and grew slightly uneasy as the Chief Inspector allowed her to continue in ignorance of what they had recently discovered.

'What do you want to know, Chief Inspector?' she asked composedly.

'I want to know what you did last night, Mrs Robertson, from when you came home from work which would be what time? Five o'clock? Until your husband was found dead? What exactly happened?'

Jo told him, speaking in a clear monotonous voice which washed all the pain out of the furious row she had had with Neil, the violence which had followed and her bus ride to Peter Masefield's cottage. Mower took notes, his head down to hide the anxiety in his eyes, and Maggie watched, rigid with tension, as Jo spared none of the details of her last battle with her husband. Huddleston seemed content to let her talk, until she moved quickly from her arrival at Peter's cottage to her decision to return home.

'A good friend of yours, is he, Peter Masefield?' the Chief Inspector broke in at that point. Jo nodded, thrown off balance slightly by this first interruption. Mower glanced at his boss, guessing what was coming next and deeply unwilling to hear either the question or its probable answer.

'How good?' Huddleston asked bluntly. Jo looked blankly at him for a moment and Maggie turned on him angrily.

'Is that really necessary, Chief Inspector?' she asked.

'You're here on sufferance, Mizz Turner,' Huddleston returned sharply. 'I'll decide what's necessary.'

He turned to Jo again.

'Should I take it that you and Mr Masefield are lovers?'

161

he asked. 'Is that why you ran to him last night, rather than to your friend Mizz Turner here?'

Jo sat for a moment in silence hardly seeming to breathe, and Mower found himself clenching his pencil to snapping point as he waited for her answer. In the end she simply nodded, almost casually.

'Yes,' she said. 'Peter and I have been lovers for a long time.'

'Did your husband know that?'

'No, he didn't,' Jo said quickly.

'You're sure?' Huddleston persisted. 'That wasn't why he gave you a bloody good thumping last night?'

'No, I told you. We were arguing about the Asian girls. He was afraid I would lose my job over that and that made him angry.' Very gradually Jo's icy calm appeared to be deserting her and she was beginning to feel the first faint stirrings of anger herself as the policeman continued to probe.

'Sir,' Mower ventured but Huddleston waved him down impatiently.

'Not now, Sergeant,' he said. 'So go on, Mrs Robertson. You went to see Mr Masefield, and then what?'

'I stayed there for a couple of hours and then I decided that I should go back and make sure that Neil had got to bed safely. It was difficult for him to manage on his own.'

'A fit of conscience, was it?' Huddleston asked. Jo flushed slightly and looked away but Maggie Turner turned on the policeman angrily unable to keep quiet any longer.

'Have you seen what that bastard did to her last night?' she asked, leaning over and pulling up the legs of Jo's borrowed tracksuit trousers to reveal the cuts and bruises across her shins.

'It wasn't just a black eye he gave her, you know. He bloody nearly broke her legs as well. She was a fool to go back. In fact she was a fool to stay with him as long as she did. Now he's dead, she's actually well rid of him, so stop treating her as if she's a murderer instead of one of the victims in this awful business.'

'Well, now,' Huddleston said quietly, well satisfied with

162

the effect he had created. 'It just so happens that it is actually a murderer I seem to be looking for.'

You old bastard, Mower thought as the two women looked at the Chief Inspector in appalled silence.

'What do you mean?' Maggie asked, her voice reduced to a strained whisper. The colour had drained out of her face now and she looked as pale as her friend.

'I mean that Mr Neil Robertson did not die in the fire at his house, as the world was obviously intended to believe. He died before that fire started. In fact he died as the result of a blow to the back of the head with a heavy instrument. I mean that I'm not here to talk about a tragic accident, Mizz Turner—I leave that to sergeants and constables. I'm here to talk about a murder. Which is why I shall have to continue to ask Mrs Robertson what you may consider inopportune questions until I know precisely what she did last night and when, right down to the precise moment she and Mr Masefield got in and out of bed together.'

The effect of Huddleston's deliberate brutality on Jo Robertson was startling and not what anyone in the room expected. She was leaning forward in her chair now, staring intently at the Chief Inspector, her eyes bright and a look which Mower could only interpret, with a sense of shock, as excitement on her face.

'Neil was murdered?' she asked in a breathless whisper. She's pleased, Mower thought incredulously. I don't believe it. The other two were also looking at her in astonishment.

'I'm afraid so,' Huddleston said with a ponderous attempt at sympathy.

'I thought I'd killed him,' Jo said patiently, as if to a group of particularly obtuse third-formers. Neither Sergeant Mower now Maggie could disguise the alarm in their eyes at that but Huddleston merely nodded heavily, as if Jo had simply confirmed some minor detail.

'Do you mind explaining that remark?' he asked, after a moment's pause.

For an instant Jo looked slightly puzzled, as if she could not understand the tension which had seized them. Maggie grasped her arm and squeezed it hard, as if to restrain her in some way, while at the table Mower sat immobile with his pencil poised over his notebook, his mask of professional impassivity slipping to reveal the horror he felt at what he took to be a confession. Jo turned back to meet Huddleston's cold blue eyes and shook her head impatiently.

'I didn't mean literally killed him,' she said. 'I thought that the fire was an accident that happened because I left Neil on his own. I thought it was my fault. I was blaming myself. I didn't think I would ever forgive myself. What you're telling me is that someone else did it.'

'What he's telling you, Jo, is that he thinks you might have done it,' Maggie said harshly. 'Don't you have to caution people in situations like this, Chief Inspector? Isn't she supposed to be told her rights or something?' Huddleston looked at Maggie with undisguised dislike.

'At the moment I am making very preliminary inquiries into the suspicious death of Neil Robertson,' he said. 'If and when I choose to arrest someone there are procedures to be followed but we are a very long way from that, Mizz Turner, a very long way. So can we continue?' He turned back to Jo, whose face had gone cold and closed again.

'You are quite sure that your husband had not found out about your relationship with Mr Masefield?' Huddleston asked.

'No,' she replied in a near whisper. 'No, I'm sure he hadn't.' Huddleston looked at her impassively again for a long moment before asking his next question. He's not dragging this out from kindness, Mower thought helplessly, head down again. Quite the reverse.

'Were you and your husband able to have normal sexual relations?' Huddleston asked at last. Maggie drew in a sharp breath and made as if to protest but Jo put a hand on hers to restrain her. She looked Huddleston straight in the eyes.

'Yes, Chief Inspector, we were, after a fashion. Neil was a deeply frustrated man, but that wasn't the reason. What Neil resented so bitterly was my freedom to go where I wanted, do what I wanted—a freedom he was never going to have again.'

Jo broke off abruptly, suddenly on the verge of tears as she ran her fingers lightly over the bruises around her eye.

'Isn't that enough, Chief Inspector?' Maggie Turner asked angrily. But Huddleston was not to be deterred quite yet.

'Do you own a poker, Mrs Robertson?' he asked. Jo looked at him for a moment in horror which quickly turned to anger.

'No, I don't,' she said, with a hint, to Maggie's delight at the normality of it, of the acerbity with which she could devastate young people who wasted her time. 'And nor, since you obviously intend to ask, did I hit my husband on the head with anything else.'

CHAPTER 13

Peter Masefield stood at the window of his cottage and watched the late December dawn spread a grey light over Bradfield. The town was little more than a haze of obscure shapes in the winter gloom of its enfolding valley as low cloud drifted between the hills. The morning was as bleak and cold as he felt.

The sense of sheer incredulity which had seized him when Chief Inspector Huddleston and Sergeant Mower had arrived the previous afternoon to ask him questions about the events of the evening before had only slightly subsided at the end of a restless and largely sleepless night. It was Saturday morning, so there was no need to get up early, but Masefield had found it physically impossible to rest and had stumbled blearily into the kitchen to make tea before first light.

The police had lost little time in telling him that their interest was in Neil Robertson's murder, not an accidental death; nor did they hesitate to suggest that he might well figure right at the top of their list of suspects. Had he not

165

admitted early in the conversation, as Chief Inspector Huddleston repeatedly reminded him, that he was in love with Joanna Robertson and wanted to marry her? Was that not motive enough for murder, they had suggested, not very obliquely? They would, they had said with a menace that Masefield found thoroughly alarming, need to speak to him again quite soon.

His own reaction, a mixture of physical paralysis and emotional turmoil, had been intense. The incredulity at his situation remained, but had been overtaken by both anger and fear: anger on his own behalf, that he should be suspected of what now sounded like a fairly brutal crime; and fear, which he hardly dared examine, that the blazing row which Jo Robertson admitted she had had with Neil had ended rather differently from the way she had described when she had arrived distraught at his door.

Now in the pale morning light he leaned his head against the cold window-pane to try to calm his racing brain. He could not imagine Jo being driven to violence of any kind. He had seen her work with the most provocative and self-destructive children and maintain a composure which he found enviable. But then, he thought, neither could he imagine Jo as the victim of the sort of violence which he knew Neil had inflicted upon her over several years. She could, he supposed dully, have hit back, and then in a panic have tried to hide the terrible consequences of a momentary loss of control.

'Oh hell,' he said, running an anguished hand through his hair. What grieved him most about his imaginings was the possibility that Jo had come to his house, and his bed, and told him less than the whole truth. What he regretted most bitterly now, in the chill light of the morning, was that instead of going straight to talk to Jo after the police had left he had spent the evening and the long watches of the night almost paralysed with fear, turning his suspicions over and over in his mind until they had grown to monstrous proportions.

'I don't bloody believe it,' he said aloud at last, turning away from the window and picking up the phone. He dialled a number and waited impatiently for a reply which did not come. Angrily he slammed the receiver down, grabbed a coat from the back of the door, and set off at a furious pace in his car towards the town below.

When he reached Maggie Turner's flat there was no reply to his urgent peals on her doorbell, although when he looked up to the top of the house he could see that all the lights were on. He rang again more frantically and when one of Maggie's neighbours came out of the front door, he brushed past him, muttering something incoherent in excuse, and took the three flights of stairs two at a time.

Maggie's front door, he was surprised to find, was ajar.

'Hello,' he called tentatively, and pushed the door open. There was no response, and more cautiously now, the first hint of fear making him catch his breath, he went in. The living-room and kitchen were empty, and when he called again, outside the bedroom door, he heard the faintest of sounds in response.

'Maggie?' he said again, cautiously opening the door. She was lying face down on the bed, fully dressed in her familiar black tracksuit, with her hand clutched over her head as if to ward off the sight and sound of the world.

'Maggie,' Peter said again. 'What's happened? Where's Jo?'

Very reluctantly Maggie turned towards him, revealing a face blotched with crying.

'Jo's fine,' she said dully. 'She went down to Margaret's house with her mother yesterday afternoon.'

With what seemed like enormous weariness Maggie rolled herself upright and sat leaning against the top of the bed with her arms round her knees. Her dark hair was dishevelled and she had black circles beneath her eyes, as if she too had hardly slept.

'You're upset,' Peter said unnecessarily. 'You think she killed Neil.'

It was a statement, not a question, and offered with such leaden despair that Maggie winced as she took in the familiar face, grey with fatigue and ill-concealed pain.

'Of course I bloody don't,' she came back angrily. 'I'm

167

bloody sure she didn't kill him. Couldn't, wouldn't, never in a million years! Come on, Peter!'

The older man stood looking at the unexpected fury in Maggie's brown eyes, and allowed himself the shadow of a smile.

'Oh Maggie, Maggie,' he said quietly. 'That's what I needed to hear. Of course she couldn't, never in a million years. I shouldn't need you to tell me that, but I had a bad time with the police yesterday and I've hardly slept.' He sat down beside her on the bed and put an arm round her.

'So why are you crying?' he asked gently.

'Because I did something that I didn't think I would do,' she admitted, looking away. 'I told someone where Farida and Ayesha are.'

Peter looked at her in surprise.

'You told someone about the refuge?'

'Yes, I bloody did,' Maggie said defiantly, with fresh tears in her eyes. 'Two men came and . . . and threatened me, and I told them, and I know I shouldn't have, it was unforgivable, but I couldn't help it.'

She turned away from Peter with a childlike despair and flung herself back down on the bed again, crying quietly, as she must have been doing for most of the night, Peter thought. He stroked her hair gently until she shrugged him away, and gradually told him what had happened.

Late the previous evening, she said, the doorbell had rung and when she had answered the intercom, a voice claiming to be the police had asked to be admitted. Not particularly surprised, after the events of the afternoon, she had opened the front door almost without thought, only to find two men she did not know with a foot in her door and definitely un-policemanlike intentions.

'Asians? Farida's family?' Peter asked, but she shook her head.

'No, they were white. I've no idea who they were. But they wanted to know where the girls were and in the end I told them.'

'Did they hurt you?' Peter asked angrily but Maggie shook her head. Only her eyes, where fear still lingered, seemed bruised and hurt by her experience. She hugged herself tightly again.

'They didn't touch me,' she said in an anguished whisper.

'But they threatened to?'

'They threatened all sorts of things, unspeakable things,' she said. 'One of them locked the door and stood against it while the other just talked, on and on, describing what he wanted to do to me, every detail. I thought I was tough, Peter, but when it came to the point—that point—I wasn't tough at all. I would have told them everything, done anything, almost, to make them go away. So I told them what they wanted to know, and the one who talked laughed, and then they went.'

'You couldn't have rung Farida . . . ?'

'They said if I warned the girls they'd come back and begin to do the things they said they'd do. I'll never forgive myself . . .'

'Don't, Maggie. I think we all have a breaking-point,' Peter said, hugging her close for a moment.

'Perhaps Jo reached hers the other night with Neil,' Maggie said, her former confidence gone now.

'No,' Peter said firmly. 'I don't believe that. Not that she couldn't, perhaps, but that she didn't. If she'd hit Neil she'd have been as appalled as you are now. She might have come to me but only to tell me what had happened, not to tell a pack of lies about it. I don't believe that.'

'Of course you're right,' Maggie agreed. 'But what I don't understand is how anyone found out I knew where the girls were. No one at school knew I was involved.'

'I didn't know until Jo told me when she came up to the cottage on Thursday night, and I certainly didn't mention it to anyone else,' Peter said slowly. 'Which leaves Jo herself, and Neil. He was around when the girls ran away, wasn't he?'

'Neil,' Maggie breathed. 'He knew I'd taken the girls to the refuge, but not exactly where, of course. Not even Jo knows the address. You don't think those men could have talked to Neil . . .'

'And possibly did more than talk to him?' They looked at each other in appalled silence.

'They were violent enough,' she said quietly. 'I've never been so frightened. I never doubted they would do what they threatened for a moment. They had a sort of coldness about them, the coldness of killers . . . Perhaps? I don't know.'

'What time did all this happen?'

'It was about eleven when they left. I was so terrified, Peter, I just did what they said. I've been lying here all night wondering if I dare move. I could have tried to stop them but I couldn't think of any way of doing it that they wouldn't trace back to me. I never doubted for a moment that they would come back if I tried. They obviously planned to go to the refuge and grab the girls straight away. They could be on the plane to Pakistan by now.'

'We'd better go down there and see,' Peter said. 'Are you up to it?'

'Will you tell Jo? I don't think I can bear it?' Maggie asked.

'Jo—and then the police,' Peter said. 'You're going to have to tell the police as well.'

'I suppose so,' Maggie said dully.

'Bingo!' exclaimed Sergeant Mower, who was sitting at the computer terminal in Chief Inspector Huddleston's office with a text file on the screen. Huddleston looked up impatiently from the statements he was reading. They had spent an hour of the previous evening at the Robertsons' smoke-blackened bungalow listening to what seemed like an endless catalogue of entirely negative findings from the forensic team who were still, though desultorily, working there.

The fire in the kitchen had effectively destroyed any evidence there might have been to identify Neil Robertson's attacker, they had been told, a conclusion which did not particularly surprise Huddleston who had dealt with cases involving fire before. And of a weapon there was no sign.

What was even more depressing was that smoke and

water damage in most of the rest of the house meant that almost every surface was covered with a thick black greasy layer of soot which made most normal procedures either messy or impossible and sometimes both. After almost an hour amid the piles of sooty debris and the pungent smell of burnt fat and plastic beginning to sting the eyes and throat and cling to their clothes, Huddleston was ready to call it a day.

But Mower, fastidiously brushing flecks of greasy soot off his jacket, had persisted. Only Neil Robertson's study had escaped the worst effects of the smoke, having been left with the relatively tight-fitting door closed. The Sergeant had fallen on the computer there with keen excitement, only to be told that with the electricity cut off, there was nothing that could be done with it. Undeterred, he had collected up the stacked boxes of floppy discs which stood by the machine, promising a far from ecstatic Huddleston that he would look at them in the office the next morning. It was already clear that all options for leisure time over the week-end were off.

'He played games,' Huddleston had grunted sceptically. 'What's that got to do with owt?' Not that he himself had much more to offer Jack Longley when he inquired tetchily about progress before he left the building an hour later 'all dolled up' in his dinner suit, as Huddleston sourly put it after the Superintendent had departed for an official engagement and he himself had reluctantly decided to call it a day.

'I'll put money on it being the wife or the boyfriend,' Huddleston said flatly to Longley. 'It always is. They've always got a motive, and for some daft reason they imagine murder is going to be easier than divorce.

'But all I've got so far is two negative statements with no contradictions that I can find. Either she whacked him on the head before she went up to Masefield's place, or else he crept out while she was asleep after their bit of nooky and did it then. With the heat of the fire, Atherton can't give me an accurate time of death, so there's no way of knowing. And the state that house is in we'll be lucky to find a shred of hard evidence there. Our best hope is a witness to one of them coming or going. That'll take time, though someone must have seen her going up to Masefield's place in the state she was in.'

Time, he reflected, was what he personally did not have. And he did not find Longley's solicitude much comfort.

'If it's domestic you'll likely only get her for manslaughter anyway with that amount of provocation from the husband,' Longley said. 'The defence would make hay with her injuries. I'd concentrate on the stabbings, if I were you.'

Mower had listened to all this speculation with a disbelief which he did not dare share with Huddleston and which he was reluctant to admit even to himself. It sat like an unacknowledged heavy weight in the pit of his stomach. He had slept badly and gone back to the office at eight in the morning, only to find the Chief Inspector there before him. Doggedly he kept his mind on the intellectual puzzle facing him on the computer screen and blotted Jo Robertson's bruised and desolate face from his mind. By the time he indicated that his irritating fiddling with keyboard and discs had borne fruit, Huddleston was ready to grasp at any straw.

'He kept a diary, guv,' Mower said, reading from the screen avidly. 'Most of this stuff is games, as we thought, but this file is different. This is a diary going back a year or more. Listen to this: *J. late again: home 5.30. Supposed to be meeting parents after school. Asked D. to follow her home tomorrow.*'

'Who the hell's D?' asked Huddleston, drawn against his better judgement across the office to stand behind Mower's shoulder and read from the screen.

'He obviously suspected she had a boyfriend,' Mower said. 'That was last January. Now look here. *D. saw J. leaving with PM.* And here: *J. two hours late. D. says there was no rehearsal after school.* He'd got someone watching her, the cunning bastard. He's known for months that she was playing around, and who with, and he's been keeping a record on a computer file.' The thrill of the chase drove him on excitedly although the leaden feeling in his stomach was now turning into a dull pain.

'But she said he didn't know,' Huddleston said, eager now. 'So there's one little lie we've caught her out in. He'd hardly have found out and not faced her with it. Now who the hell is D? It's obviously someone at school, if they could watch what was going on there. Give the headmistress a call, lad, and see if she can identify a member of staff whose name begins with D who might have been in contact with Robertson regularly.'

'It's not a teacher, it's a boy,' Mower said when he had made the call to Margaret Jackson. 'There's a boy called David Edwards who helps—helped—Robertson with his games, some sort of young computer wizard. Mrs Jackson says he spends hours up there, neglects his school work, in fact. Lives in Grange Road, on the edge of the estate.' Mower hesitated and Huddleston, alert and responsive to every inflection in his voice, looked at him sharply.

'Aye?' he asked.

'I asked Mrs Jackson about Joanna Robertson and Masefield. She knew something was going on,' Mower said reluctantly. 'And more. She says Masefield has applied for another job, somewhere in Cumbria. Has asked her for a reference. He'd be odds on to get it and would be leaving at the end of next term.'

'Oh aye,' Huddleston said heavily. 'And what does that tell you, lad?'

Mower shrugged, his dark eyes blank, his expression impassive.

'That Mrs Robertson would be under pressure to go with him,' he said quietly. 'Or upset at the prospect of being left behind. Under pressure, either way.' Huddleston looked at the younger man sombrely for a moment.

'Aye, that's what it tells me, an' all. And I'll tell you summat for nowt, too, Sergeant, summat I learned well before I was your age, and that is that you'll get nowhere in this game if you let your emotions interfere with your judgement. Is that clear?'

'Sir,' Mower said, no trace of emotion or pain on his face as his guts gave a vicious twist.

'And now I think we'd better have a word with young

David,' Huddleston said heavily. 'He might be just the lad we're looking for.'

Before the police could get near David Edwards, they had to contend with David Edwards's mother, a pale thin woman with straggling fair hair pulled unflatteringly back from her face and a cigarette held like a permanent fixture between nicotine-stained fingers. She answered the door of her down-at-heel council house to Huddleston and Mower even before the bell had finished chiming and flew immediately into an astonishing tirade of abuse.

'Effing stupid boy,' she said, taking in Huddleston's warrant card at a glance. 'I told him and told him, time and again I told him.' She waved the visitors into the cluttered living-room where two small children still in their nightclothes were gazing at the television set.

'I told him he was spending too much time up there. I told him it weren't healthy. I even wondered—well, never mind what I wondered, he said there were nowt like that, David did—but any road, I told him, he should be out playing football wi't'other lads, not gawping at a computer screen morning, noon and night. You two, go and get dressed, I'll not tell you again!' This to the two younger children, who turned away from the screen for a moment to glance at the visitors and then as quickly turned back, their mother's verbal torrent attracting no attention at all.

'Could we have it turned off, Mrs Edwards?' Mower asked mildly. Mrs Edwards hesitated in mid-flow just long enough to use the remote control to darken the screen, to much wailing from her children.

'It's not natural, is it, being stuck indoors there with a cripple all t'time? And that woman—she was never there when she were needed, David said. A right funny set-up, I call that, a helpless man like that and a wife out all t'time instead of looking after him. These last couple of weeks it's been David has been getting him his tea, as often as not. She's been doing a bloody pantomime down at t'school.'

'Right, let's have this lad of yours,' Huddleston broke in impatiently. 'It's him I need to talk to, missus. And I'd send these two children upstairs, if I were you. They should be out in't fresh air on a Saturday morning, not sat here gawping at the television.'

The two children gave him evil looks but took the hint and left the room, although to judge by the noise which ensued, dressing was not the first thing in their minds as they clattered upstairs and apparently switched on another television set. As they went out, David himself, a sandy-haired boy, pale and small for his age, and as quiet as his younger brother and sister were noisy, sidled into the room.

He did not seem intimidated by his interrogators, though, and he told them articulately enough how he had discovered in casual conversation with Mrs Robertson at school that her husband was an expert in the computer games which obsessed him. He had, more than a year ago, wangled himself an invitation to the house, from which he had seldom been absent for more than a day or two at a time ever since.

'He helped you a lot, did he?' Mower prompted, having been left to lead the questioning partly, he guessed, on the grounds that he would cut a less frightening figure to the boy but partly also, he suspected, because Huddleston required him to prove his dispassion in this case. The Chief Inspector contented himself with a lowering presence from a hard seat at the dining table while Mower and the boy sat on the somewhat battered settee in front of the television and Mrs Edwards came and went distractedly.

'He said I could make a living at it one day,' the boy said, with the first sign of emotion in his voice. 'He were going to help me find a job later on.'

'But it wasn't just the games, was it, David?' Mower asked. 'What about the diary he kept? When did you start helping him with that?' David did not try to evade the issue.

'He thought his missus were cheating on him,' he said unemotionally. 'And she were. I found out. She and Mr Masefield were having it off. At least they were going around together without Mr Robertson knowing, so that's as bad as, isn't it? She were neglecting him and cheating on him, the cow,' he ended vehemently. 'And now he's dead and it's her fault.'

175

'Bloody hell!' said the boy's mother to whom this was obviously news, leaning momentarily over the back of the settee on one of her scuttling journeys between kitchen and living-room. Mower merely nodded noncommittally, although he felt slightly sickened by the boy's self-righteousness, helpful as it was proving to be.

'Did you tell anyone what you'd found out?' he asked. 'Anyone at school?' The boy shook his head emphatically.

'It were a secret,' he said. 'Mr Robertson—Neil—he let me call him Neil—wanted it kept a secret.' And what Neil Robertson asked, Mower thought, David would do, in so far as he was able. In a very real sense the boy had become the disabled man's eyes, and his ears and his legs.

'Tell me about the night of the fire,' he prompted. 'You were there?' The boy nodded, and described how Neil had sent him away as the row with Jo intensified.

'What was the row about? Did you hear?'

'Something about her job. I think she were going to get the sack for something at school. I'm not right sure what,' the boy said. 'Serve her right, any road,' he added vindictively.

'They weren't rowing about Mr Masefield?'

'No, I don't think so.'

'Did she know that Mr Robertson knew about her . . .' Mower hesitated, unsure what word to use with a boy so young. Huddleston had no such doubts.

'Her carrying on, you mean, lad. Did she know you and her old man'd sussed her?'

David shook his head. 'I don't think so,' he said. 'I never heard them talk about it.' Mower was sure that if he had done he would have relished the telling now.

'Not even that night, when they were arguing? Mr Masefield's name wasn't mentioned?'

'I think he liked to keep it secret in the computer,' the boy said reluctantly. 'He knew she couldn't get at it there. She didn't know how to get into the files.'

'You both liked secrets, did you?' Mower asked, and the boy nodded, with a sly smile.

176

'So coming back to that night. You left them arguing and then you came home?'

'Shouting and screaming, more like,' David said with a certain amount of satisfaction. 'And I didn't come home. Not straight off, any road.' Mower felt rather than saw Huddleston's interest quicken. Don't blow it now, he thought to himself, or he'll have you on traffic duty before the day's out.

'So what did you do then, David?' he asked quietly.

'I waited, didn't I? I'd left some notes I wanted by the computer, so I thought I'd go back when they'd calmed down. I hung about outside for a bit.'

'And could you hear what was going on inside?'

'Just more shouting and screaming for a while. And then she came running out of the back door and went off down the road. I waited a bit longer and then I rang the front doorbell.'

'And?'

'And what?' the boy said, heedless of the suspense he was creating. 'Neil let me in and I got the papers, and then I came home. I wish I'd stopped. Then I could have got him out when the fire started.' Mower allowed himself the luxury of a deep breath which he hoped did not appear to Huddleston too obviously like a sigh of relief.

'He was OK, was he, Mr Robertson, when you left him?'

The boy looked at him curiously for a moment and then he nodded.

'He were fine,' he said. 'But he shouldn't have been on his own like that, should he? Someone should have been looking after him.'

'Did you see owt else on the way home, David?' Huddleston broke in impatiently. 'Anything strange, unusual?'

The boy looked at the Chief Inspector unblinkingly for a moment before answering. 'There were a big black car parked under t'tree where I saw Mrs Robertson and Mr Masefield parked t'other night. But it weren't them. It were two men I didn't know. A Paki and a white bloke. Nothing else, I don't think. I just came home.'

'It proves nowt,' Huddleston said sourly in response to Mower's speculations as the Sergeant drove him back to police headquarters later. 'No more than she did what she said she did. Either of them could have come back later and clouted him on the head. Either of them—or both of them. It proves nowt.'

CHAPTER 14

Bradfield Women's Refuge was in turmoil. Two large vans were parked outside, half on and off the pavement, into which women were loading armfuls of personal possessions while half a dozen young children, few of them looking adequately dressed to face the chilly north wind which whipped around the corner of the house, milled about in the small front garden where the soil and grass and what looked like the remains of a shrubbery had been churned into mud by the pounding of dozens of young feet.

The house was an unkempt old Victorian stone villa set back from the road behind a couple of stunted trees which had been hacked about over the years into angular shapes no arboriculturalist would recognize. This morning the front door and almost every window was flung open, letting flurries of rain into the tiled vestibule and flapping the bedraggled curtains in the wind. A young policewoman stood in the gateway keeping a desultory watch on the activity which swirled around her as the vans were loaded and the over-excited children marshalled from house to garden and back again without discernible purpose.

Peter Masefield parked his car behind the larger of the two vans and glanced at Maggie and Jo. Jo Robertson had insisted on going with them to the refuge. As she said, with ingenuous logic, Peter would not be allowed over the threshold, although he was welcome to go with them for moral support, so Maggie would need her.

Jo was looking distinctly more like her usual self this morning, in spite of the vicious bruising around her eye,

Peter had thought thankfully when she opened the door of Margaret Jackson's flat and invited them in. Though her apparent normality, he realized, was more to do with the fact that her mother, a formidable woman who bustled indefatigably about the tiny 'granny annexe' as if organizing the domestic arrangements of a fair-sized hotel, had put her to bed with a tranquillizer the night before. The morning's equilibrium looked far from stable. Whenever Neil's name was mentioned, Jo visibly winced and turned the conversation in a less painful direction, but when she was told what had happened to Maggie the previous night she reacted with a fury which took everyone aback.

'They can't do that,' she said, standing up suddenly and clenching and unclenching her fists, as if looking for someone to punch. 'They bloody well can't get away with that. They've no right. Oh, Maggie, I'm so sorry.' She flung her arms round the younger woman and gave her a fierce hug which reduced Maggie to the verge of tears as well.

'We were going down to the refuge to find out exactly what's happened,' Maggie said, when she had extricated herself from her friend's embrace.

'I'll come with you,' Jo had said flatly and no amount of argument from her mother or anyone else could deter her. But now they had followed Maggie's terse directions and arrived at the refuge they were disconcerted by the confusion which apparently prevailed. The refuge housed at any one time a miscellaneous and shifting population of mothers and children who had left violent husbands and fathers, and usually one or two young Asian women who had taken the difficult decision to leave home for a variety of reasons. This morning the entire population of the rambling house appeared to be in a state of panic.

'People seem to be moving,' Maggie said unnecessarily. 'Peter, you'd better stay in the car while we find out what's going on.'

Peter nodded grimly in assent. He resented his classification by sex as one of life's aggressors, but did not feel that this was the moment to argue with either woman on that score.

179

Jo and Maggie picked their way carefully among the obstructions, small and human and large and inanimate, on the pathway to the house. The policewoman at the gate watched them, but with only casual interest and did not attempt to detain them. Through the open front door in the spacious central hallway, they found a scene of even greater confusion than in the garden, with piles of baggage, a couple of pushchairs with small, loudly wailing children firmly strapped into them, and sitting on the stairs a group of three young women in their late teens, two Asians and one white, clutching bundles of their belongings and engaged in a furious argument.

'We need to find Beth Corrigan,' Maggie said firmly, ignoring the chaos in the hallway and leading Jo determinedly towards the back of the building. There a door marked OFFICE stood ajar. Inside a large woman in skin-tight black leggings and a flowing, flowery smock sat on a cluttered desk with a cigarette drooping from her lip, a telephone clutched to her ear and a tiny baby cradled in her other arm. She looked up as Jo and Maggie pushed the door open and shoved a hank of abundant red hair away from her face with the receiver.

'I'll be with you in a minute,' she said to Maggie, before returning her attention to the telephone, into which she was shouting a vigorous protest.

'We need the electricity today,' Beth said. 'I've got half a dozen small children and two babies moving into that house. I know it's Saturday but they're going to need hot food and water today. Tomorrow won't do. Monday certainly won't do. Now come on, pull your finger out. I know you can act quickly in an emergency and this is a bloody emergency!' Whatever the electricity board said in reply seemed to mollify her slightly.

'OK,' she conceded. 'That will have to do, I suppose. I'll make sure someone is there to meet you.' She put the receiver down with force and turned to her visitors with a look of inquiry which turned to undisguised annoyance as she recognized Maggie.

'Jesus,' she said. 'I guess I've got you to thank for all

180

this. Did you give those bastards the address?' Her eyes were green and flashing now in fury and her accent more obviously American. She hitched the baby she was carrying, which continued to sleep peacefully, more comfortably into the crook of her arm and crossed the room to slam the door shut behind Jo and Maggie.

'What happened?' Beth asked grimly, sitting down at the desk. 'I've got six families of mothers and kids and four young single women getting ready to move out of here because the address has been blown. The cops have been tramping around the place half the night. Thanks be to no one there's another house that we were gonna open as a second refuge that we can take everyone to. But I ask you! Last night irate Asian fathers, today what? Half a dozen wife batterers and child abusers through the door? What the hell's going on, Maggie? How did they find out?'

Jo glanced at Maggie, who seemed to have shrunk physically under this assault and was obviously having difficulty in speaking. Quietly she told Beth what had happened. As she listened her expression of exasperated fury softened slightly. She hugged the sleeping child closer to her ample bosom.

'Jesus, there's some bastards in this world,' she said, kissing the baby's head softly. 'So what d'ya know? So now we have to move house, and can I get the electricity, the phone, the gas switched on? I cannot. What's with this country?'

'They came and took Farida and Ayesha?' Maggie asked dully.

'They came and took Farida and Ayesha,' the American woman confirmed. 'And how. They smashed a window at half past one o'clock and by the time we'd mobilized ourselves and clambered over the howling kids that had wakened up to find strange men in their rooms, the girls had gone. I saw the car drive away.'

Maggie and Jo exchanged a look which mixed anger and desolation.

'Did they hurt them?' Jo asked.

'I don't know,' Beth said angrily. 'They didn't yell so's you'd notice but I guess to judge from your experience they

181

might have used subtler methods. Christ, why won't men leave us alone?'

'They're probably on the plane by now,' Maggie said.

'We could check out all the flights, but then what? If they walk on to the plane without making a fuss, no one will stop them,' Jo said hopelessly. 'It's Ayesha I'm most afraid for. Farida's mother will make sure that she gets her education, but if Ayesha is sent to some village at the back of beyond she'll be like a displaced person. She's had no contact with that culture since she was a small girl.'

'Patriarchal religions—I hate 'em,' Beth said dismissively. 'They're all the same. My father wanted me to be a nun. Just because I showed no interest in boys. Did I have a vocation, he kept asking. Wouldn't I like to be a missionary? Had I been to confession? When he finally got the confession that I was sleeping with my girlfriend he flipped his lid.' She laughed uproariously at that and thrusting the now wakeful baby into Jo's arms took Maggie in hers in a bear hug which almost lifted her off her feet.

'Gee, I'm sorry they did that to you,' Beth muttered into Maggie's hair. 'That's awful, sister, truly awful.'

Maggie disentangled herself and went out into the hallway with tears in her eyes. The three teenagers were still deep in conversation on the stairs and as Maggie wandered blindly down the hall the youngest of them, a tiny waif-like girl with close-cropped hair dressed completely in black slid to her feet and tapped her on the shoulder.

'Are you Farida's friend?' she said.

Maggie took a deep breath to steady herself and nodded, looking closely at the girl for the first time. She was, she guessed, about sixteen but painfully thin, and with no more than a child's shape beneath her skinny T-shirt and black leather jacket. She was very pale, with dark rings visible beneath her eyes in spite of the circling make-up, and she clutched the stub of a cigarette between the nicotine-stained and trembling fingers of her left hand.

'I'm Shell,' she said. 'I were Karim's girl till they sent us away. But I came back.'

*

Promising Beth Corrigan faithfully that they would bring her back to the new refuge when she wanted to come, they took Shell back to the flat where Jo's mother took one look at her and instantly prescribed a regime of warm bath, clean clothes, sweet tea and egg sandwiches. She came out of the bathroom with the girl's jeans and T-shirt held at arm's length and a look of incomprehension on her face.

'She's got sores all down her arms, Joanna.'

'Oh, shit,' Maggie said and got a look of distaste in return.

'She's probably been doing things she shouldn't with needles, Mum,' Jo said gently. 'Don't worry, we'll see what help we can get her.'

'Drugs, you mean?' Mrs Bailey asked in alarm. 'You mean she's taking drugs?'

'Taken, if not actually taking,' Peter Masefield said from the corner of the room where he had taken up a watching brief. He was not sure what Jo had told her mother about their relationship and had chosen to keep a low profile. So far Jo's concern for Farida and her friend seemed to have buried the far more tumultuous emotions which he knew were just beneath the surface of calm competence which she was currently displaying. If the dam broke, as break it must some time, he was determined to be there.

'But shouldn't we do something about that?' Mrs Bailey said sharply. 'She might kill herself.'

'It's not as easy as that,' Jo said, concealing the sense of wonderment which always seized her when she came up against her mother's implacable conviction, fed by a life-time of bridge-table philosophizing and over-simplified media talk, that all life's problems were susceptible to the application of a little self-help and common sense.

'We'll try to find somewhere that can help her,' Peter said. Mrs Bailey looked for a moment as if she would argue and then thought better of it. Arguing with men was not something she did readily. At that moment Shell emerged from the bathroom wrapped in the quilted pink dressing-gown Mrs Bailey had loaned her, looking rather more like a skeleton than before, with her scant hair plastered close to her skull and the dark eye make-up scrubbed from her naturally chalk-white face.

'Sit down, dear,' Mrs Bailey said kindly. Her saving grace was that her insensitivity did not extend from words to deeds. In a crisis she would always be there with sweet tea, dry clothes and open cheque-book. 'Are you feeling better?' she asked now.

Shell nodded, looking slightly bemused by the unexpected kindnesses being heaped upon her. But her eyes were wary. Mrs Bailey bustled off into the kitchen where they soon heard the clatter of tea being prepared.

'Shell,' Peter said quietly, 'weren't you at Sutton Park?' The girl nodded noncommittally.

'Only till the second year,' she said. 'Then we moved up to the Heights and I went to St Mark's for a bit. I met Karim at Sutton, though. I remembered him when I ran into him again later at the squat.'

'Shell, you know the police are looking for anyone who was with Karim at the squat, don't you?' Jo asked. The girl's face closed up and she hugged the dressing-gown around her defensively.

'I'm not talking to t'police,' she said. 'You can't make me. They'll only make me go back, and I'm not going.'

'Back where?' Jo probed. Shell shook her head, her eyes like dark pools in the pale, strained face, as she fiddled nervously with the quilted material over her lap.

'I were in care, weren't I? In a bloody children's home. And I'm not going back.'

Gradually, over tea and sandwiches, Shell was persuaded to tell them the story of her short life. She was, she admitted, only fifteen and seriously afraid that if she came to the attention of the authorities she would be returned to a children's home twenty miles away from Bradfield. She had been treated there, she claimed, almost as badly as she had been in the high-rise family home from which she had been removed in the first place as being out of control, a persistent truant and an incipient drug-abuser.

When she had run away six months ago her first refuge

had been the squat in the town centre where she had met Karim Aziz.

'It were right nice there,' she said wistfully. 'Karim were a right nice lad, in spite of being a Paki. I liked him.'

'Was he your boyfriend?' Jo asked. Shell looked doubtful.

'Sort of,' she said. 'He weren't right interested in girls. He were out a lot o' the time. But he got me the stuff I wanted very cheap, and he slept with me sometimes.'

'Was he dealing in drugs?' Peter asked.

The girl nodded, as if surprised at the question. 'Oh yeah, he were dealing. He were selling drugs at the club place at the school. I never went there 'cos I was afraid someone I knew might recognize me and grass on me to t'police, but Karim told me about it. There were lots o' kids going there for booze and drugs on the quiet. You know what Paki parents are like. And not just Pakis either. Lots of kids. It were safe there.'

'But not safe enough for Karim,' said Jo softly, her mind flashing back to that pathetic curled-up young body, so vulnerable in death.

'Do you know who killed him?' she asked.

Shell's face closed into a mask of pain and defiance.

'No, I effing don't,' she whispered.

'But you ran away,' Jo persisted.

'We didn't effing run away,' Shell flashed back angrily. 'I didn't even know he were dead, did I? He went out one day and didn't come back. And some men came round and said the squat were coming down t'next day, demolished-like, you know, which we knew was going to happen some time because they'd taken all t'rest down, just left that row. Any road, this bloke said get out, and gave us train tickets to London.'

'London,' Maggie said incredulously. 'Why on earth did he do that?'

'I dunno why he did it, do I? But the others thought London would be a good laugh, so we all went. And Karim hadn't come back so we went without him. I didn't know he were dead till I came back t'other day and someone at the refuge said.'

185

'Why did you come back, Shell?' Jo asked.

The girl shrugged her thin shoulders dispiritedly. 'I didn't reckon much to London,' she said. 'We slept in shop doorways for a couple of nights and it were effing cold. And it were near Christmas. I thought I might get to see my mum if I came back up here. She's all right, is my mum, it's me dad who . . . Well, never mind. And I thought I'd like to see Karim again, an'all. Any road, I hitched back up t'motorway and a lass in the service station down at Conningley told me about the rufuge, so I went there. I thought I'd be safe there for a bit.'

'Shell, you've got to talk to the police,' Peter Masefield said abruptly. 'Do you know where Karim was getting his supplies?'

The girl shook her head obstinately.

'I don't know,' she said vehemently. 'I don't know owt about that. And you said if I came with you there'd be no police, you'd take me back to Beth. What are you? Effing liars or summat? I thought I could trust you.'

'You can, Shell, you can, believe me,' said Jo quickly, flashing a warning look at Peter. 'But you want Karim's killer caught, don't you? I was the one who found his body, you know. That was the most awful thing, Shell, to see a young boy murdered like that. And if you don't help to catch whoever did it, then it could happen again, someone else might get stabbed. You owe it to Karim to help find the murderer.'

Shell looked at the three adults mutinously.

'They'll send me back to Threshfield,' she said. 'They've got this room there where they lock you up if you run off. I had a friend who was in there three weeks one time . . .' She rocked herself backwards and forwards like a young child in her distress at the thought.

Jo thought quickly. 'Shell, if I got just one policeman to come here, and he could write down what you said, would you feel happy about that? Then we'll take you back to the refuge, I promise.'

Shell rocked on and on, clutching herself with her thin

186

arms which emerged like sticks from the voluminous sleeves of Mrs Bailey's dressing-gown.

'You'll stay with me?' she asked Jo at last. 'Just one policeman and you'll stay?'

'I promise,' Jo said.

CHAPTER 15

Kevin Mower was intrigued by the phone call he had just received from Joanna Robertson. He was alone in the office, Huddleston having been summoned for another conference with Superintendent Longley who was rapidly getting increasingly tetchy at the outbreak of unsolved killings on his patch, tetchy enough to have come into HQ on a Saturday morning to check on the progress of inquiries. There was pressure, the station grapevine had it, both from the Press and from the Chief Constable, and a general feeling that it would be in everybody's interests to get the whole mess cleared up by Christmas.

Mower had come back from coffee in the canteen already puzzled. Never one to miss the opportunity to chat up a pretty woman, he had taken a seat next to WPC Wendy Collier, a blue-eyed blonde who was attractive enough to merit his attention with her hair fastened back to accommodate her uniform cap, but in his view positively dishy when cornered out of uniform with her hair in a loose golden halo around her heart-shaped and thoroughly desirable face.

Wendy had told him about her morning's stint on duty outside the women's refuge, which had been thrown into turmoil during the night by the incursion of an unknown number of men who had removed two Asian girls from Beth Corrigan's care.

Wendy was angry about what had happened.

'There's damn-all we can do about it if the girls themselves don't get in touch,' she said bitterly, after accepting Mower's gallant offer of a slice of his buttered teacake. 'And the amazing Corrigan woman is hopelessly vague about

187

who the girls are—no addresses or anything useful like that. Just first names.'

'Which were?' Mower prompted.

'Farida and Ayesha, or something like that.'

'Ah,' Mower said, adding a fourth spoonful of sugar absent-mindedly to his tea but otherwise displaying absolutely no overt interest in the information. He took a sip and pulled a disgusted face.

'The muck this canteen produces is beyond belief,' he said, to Wendy's surprise. 'Well, my lovely, we of the CID don't have time to sit about gossiping all morning. Are you going to this Christmas knees-up at the Woolpack old Jonesy is organizing? I'll buy you one there, doll. See you.' He was gone too quickly to hear Wendy mutter 'You'll be lucky,' under her breath as she watched his abrupt departure with cynical disdain.

Back in the office Mower sat thoughtfully wondering who could have been so determined that the two self-possessed young Asian sixth-formers who had declined a Christmas holiday in Pakistan should be returned to the bosom of their families that they had resorted to breaking and entering the hostel in the middle of the night and effectively abducting them. It was at that point that Joanna Robertson had telephoned to ask him to meet her and, she said, someone who could tell him something useful about Karim Aziz's death. The invitation filled him with an unexpected excitement and he was not particularly worried by her stipulation that he should come alone to the appointment.

What did alarm him slightly was the interpretation that Harry Huddleston would undoubtedly put on the alacrity with which he accepted both Jo's request and her terms. He was not sure how much Huddleston knew about the circumstances of his speedy departure from the Metropolitan force, but suspected that it was more than he had so far let on. He looked at his boss's empty chair for a long moment after he had put down the receiver, and then shrugged wryly. You get nowhere in this life if you are not prepared to take a chance, he told himself as he put on his coat and left the building, so let's live dangerously.

Jo was waiting for him at the address she had given, a small flat over the garage of a large semi-detached house in one of Bradfield's most attractive suburbs. She opened the door to Mower, nervously flicking her hair across her face to hide the dark bruising around her eye. Mower looked at her curiously. She was very pale but otherwise seemed composed enough as she waved him into the small living-room.

'This is Shell,' she said, indicating the small figure shrinking into the corner of the sofa. 'Michelle Hudson.' The girl was dressed now, Mrs Bailey having washed, dried and even ironed her jeans and T-shirt for her before going out with Maggie and Peter, as Jo had firmly requested. She was sure, she said, that Shell would be more forthcoming the fewer people were around when she talked to Mower.

For her part, Shell sat tense and immobile, apart from a constant fiddling with a ring which sat loosely on one of her thin, stained fingers. She almost shrank as Mower took a seat opposite her and Jo took up a place next to her on the sofa and put a protective hand on her arm.

'I'm sorry about all the hole-in-corner stuff, Sergeant,' Jo said. 'But Shell is very anxious not to come to anyone's attention officially. She's had a slight difference of opinion with a children's home and doesn't want to go back there. But she says that she knew Karim very well in the months before he was killed and I've persuaded her that she ought to tell you about it.'

Mower marvelled, not for the first time, at Jo Robertson's self-control. He felt an irresistible urge to tell her what David Edwards had told the police earlier that morning, which in spite of Huddleston's scepticism, be believed seriously reduced the likelihood that she had been involved in her husband's death, but the Chief Inspector's decision had been to 'let it simmer' while they awaited all the forensic reports on the fire and sought any other witnesses who had been near the Robertson bungalow that night.

He did not dare take it upon himself to reassure her in any way, yet the more often he came face-to-face with Jo and the pain which, in spite of herself, lurked at the back of her eyes, the more he was convinced that she was not the person who had bludgeoned Neil Robertson to death.

He turned his attention reluctantly to the girl, and made a mental note of her youth, her frailty and all the signs of a drug habit barely under control. He flashed her his warmest and, he hoped, his most reassuring, smile.

'So you were a friend of Karim's,' he said. 'It must have been a shock for you. Can you tell me about it?'

In little more than a whisper, Shell told him what she had already told Jo.

'These men who came to the squat and gave you the train tickets—what did they look like? Would you recognize them again?' Mower asked at length. The girl nodded.

'I think so. Two big blokes in dark coats, one had a lot of gold rings.'

'White?'

'Yes, white,' she confirmed. They sounded, Jo thought, like the two men who had threatened Maggie the previous night, but so far she had failed to persuade her friend to tell the police about the incident so she held her peace.

'What was Karim dealing in?' Mower wanted to know then.

'Everything, anything,' Shell muttered. 'Grass, heroin, Ecstasy, cocaine.' The Sergeant whistled quietly.

'And mainly to kids?' The girl nodded, her face devoid of expression, and not for the first time Jo found herself filled with a sort of blind fury at the forces which pulled or pushed children like Shell, for she was no more than a child, into this bleak rootless underworld of quick fixes and squalid squats. Karim, now revealed as the insouciant wheeler-dealer she had hoped he was not, had been a loved and wanted son, which made the truth harder to accept than in the case of this near-anorexic waif whom apparently no one had ever loved or cherished.

'And do you know who was supplying him?' Mower went on.

The girl shook her head.

'He said nowt about that. He had friends all over—Paki, white, black—loads o' friends. It could have been any of

190

'em.' And not one of them willing to tell what they must have known about the six months in which Karim had dropped out of sight of the legitimate, adult world, Jo thought grimly, or acknowledge what had been going on in the school basement. The underworld's security had been tight, and she suspected that the only thing which could have secured that was fear.

'And what was Karim doing himself?' Mower asked.

'Only coke. He wouldn't shoot up. He said it were bad for you,' the girl muttered, clutching her damaged arms to herself protectively.

'Too right,' Mower said. 'And you? What do you do?'

'Nothing now,' Shell said defensively. 'Beth wouldn't take me in unless I promised to stay clean . . .' Mower looked sceptical.

'But when you do, it's needles?' he asked.

The girl nodded dumbly and Jo guessed from the look in her eyes that she understood only too well the risks she was running

'So since you and Karim split up, where have you been getting your supplies?' Mower persisted.

'I haven't, have I?' Shell flashed back angrily. 'All I've got is Karim's—' She stopped suddenly, realizing too late what she had said.

'Karim's what, Shell?' Mower asked, his face stony now, his eyes cold. 'What have you got of Karim's?' The girl looked wildly at Jo for support and Jo felt helpless to respond.

'You must tell him, Shell, if it's important,' she said. 'Karim's dead. You can't protect him now.' But she knew that it was her own safety which concerned the girl, not her dead boyfriend's. Her face had gone even more pinched and sullen as she tried to outface Mower, who was having none of it.

'Where's her gear?' he asked Jo, and did not need to wait for an answer as the girl's eyes flashed involuntarily to her battered bag which she had dropped in the corner of the room when she had arrived. Mower crossed the room quickly and picked it up, up-ending the contents unceremoniously on to the coffee table in front of them. A tangle of dirty T-shirts and underwear, a much used hairbrush and a torn toilet bag cascaded out, and in the middle of it all a heavier item, about the size of a large book and wrapped in a dirty towel.

Michelle and Jo watched silently as Mower unwrapped the plastic-wrapped package and weighed it reflectively for a moment in his hand, saying nothing. The girl twisted her ring around ever more frantically and Jo could feel that she was beginning to tremble convulsively.

'What is it?' Jo asked Mower quietly. The Sergeant's face was impassive as he glanced at her and then at the girl.

'Ask her,' he said. 'What is it, Michelle? Coke? Heroin? Tell Mrs Robertson what you had hidden in her house.'

'He asked me to look after it for him,' Shell whispered. Mower could not restrain a cynical snort of disbelief at that, but the girl came back at him immediately.

'It's true,' she said. 'He were frightened. Right scared. I think he nicked it or summat. He asked me to keep it for him till things calmed down. That's why I came back from London. I brought it back for him. That's the truth.'

'How old are you?' Mower asked more gently, affected in spite of himself by the girl's waif-like defencelessness. Jo Robertson looked at him curiously and answered for her.

'She says she's fifteen, but you could check. She says she's been before the juvenile court.'

Mower nodded noncommittally.

'I'm not going back to that place,' the girl said sullenly. 'You promised.'

'Calm down,' Mower said. 'I won't tell social services where you are if you go back to the refuge and stay there, right? Is that a deal? In the meantime I want to write down everything you've told me and I want you to sign it. And later I'll want you to look at some photographs to see if you can recognize these two men who came to the squat. Right?'

That transaction completed, Mower followed Jo Robertson downstairs and out into Margaret Jackson's wintry garden where a couple of struggling Christmas roses gave the only hint that there might be life beneath the cold black earth. At the gate she turned towards him, holding her coat tightly around her to ward off the icy wind.

For a moment Mower hesitated, one hand on the personal radio in his inside pocket.

'How are you?' he asked Jo abruptly.

'I don't think it's hit me yet,' she said, her face haggard and unnaturally pale in the freezing air. 'I'm living on borrowed time, in a sort of limbo. Can I go back to the bungalow yet?'

'Tomorrow probably. I don't think they've quite finished there.'

'I didn't touch him, you know,' Jo said fiercely, searching Mower's face for some reassurance that he believed her but finding only a sort of friendly dispassion. 'Perhaps if I had hit back he would have stopped hitting me, but I never did. I never could. Never.'

Mower looked at the appeal in her eyes and would have liked to offer some comfort, but he did not dare. And he had other things on his mind now. He pulled his radio from his coat determinedly.

'I'm sure we'll soon find out what happened, Mrs Robertson,' he said. 'In the meantime, I'm going to have to take young Michelle down to HQ. She's in possession of Class A drugs worth five figures, at a guess. I'm going to send for a car with a woman officer—'

'You bastard!' Jo interrupted him explosively. 'You promised, not just me, but her! You promised her just now. You can't do that to her. She doesn't deserve that. She tried to help.'

Mower turned away from the angry appeal with a slight shrug.

'I don't have any choice,' he said flatly, making his call. Jo listened in horror.

'Can you sleep at nights?' she asked acidly, when he had finished.

'Like a log,' he responded, an edge of anger in his voice. 'If I'd wanted to be a social worker, I'd never have joined. Look, if you want to make it easier for her, you can. You can help me get her down to HQ without a scene, or you can sit on your high horse and watch us drag her down there kicking and screaming. Either way, she has to go. I'm a policeman. I don't have the luxury of deciding which laws to enforce and which to turn a blind eye to. In any case, we're not talking scrumping apples, Mrs Robertson. We're talking hard drugs. She's pathetic, she's a junky, she's had a rough time, and she's walking around with enough stuff to devastate half your bloody school. OK, I agree she's a victim, it's not her fault, all that stuff—but I spend half my life arresting victims. She's no different from a thousand others and if I didn't take her in I'd deserve everything they threw at me when they found out—and so would you.'

They stood for a moment facing each other until, as a squad car drew up quietly beside them, Jo's shoulders slumped in acquiescence.

'Let me tell her,' she said.

Back at the station, Mower found the drugs squad inspector, Watson, ensconced in Huddleston's office with the Chief Inspector himself looking more than normally disgruntled. It was bad enough, in Huddleston's book, to have to work over the weekend, much worse to find Longley on the premises as well. The sour mood in the office fitted Mower's well enough. He was still smarting from the look of furious contempt that Jo Robertson had directed at him after she had watched him and a policewoman force a near-hysterical Michelle into the police car outside the Jacksons' flat.

'We've to cooperate, lad,' Huddleston said to Mower as the Sergeant took off his coat and examined the scratches Michelle had inflicted on his hands as she had struggled all the way down the stairs and into the car.

'We've to compare notes, share resources, put our noddles together, to see if we can make owt of nowt. I told the Super that just because a nosey schoolteacher keeps popping up in the vicinity of the bodies doesn't mean there's a connection between the murders. But he won't have it. He wants her and her boyfriend brought in so's he can try a bit of the heavy stuff. I told him if he wanted to do the old tough and tender routine you'd be only too willing to be Mr Tender, but he says if that's the way you feel you're not to go anywhere near her.'

'Christ, you didn't really tell him that, did you?' Mower said, horrified. 'Do you want me out that bad, guv?'

Huddleston and Watson looked at him speculatively for a moment before Huddleston broke into a slightly shame-faced grin.

'Don't fret,' he said. 'You'll make DI yet, lad. I'm only having you on. Where've you been, any road?'

Mower told them, and gave Huddleston the girl's signed statement.

'She's downstairs in an interview room,' he said wearily. 'The custody sergeant's sent for a doctor. She threw a screaming fit when I cautioned her, fought the WPC most of the way down in the car and more or less passed out when they put her in a cell. She'll need a medical before we question her again.'

It was Sergeant Watson who seemed by far the most interested in his tale of Michelle and the package of drugs.

'It figures,' he said. 'There's been a lot more stuff around the last six or seven months and we've had no success tracing the source. Young Aziz certainly wasn't on our list of known dealers. And if he nicked a parcel of the goodies —got greedy, perhaps, and wanted to set up on his own— it gives you a motive for the killing.'

Huddleston nodded heavily. 'Aye, but who did he nick it from?' he asked. 'Have you got any ideas on that score?'

'It's unusual for the Asians to be involved,' Watson said thoughtfully. 'Unusual, but not unheard of. I think what I'd like to do next is have a look at Arif and Son's ware-houses and have that chat I've been promising myself with Sammy Arif.'

'You'll never get a search warrant for the warehouses,' Huddleston said. 'You've got nowt to go on.'

Watson grinned and tapped the side of his nose.

'Customs and Excise will oblige if I ask them nicely,' he said. 'An import and export company? There's all sorts of things they can go in there for if they put their minds to it, and I'll make sure they do put their minds to it. They owe me a favour.'

'Right, then,' Huddleston said decisively. 'Longley wants us to be pro-active, or whatever the ruddy jargon is. You go and be pro-active with the Arifs, Ray, and take young Mower here with you to liaise. I'm not sure I trust him near the Robertson woman, for all he claims to be pure as the driven snow in that direction.' Mower made to object to this, did a quick mental calculation of the value of working with Watson, and bit his tongue.

'In the meantime I'll bring a bit of old-fashioned pressure to bear on Robertson and her boyfriend. And I'll want that lass up here to look at mug shots as soon as she's fit, so get the custody sergeant to keep me informed about her, will you?'

'I promised her no social services,' Mower said.

'Aye, well, that were a daft promise to make,' Huddleston said. 'Any road, it won't be our decision now, will it, it'll be the magistrates'. And if she's only fifteen they won't remand her to prison, that's for sure. And Ray—' The drug squad man, about to leave, turned in the doorway.

'When your Customs and Excise buddies are looking at Arif's stock and books and what-have-you, just think on. I've been trying to pin Terry Hardcastle down for more years than I care to remember. He's involved with Arif, a company director, no less, and as far as we can tell he's been strapped for cash. If there's owt there shouldn't be going on there you can bet your next month's pay cheque that he's in up to his well-fed double chin. If there's so much as a shred of evidence to justify bringing him in, do me one last favour before they put me out to grass. Give me the pleasure of taking him the bad news, will you? It'll make my Christmas, that will.'

CHAPTER 16

Jo Robertson realized that the emotion which was gradually consuming her was anger. The grief which must inevitably come over Neil's death had not yet hit her, but anger at its arbitrary and shocking brutality had. She was angry too at the suspicion of involvement which had fastened itself insidiously around Peter as well as herself and she was enraged by the tangled web which had ensnared so many young people, from Karim and Shell to Farida and her friends, in an incomprehensible mesh of death and drugs and injustice.

Her anger was compounded by a profound sense of help-lessness. She was sitting with Peter and Maggie in Margaret's flat where they had all three picked at the lunch Jo's mother had prepared before she took herself off to the shops.

'Life has to go on, dear,' she had said as she left, shopping-bag in hand, though at that precise moment her daughter simply could not envisage how normal life would ever go on again.

'I suppose you're right,' Maggie said reluctantly to the other two, after the door had slammed behind Mrs Bailey, picking up the conversation where they had left off. 'I'd better go and tell the police what happened last night. It's just that I feel so—so humiliated by it. Almost as if I had really been raped, instead of just threatened.'

'They have to be stopped, Maggie,' Peter said quietly. 'Next time it might not just be threats. Next time, for some other woman, it might be the real thing.'

'I know,' Maggie groaned. 'I've been over all the arguments why you should always report these things with my women's group so many times that I could recite them to you backwards. Which doesn't actually make it easier when it comes to the point.'

'But these two sound very like the two men Shell met at the squat. The man with the rings—'

'He was the real sadist,' Maggie said. 'The one who talked dirty and really enjoyed it. He was evil and—' She stopped suddenly as though some new horror had just struck her.

'One of the things he threatened to do was use a knife,' she whispered. 'I think I'd better go to the police now.'

When she had gone and they had listened to the roar of the little MG fade away down the road, Jo jumped to her feet in frustration.

'We've got to do something, Peter,' she said desperately. 'I can't just sit here. I'm going to see Mohammed Arif to find out what's happened to the girls. Perhaps if I talk to him again he'll see reason. He seems a reasonable man, not a fanatic.'

Peter looked at her soberly. Since Neil's death he had ached to take Jo in his arms and comfort her, but he had not dared. She had cut herself off from his so completely that he felt as though there were a wall between them. With an increasing sense of despair he simply stayed close to her, hoping against hope that sooner or later she would need him and he would be there when she did.

He felt not the slightest optimism that going to see Farida's father would alter the situation one jot for the girls, but he could see that if Jo did not take some sort of action she would burn herself into a state of such anxiety that she might do something even more reckless.

'OK,' he conceded. 'I'll come with you to see Arif. Though I honestly don't think it will do the slightest good. The girls are probably on a plane by now.'

They drove across the town through the Saturday lunch-time traffic to Arif's house, an undistinguished modern building on the edge of Southwaite, set behind a high brick wall from which someone had made a half-hearted attempt to obliterate some very recent racist graffiti with a pot of black paint. The gates were open and Peter parked in the drive behind a dark blue and opulent-looking BMW.

'Someone's at home,' he said, without confidence. They rang at the front door, which was opened by a dark-skinned

198

woman of middle age, wearing a checked overall over traditional dress.

'I'll ask if Mr Arif will see you,' she said doubtfully, waving the visitors into the hall and indicating that they should wait as she disappeared back into the recesses of the house. The hall was spacious, furnished in a curiously heavy, old-fashioned style with dark oak furniture, a wealth of brass ornaments and an oriental carpet of rich dark red and sapphire blues and deep cream.

Jo sat gingerly on the edge of a polished chair and twined her hands together nervously. Now she was actually in Arif's house she began to feel that she had perhaps after all gone too far. Where, she wondered, not for the first time, did concern end and interference begin? She was terribly afraid that she had stepped over the dividing line and, glancing at Peter, who was gazing with a worried frown at an engraving of Queen Victoria at a durbar, guessed that his misgivings were far greater than her own.

Mohammed Arif appeared himself quite quickly, still clutching a linen napkin as if he had just got up from the table. He looked at his visitors interrogatively and without warmth, and waved them into what was obviously his study.

'I'm surprised to see you here, Mrs Robertson,' he said, taking a seat behind a heavy old mahogany desk and waving his visitors into more comfortable chairs opposite him. 'I was sorry to hear about your husband. What can I do for you?' His manner was not unfriendly, simply cool and remote, as though whatever problem Jo had represented no longer particularly concerned him.

'Mrs Robertson is very worried about Farida and Ayesha,' Peter Masefield offered. 'They seem to have been taken from the women's refuge last night with some violence . . .'

Arif's lips tightened in distaste at that.

'You seem to imply that I would cause my daughter some harm, Mr Masefield,' he said coldly, glancing down at the blotter on his desk where he had written Peter's name when he had introduced himself. 'I assure you that that is the very furthest thing from my thoughts. In fact I am more convinced than ever that what I have arranged for her is in her best interests.'

'She's not a child, Mr Arif,' Jo broke in angrily. 'She's a young woman with a life of her own to lead. You can't just export her, like a piece of baggage.'

'I agree,' Arif said unexpectedly. 'Which is why I was very pleased that when I saw her early this morning Farida agreed with me that a holiday in Lahore, away from the racism and other unpleasantnesses which have blown up in Bradfield this week, would be in her best interests. It is a beautiful city, you know. It will give her a rest, a respite, and then she can decide in peace whether to continue her education here in England or not.'

'I don't believe you,' Jo said flatly, throwing any remaining vestiges of caution with her school's governor to the winds. 'I don't bloody believe you. She and Ayesha are clever, talented girls. They have everything going for them if they stay here—good A-levels, university places, the careers they want. It can't make sense to ship them off to Pakistan now.'

Mohammed Arif looked at her silently for a moment.

'You must know, I suppose, Mrs Robertson, that I could probably have you dismissed for coming here this morning and harassing me like this,' he said at last.

Peter made to intervene angrily at that but Arif waved him down.

'I won't do that, Mrs Robertson,' Arif went on. 'I won't do it because I think you, probably above all the teachers at Sutton Park, really care about my daughter, and I know she is devoted to you. I do understand that you are here because you have what you see, though misguidedly in this case, as Farida's best interests at heart. But can you honestly tell me that you believe, as a good western liberal, that this town is really an acceptable place for my clever and talented and—yes—beautiful daughter to be at this moment? With thugs and hooligans like the ones who ran riot outside your school the other day still at large? With murder and drug-trafficking happening on the school premises? I was brought up to believe that Britain was the most civilized society in the world, you know? But no more.'

Arif stood up dismissively, his thin face disdainful, but Jo was not ready to be dismissed.

'Farida is still old enough to make her own decisions,' she said. 'She has that right. She has lived most of her life here and wants to stay.'

Arif picked up a set of car keys from his desk and turned off the brass lamp which had brightened the room in the grey December light, dismal even at midday.

'Their plane leaves Manchester at seven this evening. My wife and son went over this morning with the girls and were to spend the day with a cousin of my wife's in Cheshire. I had it in my mind to go to the airport myself to say goodbye, and if you wish, Mrs Robertson, I will take you and your friend with me so that you can reassure yourself that Farida is not being put on that flight against her will, as you seem determined to believe. You can ask her yourself. Would that satisfy you?'

Arif glanced at his watch.

'If you want to come, you must decide quickly. They check in at five so we need to be on our way.'

'Yes,' Jo said firmly, glancing at Peter for support. 'Yes, I would like that.'

The full might of Her Majesty's Customs and Excise was an awesome thing, Kevin Mower had to concede as he watched Inspector Ray Watson mobilize them for a raid on Arif and Son's warehouse. He was aware from his time with the Metropolitan Police that the excisemen's powers of entry and search, often used at the docks and airports, were far wider than those afforded the police. Even here, about as far from the coast as it was possible to get in the north of England, Watson obviously had his contacts and used them efficiently. Notwithstanding it was the Saturday afternoon before Christmas, he announced that the go-ahead had been given and the joint forces of the two services mobilized to make a move by four o'clock.

Arif and Son's warehouses were bright grey and red

201

structures, without windows, anonymous among a whole industrial estate of similar buildings on the southern outskirts of the town. They were surrounded by a high chain-link fence, the only entry through which was a six-foot-high metal gate with a security hut beside it. A couple of burly men, one holding a vicious-looking German shepherd guard dog on a short leash, came to the gate as the convoy of marked and unmarked cars drew up outside.

With a great show of reluctance the security men unlocked the gate and the main doors of the warehouses. Watson gave the two men an unfriendly glance and relieved them of their keys.

'Hang about,' he instructed them curtly. 'And keep that dog under control. We'll be bringing our own dogs in.'

Mower looked at the taller of the two, taking in the array of cheap, heavy gold jewellery which adorned his fingers, mainly, it seemed, fake gold coins in heavy settings, the advantage of which in a fight it did not take much imagination to envisage.

'I think I'd like to have a chat with these two later,' he said quietly to Watson, remembering Maggie Turner's description of the man who had threatened her in the statement he had taken from her an hour ago.

'Right, they can stay here until we're ready for them,' Watson agreed at once, assigning two of his men to watch over the guards until the search was complete. The combined force of police and customs men began a meticulous investigation of the stacked shelves and crates inside the warehouses.

Arif and Son were ubiquitous importers: whatever was in demand, mainly though not entirely in the Asian community, they undertook to supply. Huge racks of textiles and cotton and silk garments from the sub-continent, looking fair to keep the Asian community's women in their traditional dress for the foreseeable future, stood next to enormous stacks of wooden boxes of spices, chutneys, popadoms and canned specialities from the Middle and Far East. One corner of the first warehouse was piled high with cane and bamboo furniture from China.

Another with cheap electrical goods from Hong Kong and Singapore. A third with richly coloured rugs and carpets from Baluchistan.

The search proceeded slowly and meticulously, and it was not before a fruitless hour had passed that the whole team moved to the second warehouse which was where they found what they were looking for. Deep inside the building, concealed by crates of dried spices, canned mangoes and exotic fruit salad, the sniffer dogs the customs officers had brought with them, undeterred by the exotic aromas all around them, began to whine and wag their tails excitedly and pull their handlers towards some packages tightly wrapped in sacking. One of the dog-handlers summoned the chief customs investigator and Inspector Watson, who was being closely shadowed by Mower.

'Something here,' the officer said laconically, hauling his dancing dog away. Watson nodded, the only hint of excitement in his manner a slightly sharper than normal gleam in his eye. He pulled a penknife from the pocket of his jeans, looked at his customs colleague for assent, and then slit open the first of the packages in the sack. The knife cut through not only the outer sacking but an inner layer of polythene as well, allowing a thin trickle of white powder to emerge.

'Oh yes,' Watson said softly, almost to himself. 'Oh yes indeed. I think, young Kevin, you could go and get your boss now and ask him to fetch his friend Mr Hardcastle down to the nick to answer a few questions about this little lot. I'll go and invite the Arifs to the party. I think we're going to have some fun and games tonight.'

CHAPTER 17

Chief Inspector Harry Huddleston had gone home, having failed to locate either Joanna Robertson or Peter Masefield as Superintendent Longley had wanted. Let them stew until Monday, he thought unkindly after a frustrating conversation with Joanna's mother who, having denied all knowledge of her daughter's whereabouts, had demanded to know how soon he thought he was going to reduce the crime wave which made it too dangerous for her to venture on to the streets of Bournemouth at night. He was now sitting morosely watching a video of England's latest unsatisfactory test performance in Australia. He did not need asking twice to switch it off when Mower arrived at the door to tell him what had happened.

'Gotcha,' he exclaimed happily, his eyes lighting up in anticipation of a long-postponed consummation. 'Gotcha at last, Terry my lad. I'll bloody well retire happy after all.' He seized his coat and after shouting something almost incomprehensible through the kitchen door, where, to judge by the cooking smells emerging, his long-suffering wife was already preparing the evening meal, he followed Mower out of the house with alacrity.

Mower drove fast to the Hardcastles' house in Southwaite, reflecting his boss's ebullient mood. It was just as well DI Watson had remembered his promise to let Huddleston bring Hardcastle in or his own life would not have been worth living for the rest of the month, he thought, with a grin. Watson himself had gone directly to the Arifs' house, intending to bring both father and son to headquarters. Mower pulled to a skidding halt on Hardcastle's drive, spraying gravel across the lawn and effectively blocking the triple garage doors, which were open to expose all three vehicles inside.

'He'll not do a runner,' Huddleston observed, with total confidence. 'It'd be beneath his dignity. It'll be ' 'nowt to say before my brief arrives' ', you can put money on it. And the best lawyer money can buy. But we'll see about that.'

'You don't like him much, do you,' Mower observed mildly. 'Why's that, then?'

'It goes back a long way,' Huddleston said, his face grim. 'He were a slimy little toad at school. He started in the family business, you know. Built up a chain of betting shops, some above board and licensed, some, we suspected, not. I thought I'd got him once when I were a young DI.

204

Brought him in and put it to him, but when it came to court the two cast-iron witnesses I'd had turned out to be made of paper after all. Crumpled up, when it came to the point. Left town. Got at, no doubt, by Terry and his mates. We never found them. The case was dismissed and I got a dressing-down from the beak suggesting I was pursuing some sort of vendetta. Put my next promotion back a good two years, that did.'

'Sounds as though he could have tried the same trick with the kids from the squat,' Mower said thoughtfully. 'Only one of them decided to come back. And I'll put money on those two yobs at the warehouse being the ones who threatened Maggie Turner, and who were handing out train tickets like confetti to the kids. I've had them taken down to the station as well, by the way. They were not happy, I'll tell you. And some uniformed fool had let one of them make a call on his mobile phone while they were waiting for us to complete the search. He's no idea who to.'

'He'd better not have warned Hardcastle off or I'll have your guts for garters,' Huddleston growled. Mower shrugged. The thought had crossed his mind and he was greatly relieved to see Hardcastle's cars all neatly lined up in the garage, indicating that the Hardcastles were both at home.

'I'll get an ID parade for those two organized as soon as,' he said, giving no indication of his perturbation. 'I don't reckon much to young Michelle in the witness-box but Maggie Turner will put them away on her own if it comes to it, and love every minute of it. Hardcastle must have loaned the pair of them to Arif when he needed to come a bit heavy to get his daughter back.'

'You say we've got warrants out for the two Arifs—father and son?'

'Ray Watson's gone straight up to their place,' Mower confirmed. 'He reckons the stuff in the warehouse is worth a couple of million on the street. They're going away for a long time.'

'Right, then, let's go and wish Terry a good evening,'

Huddleston said with heavy satisfaction. 'I've waited long enough for this.'

Hardcastle came to the door himself and invited them in courteously enough, though his eyes were dark with suspicion. He was dressed casually in red sweater and slacks, as if he had been playing golf, and he led them into the sitting-room where his wife was curled up girlishly in an armchair dressed in skin-tight jeans and another of the baggy tops, shocking pink this time, which revealed and concealed according to which way she manœuvred her curves within it. Mower nodded to her cursorily and was rewarded with a look of mock indignation.

'You again, Kevin,' she murmured archly, to the Sergeant's embarrassment. But Huddleston had other things on his mind.

'A drink, Harry?' Hardcastle ventured, waving a hand at the bar where Mower guiltily spotted the malt he had enjoyed so much on his last visit. But the attempt at a hospitable smile died on Hardcastle's lips as he watched Huddleston look around the room with an overtly vindictive gleam in his eye, taking in the booze, the opulent furnishings and what was left of Brenda's porcelain collection in its gleaming glass case.

'We'd like you down at the station,' he told Hardcastle bluntly. 'There's a warrant being requested to search this place under the Dangerous Drugs Act. In the meantime you've some questions to answer about what's already been found in Mohammed Arif's warehouse.'

Hardcastle's face hardened and his normally high colour deepened a shade but he gave little away.

'I know nowt about that. I've only been in the firm five minutes. Put a bit of capital in when he needed a sleeping partner. Ring Alf Freeman,' he said curtly to Brenda, who was slowly beginning to take in that this was not a casual visit. 'Ask him to meet me at police HQ.'

'You can still afford Alf, can you, Terry?' Huddleston inquired solicitously.

For a moment it looked as though Hardcastle would lose his cool. His big fists clenched at his side and Mower stiffened, half expecting him to take a swing at Huddleston who was waiting almost expectantly for the fuse to blow. But the moment passed and Brenda swung her legs off the chair and abruptly switched off the hi-fi, which had been playing Barry Manilow in the background.

'What's all this in aid of, then?' she asked sharply.

'It might be helpful if you came down to the station with us as well, Mrs Hardcastle,' Huddleston said. Brenda paled beneath the layers of peach and cream make-up and her lips tightened from their normal pout to a narrow line of displeasure.

'What the hell would I want to do that for?' she asked, glancing at her husband with ill-concealed fury. 'I know nowt about his business arrangements.'

'No?' Huddleston said sceptically. 'Well, you might as well tell us what you do know, love. We're not talking six pennorth of illegal betting here, we're talking a couple of million of illegal substances, by all accounts.'

At that Hardcastle turned on his heel and walked abruptly out of the room, with Huddleston in close attendance.

'Come on, Mrs Hardcastle,' Mower said, a touch of sympathy in his voice as he surveyed her state of deflation and watched her swing a fur coat around her shoulders, lock up the house carefully and switch on the alarm system before closing the front door.

'By the way,' he said quietly, as they made their way to the waiting car, 'you do know that the profits of drug-dealing are liable to confiscation, don't you? You did say all this belonged to you?' He glanced meaningfully at the immaculate lawns and borders and the low spreading ranch-style house behind them. She took her seat silently in the back of the car beside her husband but when they were about to enter the doors of police headquarters she took Mower's arm and drew him back slightly from the other two.

'They'd not confiscate owt from a witness, would they?' she asked speculatively. Mower shook his head and gave her his most encouraging smile.

'Just checking,' Brenda Hardcastle said, glancing at the swing doors which had just closed decisively behind her husband and Huddleston. 'Just checking.' She gave Mower the merest hint of a wink and followed her husband through the doors with the resilience somewhat restored to her step.

Once inside, with the Hardcastles ensconced in separate interview rooms and Brenda's new pliancy taken on board, Huddleston's ebullient good humour was only partly deflated by news of Ray Watson's less successful sortie to the Arif household. Neither father nor son had been at home, the housekeeper had told them, and had been unable to offer any information on their whereabouts. More puzzling was the discovery of Peter Masefield's car parked in Arif's drive and his name clearly written on the blotter on Mohammed Arif's desk.

'I've put out a call for the Arifs,' Watson said.

'The daughter was flying to Pakistan,' Mower offered. 'Perhaps you'd better check the flights from Heathrow and Gatwick just in case they've decided to go along.'

'And what about Masefield?' Watson asked. 'Didn't you want him?'

'I did and I didn't,' Huddleston said. 'It were Longley's idea to bring him and the Robertson woman in but I've not got enough on either of them to arrest them. Let's let that ride, shall we. We'll see them on Monday. In the meantime, let's get Terry Hardcastle sewn up tight.'

Manchester Airport was bustling with crowds of pre-Christmas holidaymakers attempting an early getaway from the bleak weather which had swept with Mohammed Arif and his companions on their drive over the Pennine motorway. The journey had been a largely silent one. Arif had put a Beethoven tape on the stereo, giving Jo, who had taken the front passenger seat, a thin, mocking smile as he did so.

Jo herself swung abruptly from her residual anger about Farida and Ayesha to a growing sense of the reality of her loss of Neil. She knew that the numbness which had so far blotted out her grief would fade. She had seen the anæsthetic effect of shock often enough to know that it would not last and she consciously feared the pain which she knew would catch up with her, probably very soon now. For the moment she clung on to her outrage and anger about the girls as a way of blotting out even deeper feelings, whether of grief or guilt she was not sure, afraid of where they would take her.

For his part, Peter Masefield sat in the back of the car, soothed by the enveloping luxury of the soft leather seats and the gentle surge of the acceleration as the car climbed effortlessly over the dun brown moors and dropped again into the grey heartlands of Lancashire. He had not wanted to make this journey, any more than he had wanted to visit Mohammed Arif. A dogged loyalty kept him at Jo's side as she sought emotional oblivion in frenetic action.

Once at the airport, Arif led them to the desk which was handling the charter flight to Karachi upon which his wife and the girls were booked. They had not yet checked in when they arrived, but within minutes they turned up, wheeling a trolley laden with baggage and accompanied by Sami Arif, casually dressed in a canary yellow sports shirt and dark slacks underneath a ski-jacket. His face darkened when he saw the farewell party.

'This is too much,' he said directly to Jo and Peter as his father greeted his mother and the girls. 'Is there no end to your interference?' He stared at the two teachers with unconcealed dislike before turning abruptly back to the girls.

'You'd better get your goodbyes over, then,' he said. 'You don't have too much time, with all the checks they do these days. You ought to get through passport control straight away.'

He is desperately anxious to get rid of them, Jo thought, as she took Farida and Ayesha's hands.

'Are you all right?' she asked. The girls nodded guardedly.

'It's just a holiday,' Farida said. 'We'll be back next term.'

'Mrs Robertson,' Farida's mother said, 'I do appreciate

209

your interest in my daughter, but you really have no need to worry about her future. I will look after her, you know.'

'And Ayesha?' Jo asked desperately.

'And Ayesha,' Mrs Arif said firmly. 'She is going to stay with her aunt, but I will keep in touch.'

'You'd better believe it,' Sami Arif broke in, picking up his mother and his sister's hand baggage. 'I really don't know why you put up with this interference,' he said to his father angrily. 'It's so bloody patronizing. Now do let's go.'

Jo and Peter watched the family group make their way through the crowds to passport control, where Farida and Mrs Arif took their farewells of their menfolk.

'Do you feel better about it now?' Peter asked, putting a tentative arm around Jo's shoulder.

'I suppose so,' she said. She watched Sami Arif curiously as he fussed around the little group until finally all three travellers had passed through into the departure lounge.

'And yet . . .' Jo said. 'Sami seems too eager, somehow. And why all the threats and violence to get them here. It doesn't make sense.'

The two men were walking slowly back towards them when Sami pulled a mobile phone from under his jacket. It must have rung, although Jo and Peter were too far away to have heard it in the busy departure hall. He appeared to say little, listening in silence to whatever message was being relayed to him, but he broke into excited conversation with his father as soon as the call was finished. They had approached closely enough now for Jo and Peter to recognize that they were speaking in Punjabi and that whatever he was saying, Mohammed Arif was saying it with considerable anger and force.

'There has been a change of plan,' Sami announced as they approached. His usual urbanity had suddenly become ragged and his eyes were glittering with suppressed emotion. 'Would you come with us to the airline desk for a moment. We need to see if we can travel on this flight.'

'Travel?' Peter said stupidly. 'Aren't you going back to Bradfield?'

'I think not,' Sami said, his voice rising slightly. 'I think bloody not.' Mohammed Arif watched his son with a slightly stunned expression but he said nothing as Sami led them through the chaos of luggage and queues and unsupervised children to the desk.

'The flight to Karachi? The charter flight?' Sami demanded of the young woman behind the desk. 'Is it full?'

'Yes, I'm afraid so, sir,' the woman said dismissively. She tapped her computer keyboard languidly. 'All seats have checked in,' she said. 'They'll be boarding shortly. The flight is completely full.'

For a moment Sami stood beside the desk with his eyes blank. Then a shudder ran through him. He seized Jo's arm in a grip so tight that she cried out in pain and with his other hand pulled a small black automatic from the pocket of his jacket and held it against her side.

'Don't make a fuss,' he said to the airline clerk in a low voice but sibilantly, so that none of the group could fail to hear him. 'My father and I need to travel on that flight. Fix it, and fix it quickly, otherwise you and Mrs Robertson and a few other people are going to end up dead.'

The VIP lounge was hot and stuffy and getting more so. For almost two hours Sami Arif, gun in hand, had been pacing up and down the deep pile carpet alternately cursing and threatening his two hostages. His father was slumped in an armchair in the corner of the room to which the four of them had been ushered with courteous solicitude as soon as the airport had realized the nature of the crisis it had on its hands.

The older man had shrunk into a state of dull bafflement the moment his son had produced his weapon, a mood from which he showed absolutely no signs of emerging. If he spoke at all it was in Punjabi to Sami, who answered in the same language. Their exchanges had been monosyllabic and neither Jo nor Peter had gleaned much about the reason for Sami's sudden lurch into bright-eyed and manic criminality.

The flight to Pakistan was, according to the television indicator on the wall which was still functioning, 'delayed',

211

which could only mean, Peter thought, that it was sitting on the tarmac while the authorities worked out whether or not to accede to Sami's request for seats on the plane for himself and his father. Communication with the outside world was now restricted to a single telephone, which rang intermittently, and the one-sided conversation they could overhear had been threatening on Sami's side and evidently placatory but noncommittal on the other.

Peter and Jo were sitting on a sofa in the middle of the room, acutely conscious as Sami paced around them that at any moment his obviously fragile self-control could snap. Every now and again he sniffed something clumsily from a packet which he kept in his coat pocket, leaving trails of white powder down his shirt. They assumed he must be taking cocaine, as the procedure seemed to screw his metabolism up to new heights of excitability.

Jo leaned against Peter Masefield limply. She had walked across the empty concourse, from which police had swiftly marshalled the holiday crowds, close behind Mohammed Arif and Peter, with her head held high and Sami's gun pressed uncomfortably into her ribs. The police officers who had materialized almost instantly in response to the crisis had been accommodating, helpful even, to the man with the gun, and had ushered the quartet without comment through the now empty departure hall, littered with hastily abandoned items of luggage, and past stony-faced officials at customs and immigration control. Not until the four of them had been left in the VIP lounge and the doors closed had Jo permitted herself to relax, and then only to lean imperceptibly against Peter when Sami waved them to their present seats.

'Shit, shit, shit,' Sami said suddenly, picking up the telephone and jiggling the rest up and down impatiently. 'They must have got someone off that bloody plane by now.'

There was no response to his call and he threw the receiver down and resumed his nervous pacing. Racking his brains, Peter tried to remember all that he had ever read about the psychology of hostage-takers. The key to survival lay in the relationship between the imprisoned and the imprisoner, he seemed to remember, but years of trying to commumicate with variously disturbed and violent adolescents gave him little optimism that he could get through to Sami in his present state of drug-induced near-hysteria.

'Try talking to him,' he muttered to Jo while Arif was fiddling again with the phone. 'It's supposed to help.'

She turned towards Peter helplessly and shrugged.

'What about?' she asked.

'What did you say?' Sami asked sharply, overhearing her whisper.

'I said what is all this about?' Jo embroidered on the spur of the moment. 'What on earth is all this about?'

Sami came closer, the automatic held slackly in his right hand, and stood looking down at the two of them with an expression of contempt on his face. He was sweating slightly and his eyes were unnaturally bright.

'You really don't know, do you? You really have been blundering about all this time without the faintest idea of what you were getting yourselves into. Well, so much the worse for you.'

'All what time?' Peter asked, trying to steady his voice into something aproaching normality.

'Since you started interfering in my affairs,' Sami said, resuming his manic pacing. 'You really should have sent my sister home when she ran away, you know. I needed her out of the way. She knew too much. As a conscientious liberal you should have known better than to interfere in Moslem family affairs. You have no right.'

'You threatened Maggie Turner to find out where the girls were,' Peter said softly. 'And Neil? Did you threaten him too?'

'Not personally,' Arif said dismissively. 'It was not intended that anyone should be hurt.'

'Neil?' Jo said. 'You didn't intend to hurt Neil?' Arif turned away from her question and shrugged again with that simple elegance which characterized everything he did, however violent. There was nothing crude about him, only a simmering evil which flashed occasionally as if from a particularly beautiful but dangerous wild animal.

213

'It was not intended that anyone should be hurt,' he said again, as if that excused whatever had happened that night at the Robertsons' house. Peter took hold of Jo's arm warningly as the implication of what Arif was admitting sank in, but after a single shudder of horror she simply nodded quite calmly and glanced across the room at Mohammed Arif.

'And Karim?' she asked, her voice under perfect control, even though the use of the name brought back that cold vision of the boy's body, curled up, childlike in death, with stark clarity to her mind's eye. 'Did you intend to hurt Karim?'

Arif stopped his pacing in front of her again and laughed.

'Karim got greedy,' he said. 'He took something he shouldn't have taken. He was a very foolish boy. Very greedy.'

'Greedier than you?' Jo flashed back without thinking, and for a moment Arif stared at her, immobile, his dark eyes full of hatred, as if on the point of striking her with the gun. Then he relaxed and laughed, and began to talk as if some self-justifying switch had been turned on.

'You simply can't believe it, can you?' he said. 'It just doesn't fit any of your nice kind-hearted liberal preconceptions. Here I am, with all the privileges that money can buy in the way of education and prospects and material goods, and instead of saying thank you very much to your wonderful society I go to the dogs anyway. No excuses like poverty, or a lousy education, or an absent father.

'What you are forgetting, of course, is that for all my so-called privileges I'm still black. The sneers are less overt, the put-downs more subtle, the barriers more like a barbed wire entanglement than the brick wall my less privileged brothers meet—but they're still there, you know, those barriers. They don't go away, just because you have money or a decent education. Just watch their faces if you want to go out with their sister. Listen for the whispers if you want to get involved financially. Wait for the put-down if you want to take a single step further than they want you to go.

'Whatever my father says about making your way in this country on your merits, it doesn't happen if your skin is the wrong colour. I owe your rotten meritocracy nothing because it's a sham, a con, and all the more disgusting for being whitewashed by well-meaning fools like you.

'So I took your business ethic seriously, didn't I? Business is business, you know? Terry Hardcastle had the contacts and I had the know-how. It made perfect business sense. And if your young thugs and hooligans want to raddle their brains with drugs why should I stop them when I can make money out of them? They can rot in hell for all I care.'

'Oh God,' Jo said, running a hand wearily through her hair. The extent of her failure to understand overwhelmed her.

'At least some of us try,' Peter said angrily.

'Not enough of you,' Arif came back dismissively. A single tear ran down Jo's cheek and she dashed it away angrily as Peter put his arm around her again.

'I'm all right,' she said.

'For Christ's sake, let her go,' Peter said. 'She's had enough from you and your friends. You don't need us both here. Let her go.'

'No way,' Arif said impatiently. 'I need you both. Now what the hell are those bastards doing about this plane.'

He returned to the phone suddenly filled with renewed anger and this time his call was answered. For a moment he listened impassively to whatever was being relayed to him from the outside world before spinning round to his prisoners again, gun in hand, and waving them both towards the phone. He thrust the receiver into Jo's hand.

'They want to hear you—to be sure you're OK. Tell them that. Then tell them,' he said, 'that if they don't get us on to that plane in the next ten minutes I will shoot your friend here in both knees. Another ten minutes and I will shoot him in the head.'

In a low voice, which she could hardly grasp was her own, Jo repeated the message and was surprised to hear the now familiar voice of Sergeant Kevin Mower at the other end of the line, though his anxiously repeated assurance that she and Peter would come out of this ordeal alive hardly registered.

'They have your mother on the line,' she relayed to Arif at Mower's request. 'She wants to talk to you.'

Whatever effect that information was intended to have on Arif could hardly have been the incoherent rage which it triggered. Arif seized the receiver back from Jo Robertson.

'Get her back on to the plane,' he screamed before turning convulsively on Peter Masefield and striking him across the head with his gun, a vicious blow which brought him to his knees, his head in his hands and blood spurting between his fingers. Jo screamed and from the receiver came the now frantic voice of Mower demanding to know what was going on.

'Tell him,' Arif said to Jo, handing back the telephone again. 'Tell him to do exactly as I ask, and do it quickly, or I won't be responsible for your safety.'

Hardly able to speak, Jo did as she was asked.

'We're all right,' she said finally, glancing in horror at Peter who was still crouching on the floor, his head in his hands, her voice reduced to little more than a hoarse whisper. 'We're all right. We're still alive.' At which Arif cut off the call, leaving the receiver swinging from its rest so that, for the moment, no further contact could be made with the world outside.

'Look after him,' Arif ordered curtly, handing Jo an incongruously large and startlingly white handkerchief from the pocket of his ski jacket. He ran a finger round the collar of his shirt and wiped the palms of his hands on his slacks. The temperature in the room was rising fast and Jo wondered if that were deliberate.

Crouched on the carpet, now splashed with blood, she did her best to staunch the flow from the jagged cut on Peter's brow before helping him back to the sofa where they had been sitting earlier. He held the handkerchief to his head and looked at her with a dazed expression which reduced her to despair.

From the moment when she had at last linked Sami Arif with Karim Aziz's murder in her mind she had had no doubt about the ruthlessness of which Sami was capable. She could only assume that the police too had now made that connection and that was why Sami has decided so suddenly to take matters into his own hands and leave the country at almost any cost. If they knew he had committed one murder, she thought dully, she supposed that another would not make much difference to his future if he were eventually to be arrested. To that extent, his threats were unlikely to be empty ones. If it suited him to use the gun which he was now holding so casually again on the other side of the room, he would use it.

In the airport manager's office which the police had taken over as the control centre for the handling of the siege, an argument had raged on and off for more than an hour. The uniformed chief superintendent from the Manchester force who was in charge of the operation listened impatiently as Mrs Arif argued passionately for her husband and son to be allowed on to the plane from which she and her two young companions had just been removed. Sergeant Kevin Mower, who had asked to take the last call from Sami Arif, put the case equally strongly, though more dispassionately, for an immediate assault on the VIP lounge before more violence followed. He had been upset to a greater extent than he would ever admit by the sheer terror which had overtaken Jo Robertson as she had described the sudden violence with which Peter Masefield had been struck down. He did not doubt, any more than she did, that Sami Arif was capable of carrying out his threat to shoot his hostages and his stomach was churning with fear.

The psychologist from Salford University, however, a quiet, mild-mannered man who nevertheless spoke with a peculiarly dispassionate firmness, disagreed. His advice had been sought an hour ago and he still felt confident enough to assert the relative unlikelihood of the hostages actually being killed in a siege situation which did not end in externally provoked violence, in spite of the fact that the first blood had now been spilt.

'You are much more likely to end up with bloodshed if you go in,' he said flatly. 'Much more likely.'

'So let them go,' Mrs Arif said.

217

'Madam, the Home Secretary himself has refused permission for your husband and son to leave the country,' the chief superintendent said. 'The decision is not mine to take. It has been taken much higher up and the answer is no. If we give in to this sort of blackmail once we'll be having an incident like this at an airport every week. Some crook or another will come looking for a flight with a gun in his hand.'

Mrs Arif turned away, a look of infinite weariness on her face. So far she had maintained a dignified calm through her precipitate removal from the airliner with the two girls, and while the nature of the offences of which her son and her husband stood accused were explained to her, Mower wondered how surprised she really was by events. It was impossible to tell, though it was now clear that Sami Arif's determination to get his sister and her friends out of the country sprang from a suspicion, at the very least, that they knew too much.

The chief superintendent looked round the crowded office as if for inspiration and his eyes lighted on Harry Huddleston who, with Mower, had been summoned from Yorkshire when the nature of the airport crisis and the Bradfield involvement was recognized.

'Chief Inspector,' he said, with a glimmer of relief in his voice, 'it would help if you and your sergeant got on with taking statements from Mrs Arif and the two young ladies. There might be something which would help extricate us from this mess.'

Mower glanced at Huddleston and opened his mouth as if to protest, but a distinctly unfriendly look from his boss choked the words off effectively before they were fully formed. Perhaps, he thought, having something else to occupy his mind would help anyway. Anything might be better than having to make another call to the couple held in the room below, from which tension flowed down the phone line like some transmittable disease, twisting the gut and straining the voice to an unrecognizable pitch. Never, never again, Mower promised himself, would he sacrifice his professional objectivity for the chance of a smile from a

218

self-contained blonde who didn't give a damn about him anyway. It was a rocky road which had nearly put his career into the ditch once before.

'Aye,' Huddleston said. 'There's a great deal I'd like to ask someone about the affairs of Arif and Son. You'll do for a start, Mrs Arif, if you'd like to come with me. Right, lad?'

Mower nodded grimly.

'Sir,' he said.

Ten minutes ticked painfully away on the digital clock next to the video monitor in the VIP lounge. Sami Arif's eyes flickered towards it a couple of times each minute and Jo Robertson found herself following his gaze automatically as the minutes clicked by. Peter Masefield had leaned back in his seat, the bloodied handkerchief still clutched to his head and his eyes shut. He was not unconscious and every now and again he gave Jo's hand a gentle squeeze as if in reassurance.

She was not reassured. Talk, Peter had suggested, but her mind refused to frame sentences which appeared to her to offer any point of purchase with the man who, she now knew, was implicated, if not actually involved, in her husband's murder. She glanced at Mohammed Arif, the totally silent member of the quartet, who still sat in his corner, his dark eyes sombre and evidently turned inwards to a private world of some pain. What did he feel, Jo wondered, a man who had apparently made such a success of his life in his new country, a man respected by his own community and the wider one, seeking to flee now with his reputation in tatters and arrest and detention the most likely end to the immediate nightmare?

'Why?' she asked, almost involuntarily, addressing her question to the silent man in the corner. His eyes flickered in her direction for a moment, but he did not reply.

'Shut up,' Sami Arif said sharply. 'What you should be doing is hoping that your friends are doing as I ask. I don't think I've got a handkerchief large enough to mop up the next blood-letting.'

Peter's grip on Jo tightened again and she lifted his hand

219

briefly to touch her cheek. Arif spun away from them again and resumed his caged-animal pacing. His hand was on the telephone receiver even before the clock had indicated that his ten-minute deadline was up.

'Are you there?' he asked harshly. 'Do we board that plane now or not?'

The answer he received, it was immediately clear, was not the one he wished to hear. He waved at Jo and Peter again with the automatic and reluctantly they moved across the room to stand by the telephone. Mohammed Arif too, grey-faced and strained, seemed suddenly to shake himself out of his reverie and moved over to join the group by the phone. Sami Arif thrust the receiver into Jo's hand again.

'Describe to them exactly what I am doing,' he said, his voice pitched high, on the edge of hysteria. Roughly he pushed Peter Masefield, still dazed and unresisting, to his knees and forwards across a chair and placed the gun against his head. He nodded at Jo and with difficulty she told her interlocutor, whose voice she did not recognize this time, exactly what was happening.

'Let them on to the plane,' she whispered. 'Please, please let them on to the plane. He'll kill Peter if you don't.'

'Hold on,' the voice said quietly. 'Hold on, Jo, we're coming.'

She glanced wildly at the door, distracting Sami Arif for a second, but it was the older man who suddenly took charge, his thin face gaunt with strain but the authority back in his bearing and his eyes.

'Sami,' he said firmly. 'This is enough.'

Sami swung round, the gun faltering for a moment as he faced his father.

'Give me the gun, Sami,' Arif said, his voice regaining some of its old edge. 'This is enough. You have humiliated me enough.'

Sami shook his head and laughed wildly.

'You have to come with me,' he said. 'You have no choice. We have to go together.'

'There is always choice. I have no need to go anywhere. I have done nothing wrong,' Arif said. 'Give me the gun.'

220

Sami shook his head again and turned back towards Peter Masefield, the automatic cocked menacingly as he brought it back towards his temple. At that moment the door of the room burst open and four armed policemen hurled themselves through it into firing positions on the floor. Simultaneously, Mohammed seized his son's shoulder and spun him round away from Peter Masefield. He took the full force of his son's shot in the chest.

'Get down!' someone shouted, and Jo instinctively hurled herself across Peter in a sort of rugby tackle which landed them both on the floor, rolling away from Arif, as more shots rang out, to be followed by a long silence which she thought would last forever.

Cautiously she looked up from the carpet, taking in the scene with the clarity of a black and white photograph shot on a frosty day. The slight mist which surrounded them, she realized afterwards, was gunsmoke, the smell unfamiliar and never to be forgotten, and the silence the ears' defence after the deafening explosion of gunfire in a confined space. Peter was still beside her, holding a hand to his head but apparently otherwise unhurt. Sami Arif had been hurled across the room and lay in an ugly crumpled heap below a wall smeared with blood, his canary yellow shirt a patchwork of dark stains. Very close by, almost beside them, Mohammed Arif lay on his back, his eyes open and a large bloodstain slowly spreading across his blue shirt-front. The black automatic, small and harmless-looking now, almost like a toy, lay discarded for a moment on what seemed like an immense expanse of white carpet before being scooped up urgently by one of the blue-uniformed figures who had burst into the room.

Mohammed Arif caught Jo's eye and appeared to try to speak as none too gentle hands began to examine his wound. Cautiously she pushed herself upright and moved nearer and knelt beside him, leaning close to hear what he was trying to say.

'I'm sorry,' he whispered. 'Believe me, I didn't know.'

Jo looked into the dark eyes, pleading now, and nodded. 'I believe you,' she said. Arif nodded, a trickle of blood

221

appearing at his lips, and he closed his eyes with infinite weariness. From somewhere a stretcher appeared and urgent hands lifted him on to it. In the confusion of questions and sympathy and first aid which followed for her and Peter, Jo remembered afterwards that it was Sergeant Mower who had appeared at some point, looking almost as worn as the hostages themselves, and told them that Mohammed Arif had been dead on arrival at hospital.

'It was his son who shot him,' he had added in surprise.

'Yes,' Jo said. 'That's right. That was the bullet that was meant for Peter.'

The Sergeant had put a sympathetic hand on her arm. Only hours ago the gesture would have seemed significant to him. Now it seemed simply natural.

'You'll be all right now,' he said.

'We'll be all right,' she said, with the ghost of a smile. 'Thanks.'

The last of the youngsters straggled and jostled down the school drive towards the gates on the last day of term, anorak collars turned up against the wind which held the hint of a promise of snow, school bags swinging desultorily, here and there dark heads and blonde heads huddled over greetings cards and small presents, brown eyes and blue alive at the prospect of the holiday to come.

Jo Robertson and Peter Masefield stood together at the staff-room window watching them go. They had come into school simply to say their goodbyes before a holiday during which they would bury Neil Robertson and begin to remake their lives. Peter, a plaster covering the cut on his temple, put a hand lightly on Jo's shoulder.

'It's over,' he said quietly. She nodded and shrugged slightly. The police, it emerged, had been recording events in the airport VIP lounge, so that Sami Arif's admissions had been taped for posterity although he himself was no longer available to stand trial with Terry Hardcastle and his bully boys on charges of drug-trafficking, intimidation and murder.

'I just wish Farida was staying,' she said. 'Though I can

222